A Demon's Cry

Ray Morgan

ISBN: 978-1-8382828-3-7
Night Fox Books

A Demon's Cry
Cry

The Occultus: Book 2

RAY MORGAN

Other books from
Ray Morgan

Nate Godwin Series:
The Occultus
A Demon's Cry

Other:
Soul of Fire

1

Nate

Being outside at night is rarely a good idea. You never know who you're going to run into. But as I came to rest at the bus stop in a quiet English town I didn't even know the name of, and watched the cars pass me by on that cold December evening, I wasn't worried about what dangers could be lurking in the dark. If anything, I was too busy cursing the falling snow and the bitter air it brought with it to think about what possible trouble could befall me in some random town I was merely passing through. So as the rumbling of a car settled beside me, window wound hallway down, I didn't think much of it until I turned to look.

"Hello, Demon," the driver of the dark coloured Volvo voiced.

"Hi," I said brightly in return.

Hunters. Persistent bloody blighters. Good thing this one wasn't trying to kill me. At least... I hoped he wasn't. That would turn our reunion awkward real fast. Nothing quite says 'how've you been?' like a knife in the back. T'was the season of giving after all, and a knife was often more useful than the piece of coal I usually found in my stocking each year.

"Are you getting in," he questioned, "or are you just going to stand there all night?"

The question shook me from my thoughts, waking me up enough

to bring me back to the here and now. Christmas Eve, the rare kind where snow had fallen for once, enough of it to guarantee a nice white blanket for all the good kiddies who would wake up bright and early the next morning. And there I was, in the dead of night, standing ankle deep in the stuff, shivering my demonic backside off at a bus stop, staring at the heap of junk car before me and the hunter sitting smug in the driver's seat. Daniel. A mere bairn himself in reality, but instead of being tucked up in bed waiting for 'Santy Claus', here he was with a question in his eyes and a barely concealed smile tugging at the corner of his mouth.

I was cold but still stubborn as hell itself and certainly not about to let Daniel have the satisfaction of seeing I was even the slightest bit happy to see him.

"Actually, I'm waiting for a bus," I answered in a drawl, low and bored, shoving my hands deep into the pockets of my long cloth jacket. It helped keep some of the cold away, but let's be real, it was nowhere near as warm as a roaring fire or, and I hated to admit it, the heated Volvo before me. Even if it was a heap of junk.

"It's Christmas Eve," he argued.

I shrugged. "I can wait."

"You do realise the last bus probably left like an hour ago? You'll be stuck here 'til Boxing Day if you keep this up."

With a sigh, shoulders slumping, I made my way around to the passenger side, calling out to him as I went, "I'm going to regret this, aren't I?"

"Probably," was his answer, and he couldn't hide his smile this time, knowing he had won.

I let go of a put-on grumble and climbed in, the heat immediately hitting me, as well as the scent of coffee. I spied the culprit of the scent immediately. A disposable cup sat in the cup holder by the gear stick. I couldn't help but wonder how many sugars the kid had dumped into his drink to gain his look of 'I'm so energised right now but I could drop at any minute'. I decided it was probably best not to ask, doing so could result in an early sugar/caffeine crash if he was reminded of how tired he was—because he certainly looked it. I could see it in his eyes, the usual bright blue dulled by the bloodshot red that took over his whites. No choppy blond fringe of hair blocked my view of them, unlike the last time I had seen him. That must have been a month or so now, back when I left him and Charlie up in Scotland—somewhere Danny Boy should have still been.

"Why aren't you in Scotland?" I asked, shaking the snow from my hair and allowing myself a satisfactory smile when I saw some of it splash the kid.

He couldn't stop the roll of his eyes, but by God, he sure tried to hide it. There was no answer at first as he shifted the car into gear and pulled away from the bus stop. Something was different about him, and not just the hair. Looking at him now, he was no longer the baby-faced hapless hunter who had tried, and failed, to exorcise me when he first met me the November just gone. He still looked about twelve years old, even if he did claim to be eighteen, but there wasn't as much hesitation or self-doubt as before.

Damn, maybe I had rubbed off on the kid more than I realised.

"I have my reasons," he eventually answered, the words going almost unheard as my attention was too focused on my ponderings, eyes narrowed, watching the kid as he watched the road.

"And I presume you're going to tell me what those reasons are?" I also presumed they involved me somehow, or else why would he bother seeking me out miles upon miles away from the church up in Scotland, where he was supposed to be hiding? After all, he and Charlie were still wanted by angels and demons. Speaking of Charlie... "And where's Charlie? Where's she hiding? The boot?"

"She's still with them," he answered, tone low and evasive.

By 'them' he meant the Occultus, a group of people who were adept at concealing things. They *were* supposed to be a magical amulet that should have been in my possession due to my deal with Daniel, but somehow things never seem to work out quite how you plan them to. My gut told me the same thing would be true of this situation. Whatever reason Daniel had for picking me up out of the blue, it would leave me just as empty handed, and probably just as broke, as the last time.

"At least one of you has some sense," I scoffed, nodding my head probably a bit more excessively than I needed to and crossing my arms over my chest. "I didn't go through all the trouble of saving your arses for you both to throw it all away."

Given their gifts, the kind that made you wanted amongst both the angelic and demonic communities, Daniel and Charlie were *both* supposed to be under protection by the Occultus. It wasn't exactly freedom, but it took the target off their backs a little at least. The price you pay when you can truly see angels and demons for what they are. But perhaps, with Amon trapped somewhere in the Earth's crust, they would be somewhat safe for now. Still, that didn't mean others wouldn't follow where he left off.

"I know… I just—I couldn't stay," he finally said, and I could hear the frustration clear in his voice and see it in the way his grip tightened on the steering wheel as he spoke.

Resolve. That's what it was. Determination and resolve. That's what had changed in him. Sure, he had always been driven. He wouldn't be where he was, or have survived what he had, if he wasn't. He had always wanted to be the good guy, the one who slayed the big bad demons and sent the nightmares back to the place they came. It had been a naive sort of bravery on his part, the kind that would have gotten him killed if the demon he tried to slay hadn't been me.

But now the naivete had dwindled.

"And that's why you're here?" I asked, slow and cautious.

Sure, the kid had been a pain in the arse for me, and he had brought Amon screeching back into my life. But he kind of grew on you. He grew on me.

It took him a moment to answer. One very long, drawn out moment, during which I figured he must have been attempting to decide what to actually say. I already had an idea of what that would be, but he needed to say it for himself. He had come to a decision, and now he was pursuing that decision.

"I want to find the demon that killed my dad."

"And you, what? Want my help?"

He said nothing at first, just shifted silently in the driver's seat.

"I remember what happened last time I helped you," I continued. "I still have nightmares."

And scars. One in particular actually. The wound in my side never had fully healed, despite my demonic nature. A silent reminder that I wasn't indestructible—there were weapons out there that could hurt me and hurt me good. Blessed blades; they're a real bitch and a half.

"You're a demon," he started, "and the way I figure it—if you want to take down a demon, it's best to have another demon as back up."

"And you chose me." It wasn't a question. It didn't need to be. And it didn't need an answer. We both knew it to be the truth. So when he didn't say anything else, I simply shook my head and let go of a deep sigh. "And do they know where you are? The Occultus? Do they know what you're planning?"

His silence told me the answer was no.

"Does Charlie?"

He shifted uncomfortably in his seat at that, hands adjusting on the wheel as he took a right turn. It was only when he straightened up that he finally answered. "I left her a note."

"A note?"

"I didn't exactly have a choice."

"And pray tell, why didn't you have a choice?"

He breathed out and scrubbed a hand up and through his hair before returning it to the steering wheel. "She would have tried to talk me out of it. She would have hidden my keys or something."

My brow burrowed a little at that. Charlie was as stubborn as I was and as determined as Daniel. She was a fighter. She wasn't the type to hide away from everything. In the short time I had known her, I knew that to be true. The Charlie I remembered would have demanded to come with him. The Charlie I remembered *would* have been hiding in the boot.

"I think she's afraid," he continued, tone softer this time.

"Charlie doesn't get afraid." She was bold, and annoying, and had tried to kill me with a broken piece of bedpost the first time she had seen me. Fear wasn't something she allowed herself to feel.

"Last week... it was the two-month anniversary, and I think it hit her badly."

Anniversary? I looked to him with confusion, but it soon dawned on me. It was when her boyfriend died. Or rather, it was when she had been forced to kill him for her own protection—the man she loved possessed by a demon hell bent on killing her first.

"She doesn't have anyone else, and I don't think she can face losing the people she does have left." There was guilt lining his words, but he swallowed it thickly and seemed to shake negative thoughts from his head, focusing once more on the road ahead.

"So, it's just me and you then?"

"You, me, and this," he answered, digging into the pocket of his jacket to pull out a key card I remembered well. The one to the Harkanians' headquarters.

"Once more into the dragon's den?" I questioned, and I had to admit, I felt my spirit lift for what was probably the first time in weeks, a small smile flickering across my lips at the excitement of it all.

"There must be records of what happened. They're too thorough not to have kept any."

"And you're hoping those records will tell you what you need to know about the demon?"

"It can't hurt to try."

I bobbed my head in agreement and stretched out in the seat. "Manchester. That's a pretty long drive. You planning on driving all night to get there?"

That would explain the coffee. He was gearing himself up for an all-nighter. Not that he looked like he would be able to make it.

"Actually... no."

"No?"

"There's somewhere I need to go to first."

"Right...?"

"A lot of my dad's old stuff is there."

That didn't help me at all. But I said nothing at first, just rolled my eyes and let go of a yawn, until the silence got too much for me. "And where is this place?"

"It's just under an hour away."

Again, that told me nothing. "Well, I'm glad at least one of us knows where you're going."

He didn't rise to the bait, just continued driving onward, and I continued to watch him. Had he really grown so much within just the space of a month? I couldn't help but wonder if he hadn't told Charlie for another reason too, aside from the fear of her trying to stop him. Maybe he was afraid she wouldn't. Maybe he was afraid she would have come along for the ride. By simply leaving her a note, he had taken the choice away from her, leaving her with no other option but to stay with the Occultus, where she was safe. After all, she wasn't the only one that didn't have anyone else. With both his parents dead, Daniel didn't exactly have much family left in the world—none that I knew of. So maybe he was just as afraid as Charlie was about losing someone else. They had developed a bond after all, there was no denying it. Yin and Yang.

"How did you find me, anyway?" I asked, choosing to change the topic in hopes of getting actual answers.

"Serena," he answered, and really? Was I surprised?

"Should have known." I scoffed. "Let me guess, she's the one that planted the idea in your head in the first place?"

"Actually... no," he admitted, and he looked somewhat sheepish.

"So now you're coming up with your own suicidal missions?"

"It's not suicidal," he defended.

I shrugged. "But it is dangerous."

Maybe I imagined it, or maybe it was just a trick of the light, but I thought I saw the corner of his mouth hitch up for the briefest of moments into a small smirk. "Are you complaining?"

*****

Just as Daniel said, we were there in less than an hour. Wherever there was. It certainly wasn't much to look at, an old rundown building out in the middle of the countryside. It was secluded enough, hidden by trees and winding roads, that we would have privacy for whatever it was Danny Boy planned on doing there, but given the heavy snow on the ground and the decrepit look of the place, it certainly wasn't inviting.

Even when the car came to a stop, Daniel kept the engine running, the headlights helping to illuminate the area around us somewhat. Whilst it did the trick, in a way, it did cause the shadows to lengthen out across the ground, innocent bushes and branches becoming twisted fingers clawing at the snow.

"We should stay the night," Daniel said, but even he didn't look convinced, and I certainly didn't feel it.

"You know, I think I saw a hotel a few miles back along the motorway. Maybe we should head back there and come here in the morning, or the afternoon, when it's warmer."

"It's not as bad as it looks."

"Really?" I asked, sceptical. "'Cause it looks pretty damn bad."

He huffed out but otherwise ignored my comments, choosing to climb from the car instead. He switched on a torch he grabbed from the car and led the way, leaving me to follow after, my pace much less enthusiastic.

"Exactly why is your dad's stuff out here? In the middle of nowhere?" I questioned, coming to a stop several feet away to stare more intently at the looming building. It was just an average sized cottage style house made of stone—each one different in size and shape and colour, making it look like a mismatched hovel with an overall greying look, despite the odd yellow and red bricks. The tiles on the slanted roof looked like they had once been red, but the colour had been washed out after years of being beaten on by rain, and several were cracked, or missing completely.

"Why not?" he argued, which would have been valid except for the gaping hole I could see in the far right of the roof and the fact several of the wooden windowpanes were missing glass.

"Not the most secure of places," I answered, making to take another step forward only to find I couldn't.

Daniel huffed out and swung around to glare at me. "You can always sleep out here if you'd prefer?"

I took another look at the surroundings and the house itself, more carefully this time. "At this rate, I might have to."

"You..." he started, but the words fell away in his frustration, and he rolled his eyes. "Did you suddenly remember you have a fear of creepy old buildings or something?"

"No, but I did just realise your dad was paranoid about not letting the wrong kind of people into his secret club hideout."

His brow furrowed for a moment and I could see the confusion as the cogs turned until it dawned on him and he realised what I was implying. There was some sort of protection set up on the place, against the likes of me. Now I noticed it, I could practically feel the hum of it hovering in the air in front of me. Whatever the charm was, it worked like a magnet—except not in the typical sense. More like when you tried to hold two of the same poles together. They repelled each other, just like the charm was repelling me. It was physically impossible for me to move forward.

"I guess being a demon doesn't always have its perks," he said, considering me before turning back to consider the house. "There has to be a way to break it. I'll check inside, see if I can figure out what's causing it."

"Great," I drawled, letting my shoulders slump. "And I guess I'll have to check out here, try and find a weak spot or something."

He nodded absently, which I took to mean he was only partially listening to me as he made his way to the front door.

"Or, and I'm just throwing this out there, we could always go back to that hotel I saw. I mean, it's late, it's cold, and we would probably just be better off coming back tomorrow..."

No response.

"Or I could even wait in the car!" I tried, calling out to him as he disappeared into the shadows of the house. Again, he said nothing, and I let go of a sigh. Somehow, standing out there in the cold and snow, it didn't feel much better than standing at that bus stop.

"Or maybe I'll just talk to myself," I muttered under my breath, looking left then right, attempting to decide which direction to start in. Moving around would keep me warm, or at least warmer than I was. Get the blood pumping. So that was what I did. I made it halfway around before I came to the conclusion that unless Daniel was having better luck inside, I wasn't crossing that barrier.

Every inch of it was as strong as the last. High, low, left, right. It wasn't giving in at all. No weak spots. No cracks I could slip through. And it continued on like that all the way around back to where I started. Daniel's father had not been messing around when he put up protection on this place. Maybe there was something there after all.

A crunch in the snow behind me caused me to pause in my thoughts, my body stilling, my ears straining, suddenly paying attention to what was behind rather than what was in front. It wasn't Daniel. He hadn't left the house. It could have been an animal, some lost deer or brave rabbit, but I wasn't that lucky. I would never be that lucky. So I started turning around, even before the stranger start to speak.

"You're on my land," they said, voice strong and distinctly feminine. Accusation and warning laced the words, and I wasn't even surprised to find myself facing the barrel of a shotgun when I turned completely to face the newcomer. She stood about twelve feet away, but with such a sturdy hand and such a dangerous look in her eyes, I knew the distance wouldn't matter. She was a good shot. I could tell just by looking at her.

"Didn't know this was private property," I answered, holding my hands up and looking her over carefully, assessing the situation. She was a threat, that was for sure, but she was human. A few pyrotechnics, a bit of telekinesis, and I could send her on her merry way. Maybe scare her with a fire starting in the bush beside her... And since when had I started thinking like that? She had a gun held at me. My simplest option would be to kill her. That would be the easiest and safest option, but something held me back.

"Well, it is, and you shouldn't be here."

"Right then, that's me told," I answered. "So, if you would just lower the gun, and then I can get out of your hair. No need for anyone to get hurt."

But she shook her head, and even in the thick of the shadows I could see a dark smile on her slips. "You're not going anywhere. I know what you are."

"I'm a lost traveller," I tried, but she wasn't having it.

"You're a demon, and you're going to tell me what you're doing here, or I'm going to fill you full of buckshot."

So that was the way it was then. I was beginning to think a random burning bush wouldn't do the trick to scare her off after all. Knowing my extremely bad luck, it would probably just make her more inclined to shoot me. Unless she had a sudden change of heart, I was going to have to get tough. Daniel wouldn't be best pleased, but I didn't exactly feel like getting shot in the chest, or worse—the head. It wouldn't kill me, but it would damn well hurt, not to mention the small fact I didn't have any other shirts if this one got ruined.

"Maybe you should put the gun down anyway," I said, straightening up to stand tall, my arms hanging loosely by my side, ready. No point playing innocent anymore.

"Why would I make it any easier for you to try and kill me?"

A slow smile crawled across my lips. "I'm giving you a chance for me not to kill you."

She shook her head. "The only time a demon doesn't go for the kill is if it benefited them somehow, so if you're hoping I'll tell you how to get whatever it is you're here for, you're mistaken."

The thought hadn't even crossed my mind, but now she had said it, another thought did. Who was she, and how did she know about this place? Did she know Daniel's father? If that was so, I definitely couldn't kill her. Whatever Daniel came here for, she might have information on it. Damn kid. It would have been so much simpler if I could have just taken her out.

"Nate!"

Speak of the devil.

Daniel's voice rang out from behind me, worry etched into it. Ice-covered snow crunched beneath his boots as he raced toward me, and I would have laughed at his startled shout when he slipped in his hurry to reach me, if not for the woman and her gun. Although it would have been hilarious to watch him flailing about on the slick terrain, I didn't see his clumsy attempt to get to me, but what I could see was the shock on the stranger's face and the way her shotgun swivelled toward Daniel on instinct at the loud noise. I could sense her muscles tightening on the trigger before she fully pulled it, and I pushed forward with my own energy to counteract the result. The shotgun went upwards, she flew backwards and hit the ground, and Daniel arrived by my side uninjured.

"What the hell are you playing at?" I berated him, turning on him to look him over and taking in his pale features. "She nearly shot you!"

"She was going to shoot you!" Daniel argued, losing the frightened deer look from his eyes and regaining that look of pure frustration with me.

"I heal! You don't, you bloody idiot!" I looked up to the sky and let go of a heavy breath. "Next time you try to play the hero, Danny Boy, try remembering that you're only human, before you go and get yourself killed."

He didn't have a chance to answer. The woman begun to stir from where she had fallen. I expected her to reach for her gun and try again, but she didn't. Instead, she spoke up with a softer tone in her voice.

"Daniel?" she questioned, and I swear, I could hear tears.

Daniel pulled his gaze away from me to look to the fallen woman, his brow burrowing as he considered her before his eyes widened with surprise. "Aunt Suzie?"

I stalled. My mouth opened and shut several times before I managed to find any words, and even then, they were limited, a cheap repetition as I parroted Daniel. "Aunt...?" I questioned, swinging to look at the woman as she pulled herself to her feet. "Aunt?! She's your aunt?"

She looked cautiously between Daniel and me, her gaze flitting toward the shotgun momentarily. Was she really still planning on trying to shoot me? Back slightly hunched, she held her palms out flat but facing downward, taking a slow step forward, the same way you would when approaching a dangerous animal you needed to get around.

"Daniel, you should come over here," she said. Her tone was as careful as her each and every movement, tension running through her.

She thought I was a threat! I just saved her nephew from being shot, by her, and she thought I was a threat! Well, I suppose it was an improvement. At least somebody seemed to think I was. Every other human I met of late thought I was some kind of cuddly demon with horns made of marshmallows or something.

"It's fine," Daniel said, relaxing and shaking his head.

But she wasn't convinced. In one swift movement, she surged forward and grabbed her shotgun. Within the next moment, she was aiming it at me once again, and Daniel darted in front of me, arms splayed outward. As far as family reunions went, I figured it could have gone worse.

"Daniel, he's a demon," she said, wavering in stance. She was probably afraid she would accidentally shoot again and this time she would hit her nephew. "Whatever lies he's filled your head with, none of it is true."

"Nate is a friend," Daniel answered, and that was the most shocking thing I had heard all night. Friend. And it wasn't just the word either. There was honesty behind it. He actually believed it. It wasn't just some line to get his crazy aunt to drop her gun.

"Demons trick you," she continued.

"And they lie and cheat and steal and scheme," I finished for her. "Believe me, I've tried to tell him, but does he listen?"

He grumbled and threw a brief glare my way before returning his attention to his aunt. "Aunt Suzie, please—trust me. He's going to help me track down the demon that killed my dad."

"Daniel..."

"Do you really think I would have brought him here if I thought he was a threat?"

"Hey!" I complained. "I should be insulted. In fact, I *am* insulted. I am very much a threat. What is it about me being a demon that you just don't get? I could have killed her! I nearly did!"

Suzie raised her shotgun again, her grip tightening, causing Daniel to reposition himself once again so he was completely blocking her view of me. Or at least, almost was. He was, after all, at least a head shorter than me. But still, it was a good effort.

"You're not helping, Nate!" he whined. "Forget about your ego for five minutes, please."

I huffed out and sulked, shoulders slumping. "Fine," I grunted. "Tell her how I'm not a big bad demon. Ego or not, she still probably won't believe you."

Yet, even as I spoke, she began to lower the shotgun, her head cocking to the side. She was as crazy as the rest of them. "His stuff isn't there anymore," she said, and though her eyes never left me, I knew it was Daniel she was talking to.

"Where is it?" Daniel asked, voice strained, desperation shining through.

"I moved it all up to the house, thought it would be easier to keep an eye on it. The charm only stops demons from getting inside, and we both know they aren't the only ones who want to be in. It was only by chance I saw your headlights and knew someone was here."

I wondered if she was referring to the Harkanians with her vague riddle of an answer. It wouldn't surprise me. The hunter organisation that Daniel's father once belonged to certainly wouldn't have batted an eyelid at breaking into someone else's property. I wasn't one to judge, given my track record, but considering they were supposed to be the good guys—well, it didn't exactly give the best impression.

"Is it all there?" Daniel asked.

"As far as I know." She looked to me, then back to Daniel.

"Maybe your 'friend' should wait in the car...?"

"I said that too!" I said, nodding excessively. "But he just completely ignored me. Like usual."

"He's safe," Daniel answered instead, again proving my point that the kid just blanked me. I might as well have been talking to myself half the time. "I swear, Aunt Suzie. Trust me."

She gave one curt nod. "Fine, but I'm keeping tight hold of my shotgun."

2

Daniel

It had been at least half a year since I had last seen Aunt Suzie. She had been sleeping on the couch, clutching the keys to my dad's car in the hopes doing so would somehow keep me from leaving. I had replaced the keys with a crumpled up note instead. Seemed I was getting good at that. Leaving notes and disappearing while those who cared about me were sleeping. Charlie looked as peaceful as Aunt Suzie when I placed the note on her pillow earlier that day, before dawn had broken and the cocks could crow and birds could start their morning chorus.

Aunt Suzie's house was further up the hill, just beyond a line of trees overlooking the shack my dad used to store his things. It was on old farmhouse, but Aunt Suzie had allowed nature to take over the surrounding land, having little interest in raising animals or crops. The closer we got, the more I could see nothing had changed. From the white painted wooden door, with a golden knocker, that led into the narrow hallway entrance of the home, to the old wallpaper along the hallway, pinkish and cream with flowers here and there in plain ovals, breaking up the thick stripes. The mahogany side table and bookcase filled with cookbooks that were never touched and gardening books collected with the intent to be used but had somehow become as forgotten as the overgrown garden that surrounded the grounds. She was a collector of hobbies, my aunt.

One Christmas it had been knitting. I still had the woolly jumper she had given me. Or rather, Charlie did.

Christmas. That was something that was missing.

Growing up, my dad always tried to make an effort. My aunt helped too. But as years passed and my dad became more and more secretive about the Harkanians, when he no longer took me for visits even though I begged, and when the late nights became later nights, and sometimes not at all, and Christmas became an afterthought, Aunt Suzie still tried. Her house would be green and red and gold, and it would smell of cinnamon and spiced apples, and it would feel warm and cosy despite the cold winter winds outside.

None of that existed here now.

It was almost like Christmas itself didn't exist. Even though it had been the furthest thing from my mind over the past weeks, walking into the home away from home that had always been filled with so much, I suddenly felt its absence more than any year before.

"I'll put the kettle on," Aunt Suzie said, propping her shotgun up against the wall long enough to take off her thick winter jacket and hang it up on the coat rack fixed to the wall.

"I think Danny Boy has had enough caffeine for one day," Nate answered, coming in last and shutting the door behind him. He ran his hands up and through his hair, rubbing out all the snow that had fallen there. He eyed the coat rack but didn't seem as inclined to give up his coat. It was one of the few possessions the demon seemed to treasure, that and the small silver lighter he kept in his pocket at all times, except for when he toyed with it on occasion. Whenever he did, it often gave me the impression that he didn't even realise he was doing it.

I pretended I didn't hear him and gave Aunt Suzie a smile. "I'd love a tea, maybe?"

She smiled back and seemed to relax somewhat. "Three sugars or four?"

"Three... or four?" Nate questioned, turning on me, and I could immediately feel the heat rush to my cheeks. "Are you trying to overdose on sugar?"

Instead of giving a definitive answer or acknowledging Nate in the slightest, I shrugged and gave a quick, "whichever", before disappearing from the hall and into the living room of the house. Again, it was exactly how I remembered it. Not a thing out of place. And yet, I felt like a stranger there. The place I had stayed so often when my dad was at work, the place I had viewed as a home, made me feel out of place. Had I changed that much? Or was it something else?

I stood there, in the doorway, staring in at the small front room. The plush couch in front of the fire had been where Aunt Suzie slept when I had snuck down the stairs with my bags filled with stuff. She knew I was going to try and runaway, and she stayed up all night to try and stop me. She didn't stand a chance. It was too important that I leave.

A sharp jab to the back pulled me from my thoughts and I turned to glare at Nate. "What was that for?"

"Stop feeling sorry for yourself," he said, brushing past me with ease and making his way toward the couch. He lounged across it with a contented smile, closing his eyes as he basked in the heat of the open fire. Turned out he decided to leave his coat in the hall after all as he wasn't wearing it anymore, but I imagined it hadn't been an easy choice for him. Strange, because he always seemed to make everything look so easy.

I couldn't even bring myself to step further into the room, and there he was, making himself at home like it was exactly where he was meant to be in that moment and nothing anyone said would change that. Maybe it was all part of being a demon, or maybe it was just part of being... Nate.

I couldn't quite explain it, but it was the sight of him relaxing, the feel of familiarity that came with it, that had me feeling more comfortable. I claimed the armchair near the fire and sunk into it. It wasn't until my eyes closed also that Nate decided to speak.

"So, what is it you're really looking for here?" he asked.

I didn't open my eyes, but I could feel his gaze on me. I chewed my bottom lip, a small breath escaping past, and sat forward, now open eyes considering the murky pink carpet. "Answers."

"What if you don't like them?"

I looked at him through a narrowed, questioning gaze. "Why wouldn't I?"

He gave me the once over then shrugged. "I'm just asking," was all he said, but I could tell it wasn't all he was thinking. Whatever that was, he wasn't letting on.

"You wouldn't understand," I answered, shaking my head, the fire drawing my attention there.

I saw his gaze drop from the corner of my eye, a thoughtful but sad look playing across his features and etched into his brow. For a demon, he sometimes had a habit of looking very human. "No, you're probably right."

I took pity on him. "My dad had paperwork he used to keep away from 'the office'. I thought, if I could get another look at it, I could maybe make sense of everything I already know." Which, admittedly, wasn't a whole lot.

Before I had done my disappearing act on Aunt Suzie, I had looked through what I could find, but there were pieces missing. All I really knew was that my dad was working on something and it left him acting paranoid. I could still remember one of the phone calls to Aunt Suzie. I listened in using the phone in her office while she told my dad I was getting restless and was ready to come home. He hadn't said why, at least not in the conversation I heard, but he had said it wasn't safe. Somehow, the Harkanians were involved, and I was going to figure it all out, once and for all.

"You mean now you've grown up a bit more?" Nate asked, a smug smile sitting on his face as his right eyebrow quirked upward.

My own face twisted up in return, and I let out a grumble. He was probably right, but I wasn't going to admit that. Not to him. It would give him too much satisfaction. I couldn't deny the element of truth in his words though, not in my head or heart. The year before, when I set out on my own, I was determined to make every last demon pay for what happened to my dad. I didn't care if it was the right demon—every single one of them was going to burn in hell. Then, at some point between meeting Nate and being stuck up there in Scotland, there'd been some weird moment of clarity.

It didn't matter how many demons I got if none of them were the ones responsible for my dad's death. Then there were the Harkanians. They had been involved, and ignoring that would mean letting them get away with it. My dad deserved retribution if nothing else. If I was going to get that for him, I needed to start being smarter.

"Here we go," Aunt Suzie announced from the doorway, carrying a tray of drinks. She brought three, despite Nate having declined her gracious offer of hospitality.

I sat straighter in my seat and offered her a smile. Why did it feel so awkward? Was I really so afraid that she was angry with me for running away? "Thanks," I said, taking the cup she offered to me.

She offered Nate a second cup, but he eyed it suspiciously and didn't even attempt to take it from her. I couldn't blame him. After all, I couldn't guarantee she hadn't laced it with holy water or something. She snorted and placed it on the table beside the couch instead before finally taking her place in the last seat by the fire, cup in one hand and shotgun rested over her lap. She breathed in her tea and then looked at us each in turn.

"When's the last time you slept?" Aunt Suzie asked, and whilst her tone was authoritative, her eyes softened.

I shook my head and pretended that I couldn't feel my eyes

stinging from tiredness or feel the threat of exhaustion every time I breathed too deeply. The effects of the three, no... four cups of coffee, were beginning to fade, but now I was on the move, now I was doing something, I didn't want to slow down. Once the tea in my hands was in my system, I would be fine and raring to go again, and I wouldn't have to lose any more time.

"I just had an early start, that's all," I answered, looking away and down into the cup. I could see the steam rising up off of it and feel the heat seeping into my fingers and palms. Give it a few minutes and it would be cool enough to drink.

"Liar," Nate snorted, and I tried not to roll my eyes at him.

How could it be that I was such an easy book to read? They could both see sleep wasn't a priority for me, and I was so bad at hiding it. I never was all that good at lying. My face always gave me away. Though, now I supposed it was the redness of my eyes and the possible dark circles beneath them. I barely managed to sleep the night before, and I needed to be sure to be up and out before Charlie woke up, or even worse, before any of the brotherhood woke up.

I could feel my chest tighten at the thought of leaving Charlie up there, alone with them. We knew them as the Occultus before we officially met them, but these days they referred to themselves as a brotherhood. Charlie wasn't a fan of the term, deemed it too archaic, but I found it fitting considering how much they behaved like Big Brother. Eyes everywhere. Constantly watching. I could barely even use the bathroom without one of them keeping a close eye on me. It was for my protection, of course. But if they were watching me all the time, I would never find out the truth about what happened to my father.

"You should rest," Aunt Suzie went on to say.

"I'll rest later," I answered. "Once I've looked through my dad's stuff."

She gently shook her head, not denying me the right, but simply in disapproval. "You'll run yourself into the ground, Daniel. If you really want to go after those responsible for your father's death, you need to first look after yourself."

"I'm fine!" I all but shouted, feeling ashamed of it almost immediately. I hung my head, heat spreading across my cheeks and burning at my ears. "I'm fine. I swear."

A gentle sigh. "Then at least relax for five minutes to enjoy your tea."

"The crazy old lady is right, Danny Boy," Nate chimed in, and I could hear the grin in his voice. "Besides, I'm enjoying this fire too much after being outside in all that snow. Five minutes won't kill you."

I nodded at that. "Fine, but no longer."

Blowing at my tea, I tested it. If I took slow sips and kept blowing, I could have it finished it five minutes. I took my first sip then, enjoying the taste of sugar and caffeine. Aunt Suzie continued to nurse her cup, and Nate even picked his up briefly, if only to sniff at it, before putting it back down on the table.

By the time I was finished my cup, I could feel myself getting heavy, my eyelids threatening to close and stay closed. I shook my head in an attempt to wake myself. I needed to get going. If I got moving, I would wake up again. My brain would kick into gear and adrenaline would rush through my body. I pushed up, attempting to stand. I didn't even make it a single step before I stumbled.

Nate was there immediately, that grin on his face as he held me up. "Easy there, sleepyhead."

"M'fine," I tried to say, but I wasn't. I was barely hanging on, and even as Nate lowered me onto the couch he had claimed for himself, I could feel myself slipping. I could feel sleep claiming me, darkness taking hold, and then I was gone.

*****

I couldn't pinpoint an exact time when the dreams started, but it was somewhere between first meeting Serena and discovering Nate and Charlie. Although, in truth, 'dreams' was a generous description. Nightmares would be more accurate. They didn't happen every night, but they happened regularly enough to stick out in my mind. Sometimes I would be me, screaming out for Nate or Charlie, unable to help them against the demons and angels, and sometimes... I wasn't exactly sure who I was. Or where I was. The only thing I ever knew for certain was that I was dreaming.

This was one of those times.

Everything was muted. The world around me was grey and blurry, nothing really distinctive, the buildings more like outlines than actual shapes. The crowds of people were more like shadows passing by, but more solid, until I held my hand out to catch one between my fingertips only to find that it slipped through, like mist. Their words were indecipherable, like they weren't speaking any language I knew, but something else. Everything moved fast and slow at the same time, and I just stood there, in the confusion of it all, looking around, hoping to see something familiar.

But nothing ever was. Nothing ever truly made sense to me. So, I ended up just walking instead, making my way through the mass of dream people that cursed me in their weird language and shouted at me, even though they were nothing more than blackened air. The panic I felt rising inside of me wasn't mine. It felt alien, distant, but there all the same, and it continued to grow as my feet pounded against the tough grey ground and my eyes searched for what my mind didn't even know existed.

"Are you lost?" asked a voice, bringing me to a halt.

I turned to look at the owner, but they were just as shadowed as the rest of the people around me. Their face was like a blank mask, head tilted to the side. I shook my head and took a step backward.

They laughed lightly and dropped to their haunches, holding their hand out for me to take.

"Don't be afraid... I won't hurt you."

"I'm not supposed to talk to strangers." The answer of a child, and yet it slipped past my lips.

"A stranger is only a friend you haven't met yet," he said, and the mask shifted slightly, enough for me to see a friendly smile. "We can be friends, can't we?"

I shook my head, determined. "Tommy wouldnae like that."

"It can be our secret," the man offered in a hushed voice, like it was a game. "He doesn't have to know."

Hesitation, doubt. My mind screamed no. It screamed for me to run. Everything about the strange, shadowed man was wrong. He was not the friend he offered to be. But the dream me, the me that wasn't me, but was a child in a strange place, that me was tempted, and it was that me that had control.

"I don't know..." the child in me said, eyeing the man and his still outstretched hand.

"It can be a game," the man said. "You like games, right? Everybody likes games."

A slow nod, but no answer.

And the whole time, all the other shadows just passed us by. None of them afforded a single look our way. None of them cared for the man that didn't feel right and the child that was too naive to know you didn't become friends with someone like that.

I took a step forward. His smile turned into a widened grin.

"Good boy," he said, patient and waiting. "That's it."

My hand lifted of its own accord, reaching out for his. And by then, I knew it was too late. The grin became wicked, pearly white teeth becoming sharp fangs, and outstretched hand turning to outstretched claw, with sharpened, inch-long nails that dug into the flesh of my forearm as it gripped hold tight. His eyes became darkened pools that spun and swirled, drowning me in them, making me lose my breath and my ability to think straight.

I was trapped there, and even though I struggled, he wouldn't let go.

"It's okay," he said, voice sounding more like a hiss now, scratchy and low. "We're going to be great friends."

I wanted to scream, to cry out for help, but nothing left my mouth, even as I opened it wide and could feel the pain of the scream tearing at my throat. There was no noise. There was no rush of feet to help me. There was nothing and no one. The man, more like a snake or lizard now, leaned closer until his face was mere inches from mine, his breath hot and rancid on my face.

"I'll be watching," he said, "and when you're ready... Oh, the fun we'll have. You're mine... and they won't stop me from having you."

"Please," I tried to say, tried to beg, but he only held on tighter.

"Don't fight me," he said, placing his free hand on my chest over my heart. It made me feel dirty, like his shadows were seeping into me somehow. "Never fight me, and the world will be yours. Oh, how the world will be yours, little Natty."

3

Nate

Well, one thing I knew for certain was Aunt Suzie was one tricky devil. I had to hand it to her. Drugging her own nephew. That was one sly move. I would have warned him, but the kid needed the sleep. He was the palest I had ever seen him, and considering how pale he already was, that was saying something. Now though, he was peaceful... Somewhat anyway. I looked down at him as he drifted away on the couch and gave my head a light shake. The idiot. He had run himself down. If he truly wanted to get revenge, he had to look after himself first.

"I should exorcise you," Aunt Suzie said, bringing my attention toward her and away from Daniel.

I raised an eyebrow at her. "You could try."

She was a somewhat stout woman, short and a little plumpish, with dark hair that had started greying for a long enough time to give her whitened highlights throughout, but it was still all very thick; long and loose waves framing her face. Her features were soft, like Daniel's, and her eyes as blue as his. You could see the family resemblance. It made me wonder if her reflexes were as fast as Daniel's. The kid looked like a damn puppy, harmless despite all the yapping, but he was quick and fearless.

Aunt Suzie definitely had the fearless part down. I had no doubt in my mind she would shoot me with that shotgun of hers if she thought

I was a threat. It was just a little bit insulting that she hadn't tried again since her accidental shooting out by the cabin. Once over, when people knew what I was, they tried to actually kill me. They didn't talk about it. They saw I was dangerous and took the opportunity whilst they had a chance. Either I no longer looked as dangerous, or people were becoming desensitised to it.

"What do you want from him?" Aunt Suzie asked, and her words were cautious and cold. In her mind, there was no way I was doing this out of the goodness of my heart. I was in it for something.

A sly smile slipped across my lips as I continued to watch Daniel sleeping. "We made a deal."

I immediately felt her still, a sharp intake of breath from her. Her fingers twitched and hovered over the shotgun. "I'll kill you first," she said, and there was no hesitation there. She meant it. If the shotgun didn't do it, she would find a way. She would keep her nephew safe.

"Relax," I said, without even looking to her. "His soul is his own. He's not so stupid that he would give it up so freely."

He was, however, naive enough to think that nothing would ever make him give it up. As pure at heart as he was, as good as his intentions may be, one day, he would encounter a situation that would make him waiver. There was always something. It didn't matter who you were. Whether it was for greed or for love, there was always a price. And maybe it was my own naivete that had me hoping Daniel would never have to learn what his was.

God, since when did I become so sentimental and soppy? Since when had I started caring about someone other than myself? If this carried on, I was going to be in trouble. Giving a damn about others, that was how you ended up dead.

"Then what?" she asked.

I huffed out and took my place in the chair Daniel had vacated. "The deal was, he gets my protection."

"In return for what?"

I met her gaze. "Something so powerful and so brilliant I'd be a fool not to want it."

Lies. Pure and utter lies. The deal we had made before had been for a trinket that turned out to be non-existent. That in itself made our deal void. The laws that governed demon contracts would have terminated the deal as soon as the truth had come to light, and if that hadn't been enough to do so, then we had both already fulfilled our halves of the bargain enough to deem the contract finished. If I was to tell Aunt Suzie as much though, she would never believe me.

I was a demon. Why would I willingly help some hapless hunter? The truth was it went against everything I was about. The quiet life. Being selfish. Avoiding responsibilities. It contradicted my very nature. And yet, here I was. Even I couldn't explain it, so there wasn't a chance that Aunt Suzie would believe it.

A sad look formed in the deep burrows of her brow as she chewed at her lower lip. Her next words weren't meant for me, but I heard them all the same, a whisper released on a breath. "Oh, Daniel, what have you done?"

I just snorted lightly in reply and shook my head. She had no idea. She thought he was a fool, but she didn't have a clue. I wouldn't deny he was foolish to an extent, but his heart was good. That wouldn't change. He wouldn't do something if it conflicted with what his heart told him. If she knew that, she would have been proud. If she knew the effect the kid had on people, she would have been smiling.

Daniel groaned and my attention once more went to him, his face twisting up. At first, I thought he was waking up, but it didn't take me long to realise he was just dreaming. He shifted on the couch, unsettled, and I instinctively began to move forward, to make my way to his side, but I stalled at the last moment, Aunt Suzie beating me to it. She was on the floor beside the couch in no time, running her fingers up and through Daniel's hair. She shushed him, uttering calming words, soothing him, and she didn't stop until long after his features had softened again, whatever bad dream that had been ailing him leaving to be replaced by nicer, happier dreams, probably featuring rainbows and unicorns.

"You knew he wouldn't sleep," I said, watching her with Daniel. "At least, not without a little intervention."

"He's always been stubborn," she answered, and I could see that about him. She turned to glare at me, fierce and protective. "If you harm him, in any way, I will hunt you down and kill you."

I felt like a potential date for some overprotective father's young princess. The glare, the shotgun, the sharp warning. All that was missing was Daniel's prom dress and me waiting to fix a corsage to it. "If your next step is to tell me to have him back before ten, then I'm not sure I can manage that, but I will promise not to feed him after midnight if that helps."

There was a grunt of aggravation and a look of confusion as she no doubt tried to figure me out. "What kind of demon are you?"

At that, I had to grin. "One of a kind."

She raised an eyebrow at me, not impressed. Seriously, I swear, no one had a sense of humour anymore. It was one thing for everybody to be losing their fear of demons, but losing their sense of humours too? It was tragic. The start of the end of the world if you asked me.

It was a little while before she spoke again, and when she did it was gentle. Not for my benefit, but for Daniel's. She cared for him a great deal. I guess not all humans are as selfish as I always thought they were.

"Where has he been?" she asked, and it probably killed her having to ask. It probably caused her heart to ache knowing that a demon knew more about her nephew's last year than she did.

"Here and there," I answered. "But he spent the last month up in Scotland."

"Scotland?"

"It's a country up north from here—if you go past Manchester and Newcastle and you just keep driving—"

"I know where Scotland is," she interrupted with a huff. "I just don't understand why he was there. What's in Scotland?"

My eyes shone with mischief as I already began to list the numerous sights and landmarks in my mind, but when she narrowed her eyes at me, 'the Kelpies' no longer sat on the tip of my tongue, replaced by a more serious answer. "Protection."

"He has protection right here," was her answer. "I would protect him from anything."

"But you're not a hunter," I shot back, because despite it all, the bravado, the shotgun, the knowledge of everything, I knew in my heart she wasn't a hunter. Her brother may have been, and Daniel may have been trying to be, but she wasn't. "You can't protect him."

Her face twisted up and she shot up from the ground. Maybe her reflexes *were* as good as Daniel's. "He is my family, and family protect each other. Whatever games you're playing with him, you can't make him forget that."

"I'm not playing any games," I answered, not fazed by her reaction. "I'm just stating the truth. You can't protect him from something you know nothing about. You ever heard of the Occultus?"

"It's not real—it's just a myth."

"There's always an element of truth in myths. Finding out what part is the truth is the trick." I looked to Daniel, watching him in his slumber. "Turns out, it's not an amulet but a group of people that protect and hide things. Daniel is supposed to be under their protection—that's where he's meant to be right now."

Her attention returned to the kid, her body slackening, losing its tension. "What was he hiding from?"

I scoffed at the thought. "Turns out he's a wanted man... in a sense. The kid has a gift, and there are those out there who don't want him to have it."

That was what happened when you could truly see angels. Angels wanted you dead, and demons just wanted you so they could turn you into a puppet. The kid had had it rough, but he had been strong through it all. In fact, if I had to say, I would say he had found his strength through it. He and Charlie worked as a good team, which just left me wondering again why he had chosen to leave her behind. She was his opposite. She could see demons. That could only be an advantage. But instead, he was trying to keep her safe.

Aunt Suzie didn't say anything else, she just sunk down to the floor next to the couch once more and looked over her nephew. She had known he was special, I could see that much, but she didn't have a clue as to just how special he was. Well, at least she seemed to have forgotten about the shotgun for now—that meant it was less likely for me to get a chest full of buckshot if I decided to shut my own eyes for five minutes.

It was certainly serene and cosy enough for me to want to try. The fire crackled, the warmth of it spreading out into the room, the light of it dim enough to make a person drowsy. In the hallway, the grandfather clock rang out, announcing that it was midnight, and I couldn't help but crack a smile.

"Hey, Aunt Suzie," I said, drawing her attention once more and taking in the light frown on her face. "Merry Christmas."

*****

It was still dark outside when Daniel began to wake. I was watching the flames in the fireplace as the fire continued to burn bright, a few fresh pieces of wood now breaking up and beginning to crumble in the heat. Log fires would always remain one of my favourite things. They were more than just heat. The crackle, the sight, it all helped in staving off both the darkness and the cold. That was the problem with winter, it was always so cold. It didn't matter whether you were outdoors or in, it was always so bloody freezing, and I'd never been a fan of the cold. It reminded me too much of a place a little too far south; a place where fire can freeze you and ice can burn you, and the emptiness... it can swallow you whole, and when it does, it will never let you go again. To most, it's just a myth to keep them on the straight and narrow. To me, it was a bad memory that I could never seem to shake. I supposed that was why I found myself entranced by fire so much.

Daniel groaned from his place on the couch and the couch creaked under his movements. I pulled my gaze away from the fire and looked to him instead. The furrowed brow told me he was still trying to put all the pieces together, and the hand to his head told me that he was struggling to do it.

"Morning!" I said brightly, a grin settling on my features.

He looked to me through the grogginess still clouding his vision and thoughts. "What happened?"

"Aunt Suzie slipped you a little something to help you sleep," I said, motioning toward her with a nod of the head. She was out of it in the other chair, head lolled against the high cushioned back of the chair and shotgun now placed well out of reach so she couldn't accidentally shoot anyone. I had given her about half an hour of sleeping before I'd pried it from her grasp and placed it by the doorway to the kitchen instead.

Any anger playing across Daniel's face was short-lived, and he breathed out, looking over at the sleeping form of his aunt. He pulled the thick blanket from himself, the one Aunt Suzie had fetched and draped over him, and placed it over her, making sure it was snugly in place before he returned to the couch.

"Feel any better?" I asked, and even in the darkness I could see he wasn't as pale anymore.

"I feel like I was hit by a train," he answered, scrubbing his hands across his face. He sighed and fell backwards, slouching a bit more and allowing his gaze to wander the room.

"Nightmares will do that to you," I said with a shrug, not failing to notice the way his gaze instantly fell downwards, avoiding mine.

"How did you know?"

"Kind of obvious when you're groaning on and twisting about in your sleep."

He was silent. Sullen.

"What was it?"

At that, he shook his head. "Nothing..."

"You're a bad liar, Danny Boy."

A heavy breath. "Just bad dreams, that's all. I can barely even remember them now."

I scoffed. "Sure, but if you suddenly forget you have dream amnesia—"

"Then what?" Daniel interrupted, looking at me with a raised eyebrow. "You offering to be my demonic counsellor?"

"When you put it like that..." I answered. "Yeah, maybe you should take it up with Serena. She's more the counselling type. Comes with the holier than thou angelic job description."

That said, out of all the angels I'd run into through my many years, Serena had been the only one who hadn't repeatedly try to kill me. Sure, she threatened every once in a while, but that was all part of our friendly comradery.

"I'm fine, Nate," Daniel continued, and his gaze fell once more. "They're just bad dreams."

Neither of us believed that. But I wasn't going to push the kid. I stretched out in the seat instead in exaggerated movements and groans. "Then maybe you want to try waking Aunt Suzie—I think she might actually kill me if I try."

"Shotguns can't kill you," he pointed out, tone dry and

unimpressed.

"No, but looks can, and quite frankly, I'm surprised I'm still alive and kicking right now with some of the looks your aunt has got stockpiled up. She's a pretty scary woman."

He rolled his eyes. "Let her sleep, she probably needs it."

"But I'm hungry... and I'm about ten seconds away from raiding her kitchen for food." I spread my arms out. "Do you have any idea how long I've sat here waiting for one of you to wake up. Six hours is an awfully long time for someone like me."

"You mean someone with the attention span of a five-year-old?"

"Exactly!"

He shook his head and pushed up. "Just... stay here and don't wake my aunt. I'll go see what food I can rummage up. And I mean it, don't wake her up."

"I wouldn't even dare," I answered.

Not waking her up was the easy part. Staying where I was—that was a little trickier. It lasted for a whole five minutes before I found my way into the kitchen to watch Daniel as he searched the cupboards and fridge and started the motions for making breakfast. Eggs, bacon, sausages, a few tomatoes. It was the feast of kings. Kind of.

"What, no turkey?" I asked, leaning against the doorway.

He flinched and swung around to glare at me at the sound of my voice breaking through the silence, but he caught himself at the last second and swung to glare at me. "What are you talking about?"

"Turkey," I repeated, watching as he returned to work. "You know, it's kind of traditional."

"Traditional?" he asked, not fully grasping what I was saying. "What? For demons?"

"For Christmas."

He stilled. The kid hadn't even realised it. "Christmas..." he breathed out, like it was a long-forgotten memory.

"You forgot," I teased.

"I didn't," he lied, grumbling under his breath. "I knew it was Christmas time... I just... I forgot it was today."

"I think Aunt Suzie forgot too," I said. No Christmas tree. No tinsel. No lights. Hell, not even a single piece of holly. "Hopefully the Harkanians won't have though."

He paused to look at me, knowing I was hinting at something, but not quite following where I was going with my train of thought. "And why's that?"

I shrugged. "Just thinking... Christmas Day, you know. Time to be with your family, stuff your face with Christmas dinner, turkey and all the trimmings, then pass out from overeating..."

"I'm guessing you have a point somewhere, but I'm really not getting it yet."

"Well, you know—Harkanians, being a largely Christian operation, they're bound to be pretty quiet today. I imagine most of them should be home celebrating."

"So, what you're saying is that, if we're going to break in and go looking for information, we should do it today?"

"Nah, actually I thought we could go out and find a turkey and have our own celebration—pull a few crackers, open some badly wrapped presents, sing carols on the doorsteps of non-existent neighbours."

"Your level of sarcasm is overbearing sometimes," was his very dry, very bored response.

"So that's a no then?"

He feigned frustration, but I could tell he loved it. "Why did I decide it was a good idea to ask you for help again?"

"Because you've missed me," I answered with a beaming grin. "Go on, admit it. You missed me. You actually grew to like me, a demon, and you missed having my sparkling wit and amazing sense of humour around."

He said nothing. He didn't even deny it. He just continued on with making breakfast, piling up three plates full of salty, greasy goodness, and filling three cups with non-poisoned coffee. He added four sugars in his. I counted, and I couldn't help the small smile that crept onto my face, but I said nothing. The kid had a sweet tooth.

Aunt Suzie was still asleep when Daniel carried the coffee through into the living room for her. He lowered himself to his haunches in front of her, gently waking her with his free hand and soft words.

"Alan?" she questioned, sleep still sitting behind her eyes. When it had cleared, a small smile crept onto her face, and she placed a hand on Daniel's cheek. "You looked just like him then..."

Daniel didn't acknowledge her, swallowing thickly instead and handing her the coffee. "I made breakfast, you should come and eat with us."

Her eyes found me then, and I could practically see her thoughts. Part of her had hoped I had been part of her dreams and I would be gone when she woke up. Tough luck for her. But she pushed past it, for Daniel's sake. "I'll just tidy myself up, then I'll be right there."

"Okay, Aunt Suzie," he said softly, and then he returned to the kitchen where the breakfasts sat on plates around the oak table. He may have missed the stray tear falling from his aunt's eye, but I didn't. Family. It could be the death of you.

By the time she joined us at the table, you couldn't even tell she had been crying. The tears had been washed away and her hair tied back into a long plait that draped over her left shoulder. She had a small box in her hand. Nothing fancy, just plain and brown, worn around the edges and faded a little. She toyed with it at first before breathing in and smiling to Daniel, placing it in front of him on the table.

"This was your father's," she said. "It's only right that you have it."

He sat for a moment, confusion causing his brow to burrow,

before slowly opening the box. He pulled out a small golden pocket watch, barely bigger than a few inches in diameter. From what I could see, it was covered in a leafy pattern, intricate and beautiful, kept dust free and safe from wear by the box. He carefully opened it and a smile played at his lips, tears forming in his eyes but refusing to fall. "With all my love, Sarah..."

"Your mother gave him that watch for their first anniversary... the year before you were born. When she died, he refused to wear it. He wanted to keep it safe. But something like that, it shouldn't be forgotten about in some old woman's house, collecting dust." She smiled at him. "It belongs with you, so you can remember them both."

"Thanks, Aunt Suzie..." He toyed with it a moment longer before taking it firmly in his grasp and slipping it into the pocket of his jeans where it could sit safe and sound, and close by. I could tell he was reluctant to let it go, but he eventually managed to pull his hand free, and was left staring at the empty box it had resided in.

"Maybe it will help you feel like they're close to you, watching over you." She smiled sweetly, her gaze drifting toward some forgotten memory. "I wish you had had the chance to meet her," she said, and then her attention returned to Daniel. "You're a lot like her you know—gentle, kind... You even have her hair, but you have his eyes."

I squirmed in my seat, shifting uncomfortably, and gave a harsh clearing of my throat. "Heart-warming, truly," I said, "with just the tiniest dash of awkwardness."

Daniel shook his head in disapproval. "Ignore him," he said. "He's always like this."

"Yes," I said, all attitude, "ignore me. It's what he always does. I swear, the kid has no respect."

"You're a demon," Aunt Suzie reminded me, as if that explained it all away.

"But I'm still an elder, and you should respect your elders."

Daniel, of course, just did what he was good at and completely ignored me, choosing to continue on with eating his breakfast instead. I swear, that damn kid... if he wasn't so damn likeable, I would have killed him by now.

4

Charlie

The library was as peaceful as ever, the perfect retreat when my mind was full. Usually, I could spend hours upon hours there, walking between the dark wooden bookshelves that stretched up at least a good foot or two above my head, or sitting at the tables set right towards the back. It was exactly the kind of library I imagined would be in a place like this, this being an old monastery hidden in the grounds behind the All Saints Church that the Occultus used as their front.

There were very few modern-day amenities in the church or monastery, with only one television located in the common room on the ground floor. It was like stepping back in time, using candlelight to wander through vast hallways that felt empty and cold. Luckily, the bathrooms weren't so outdated. If they had been, I doubted I would have survived the first week. As for everything else, it was easier to forget about it when I came to the library to read. It was a haven for me. With how much my life had changed so drastically in the last year, this small escape made it easier for me to embrace it, even if only a little. The books reminded me of the ones we had found at Coulby's place, most old and leather bound, thick with dust, a musky scent lingering on pages that hadn't been turned in years.

We'd only met Coulby briefly in our search for the Occultus. Daniel found his name in the Harkanian's database, and we caught up to him in London. Sometimes I wondered if he would still be alive if we had gotten there a little sooner or if we had kept an eye on him. There were so many questions I would ask him, most involving the books we had 'borrowed' from his apartment as we fled. One of those books stayed by my side, quenching my thirst for knowledge and helping to distract me from my new life, allowing me to embrace it, even if only a little.

But today... today I just could not concentrate.

It was all Daniel's fault. Damn him. I glanced toward the scribbled letter on the table in front me and cursed him again. He had left it for me the morning before and had disappeared without a trace. I should have known. In fact, I think I did, at the back of my mind. It was only a matter of time. It was just... I was supposed to be with him when it happened. Now I was trapped here alone.

"Daniel Jayden," I pushed out under my breath, hard and unforgiving, "when I get my hands on you, I am going to kill you."

He had spoken about it, going after the demon responsible for his dad's death, but I'd told him it wasn't time. Serena and Nate had left us here, with the Occultus, for our own protection. It wasn't ideal. But they had risked so much for us. How could we let it all be for nothing? To leave and go on some wild goose chase? It wasn't safe.

"It will never be safe," Daniel had said. And I knew he was right, but still...

God, it was just so frustrating. How could he just leave me there? Damn him.

"Just you wait, Daniel," I said, leaning back in my seat and looking up toward the high ceiling that I could barely even see in the dim light of the candlelit library. I ran my hand through my hair and sighed at the shortness of it. I still wasn't used to it.

After about a week or so of being with the Occultus, I decided it was time for a change and had cut and dyed my hair. Where there had once been long curls of blonde, now there was choppy short mahogany hair. Before, my fingers would get tangled in the mess of it all, but now, with the new cut barely reaching past my chin, they didn't have the chance. It was all part of the new lifestyle. It served a dual purpose—to help me embrace my new way of living, but to also protect me from anyone who might recognise me.

It wasn't just demons and angels we had been running from. The police were still hunting me down. Sure, the media coverage had died down, but my face had been all over the news the previous months and there would always be that one person who looked a little too close for a little too long. That's what happened when you murdered your boyfriend in cold blood. They didn't care that he had been possessed by a demon and had tried to kill me first. They didn't believe me.

But it was amazing how much a new haircut could change the way you looked. I barely recognised myself in the mirror some days. Hopefully that would mean others would have the same trouble. If I didn't look like the girl on the news, then no one would have a reason to call the police simply because I walked into a shop to buy a coffee and a pastry. Not that I really got the chance to go out. The Occultus were too careful for that. They had been entrusted with our care, and they took that very seriously.

"Ah, there you are, Charlie," came a voice from up ahead, and I lifted my head to see Aiden approach with a bright smile on his face. Since the day we had met him, he had always been the one we went to whenever we needed something. He was kind and softly spoken, and he quickly became the member of the Occultus we trusted the most. "There's someone I would like you to meet."

He beckoned me to follow him, leading the way toward the entrance to the library until I could see the woman that stood there. I took her in with a deep breath. She was imposing from the air about her to the way she held her body, tight shoulders held high, back lean and straight, and the muscles of her arms clear with the sleeveless black shirt she wore. Her height matched Aiden's easily, which was not an easy task. Thick black tattoos took up the place of hair on her shaved head but given the darkness of the library and the darkness of her skin, it was difficult to make them out properly from where I stood. Even so, I could tell they weren't there simply for decoration. It was my first time ever seeing her but I sensed everything about her had a purpose. She struck me as that kind of person.

"Charlie," Aiden started, "this is Sister Myka. She was eager to meet you when I told her about you and your curious nature."

Myka nodded, looking me up and down, but even though her steady gaze never left me, her next words were directed at Aiden. "I had heard you had taken charges."

Her voice was deep, thick with a foreign accent I couldn't quite place, which only served to add to her mystery.

"We offer them protection," Aiden answered with a nod.

"Even if they do not wish it for themselves?"

Where Aiden's gaze was soft, Myka's was not. She had such hard features and such piercingly dark eyes that I found myself intimidated more by the look of her than I had been by many of the demons I had encountered the year before.

"You mean Daniel," Aiden breathed out, his shoulders sagging a little.

"So the rumour is true? The boy decided to leave?"

"This life, locked up inside here, is not for everyone. But we continue to offer Charlie protection for as long as she wants it, and of course, access to the library and books. She is extremely eager to learn all that she can."

Myka merely nodded, once more looking me up and down before turning her attention toward Aiden. "Well, I believe noon is approaching and my stomach is eager for food. We will surely speak later."

Aiden bowed his head politely. "I look forward to it."

And with that, Myka gave me one last cursory glance—or glare—and strode off in direction of the kitchens. I got the feeling she didn't like me very much.

"Who's that?" I asked, moving forward, my gaze still following the direction Myka had gone off in.

"Sister Myka—she's not as scary as she looks," Aiden said, always one to try and make me feel comfortable. "She comes seeking refuge."

"From what?" My mind raced. Demons? Angels? Something else altogether? There were so many mysteries in the world, and I had barely scraped the surface.

"The cold," Aiden answered.

I frowned and looked to him. He must have seen I was less than impressed by the answer, not that I was trying to hide it.

"We often get different members passing through, and when they do, they stop and rest here awhile."

"So, she's not from here?"

Aiden shook his head. "The Occultus is a network of people. It's the only way we can work efficiently. It makes it easier to hide what must be hidden. If one location is discovered, we can move the item—or the people—to another."

"Like the thing buried at Finchale Priory," I mused, gaze cast downward in thought. I often wondered what had been hidden there and had even gone as far as to question Aiden on it in the past, but he claimed he didn't know. Part of me believed him. In fact, the larger part of me did. But there was still that small part of me that was suspicious, the part of me that was used to people hiding things.

Aiden placed his hand on my arm, drawing my attention to him once more. I blinked and looked up, staring into his face almost blankly, barely even seeing it. "Something's troubling you," he said, imploring.

I shook my head in denial. "I'm fine."

"His absence bothers you," he continued. "I'm sure Daniel had your best interests at heart."

"He still should have spoken to me instead of leaving me a stupid letter." I groaned and tried to shake my irritation, but it was going nowhere.

"You're wanting to go after him," Aiden said, no question there, just statement. Was I that easy to read?

"He's an idiot, an idiot that'll get himself into trouble," I argued.

"And if you left, then you would both be in trouble," he argued right back. "It's still dangerous for you both out there. When Serena brought you to us, she explained the situation, and though you both may no longer be the hot topic of the demon world, you are both still at risk."

"Which is why he shouldn't have gone by himself." Even though I knew it wasn't completely true, I also knew that for at least part of the journey, he wouldn't have been alone. Serena was bound to be watching out for him, and he had mentioned Nate in the letter, but still... I stood by my statement. He was an idiot.

"You cannot change his actions, and even if you wanted to, you have no means to go after him. Why upset yourself over something you can't change?" He patted my arm gently and took a step back. "Go back to your books, Charlie. Take your mind away from it. You might as well continue to soak up all the knowledge you can whilst you're here. I'll send someone up to fetch you when dinner is ready."

He didn't understand. He couldn't. He was in the place he was meant to be. But me? I was a canary trapped in a coal mine. Taken to a place I wasn't meant to be in for a purpose that wasn't truly mine. I would suffocate and choke long before those around me. Still, I relented, deciding it would be unwise to continue in battle, and nodded.

"I know," I lied, because the books weren't taking my mind away from anything at that time.

He nodded and I could feel him watching as I made my way back into the library. Rather than head straight toward the tables and the pile of books I already had spread out there, I took a detour to gather more. There were a couple of books on demons that I hadn't been able to carry along with the others when I had first gathered my materials earlier that day. Now that I was getting used to the index system used in the library, finding the books became easier, and this week I had been reading up on demons.

I pulled one out and flipped through it, then another and another, before deciding on a thick volume that had familiar symbols and names sprinkled throughout. Amon. Vassago. Dantalion. All names I had come across during my time with Nate and Daniel. My fingertips traced the symbol next to Amon's name, following the lines as I thought back to the same symbol I had seen on Nate's chest. That was where his shadows came from, the ones that all demons possessed.

Shaking the thoughts temporarily from my head, I closed the book and continued my way back toward the tables. When I got there, I found myself confronted with another brother. This one I didn't know as well as Aiden. His face wasn't memorable, and I normally would have just acknowledged him with a light nod, if he hadn't been holding one of my books up to his nose, staring into it.

"Hey! That's mine!" I couldn't help but call out. The library was beginning to become a little too crowded for my liking.

He jumped and dropped the book. It fell from his grasp and hit the table's edge with a thud before landing on the floor with an awkward ruffle of pages. When he bent down to pick it up and dust it out, I couldn't help but notice the stiffness in his movements, deliberate and precise as he placed the book back on the table and patted the front cover, ensuring it was closed and all neat and tidy.

"Interesting book," he said, head cocking to the side.

I moved forward, closer to the desk so I could start to gather my things. "Yes, it is."

"Where did you get it from?"

It was one of the books from Coulby's apartment. I enjoyed looking through them from time to time, despite already having read through most of them several times. "From a friend."

He huffed out and stuck his hands into his pockets, bobbing his head toward me and the book. "Pretty knowledgeable friend," he said.

A tight smile slipped onto my face. "Not knowledgeable enough."

"Oh yeah?" he questioned. "And why's that?"

"He's dead."

He had no answer to that, which allowed me to gather the rest of my items into my arms, including the book. I was turning away and moving off before he spoke again. "You ought to be careful," he said. "You wouldn't want to end up like your friend."

I ignored his jibe and continued on. It wasn't until I knew I was out of his line of sight that I felt I could relax. But just because I was out of sight, it didn't mean I was out of earshot. He spoke to someone I hadn't seen, voice hushed like he was trying not to be overheard.

"Do you think she knows?" he questioned, and he sounded agitated, worried.

It made me pause. I must have heard him wrong. I was just being paranoid. Being left alone with them, it was making me suspicious of them all.

"She doesn't," said the second person, this one female. She sounded more confident than the man, but there was still an edge of worry.

"But the boy..."

"What about him?"

"What if they know and he's gone for help?"

A cold shiver ran down my back, spreading out across my skin, causing goosebumps to dance across my exposed forearms. The words had me wondering why Daniel would ever need to go for help. I knew he hadn't, because there was no danger... but the way they spoke set me on edge.

"You think he would have left her here? No, they don't know."

"But the book..."

The book...? I looked down to the mentioned book, still cradled in my arms. What about the book?

"She likes to read, that's all."

What were they talking about?

I chewed at my lips, trying to steady my thoughts enough to actually act. Something wasn't right, and I didn't like it. Without Daniel here, there was only one other person I could go to. Aiden. Taking a deep breath, I rushed out of the library and headed to the stone staircase that led back down into the monastery. As I neared the bottom step, I was sure I could hear footsteps out in the corridor beyond and I hoped they were Aiden's. But as I rushed out the door my jumper snagged on the handle, catching me off guard and causing me to curse. By the time I managed to free myself, the footsteps were gone, but I pushed on regardless.

"Aiden!" I tried to call as quietly as I could, but when you're both trying to draw attention to yourself and not draw attention to yourself at the same time, it was awkward. I didn't want the wrong people to hear, or the wrong people to see. Aiden though, Aiden I could trust.

I pushed on after him, chasing him down, unable to stop myself from tripping on a slightly raised part of the slate flooring. I fell with a clatter, knocking over one of the metal candle holders as I went, books and papers falling from my hands. I hissed in pain and could already feel the throbbing in my wrist, my knees feeling suddenly wet, but I didn't stop to investigate my injuries. I would take stock later on. For now, I had to catch up with Aiden. I had to tell him what I had heard and show him the book. He would know. He would help.

I shoved Daniel's letter into the back pocket of my jeans and grabbed the book, leaving the rest of the stuff laying where it had all landed. They were unimportant right now. What mattered was the book and getting to Aiden. I rushed forward again, my footsteps heavy on the stone floor, and threw myself around the next corner, feeling my heart quickening. There he was, at the end of the hallway. Just within range if I shouted now.

I opened my mouth to do just that, but before anything could come out, before I could take another step, a hand over my mouth silenced me. A second hand gripped my arm and pulled me back into the shadows of an open and unlit doorway. I tried to struggle against the grip, but the owner of the hands was large and strong. Far stronger than I was.

"Quiet, girl," she ordered in that deep and powerful voice of hers, forceful and just as strong as her grip. She pulled me backward until I was completely within her grasp, unable to escape. But even as I tried to scream, I could still make out Aiden down the hallway. So very close but so far away.

If I had just been quicker...

"Brother Aiden!" a voice called out, and Aiden turned to face the owner.

I couldn't see their face, and I never got to hear their name as it died on Aiden's lips before he even got a chance to say it, the beaming smile on his face dying too. Having a dagger shoved into your abdomen would have that effect on a person. My heart dropped, my world spinning, my body freezing up at the sight of Aiden. When my senses returned, I tried to fight the grip my captor had on me so I could rush forward and help, but she wasn't giving in.

"I'm sorry, brother," the other stranger down the hall said, pulling the dagger free and allowing Aiden to fall to his knees. "You would have gotten in the way. It's easier this way. More merciful."

I tried to call out, but my voice was just a muffle behind those fingers. The tears were already stinging at my eyes, my throat threatening to close up in anger and grief. I could barely believe it, expecting to wake up at any moment to find Daniel shaking me from what had to be a bad dream. But it wasn't, and the only hands holding me were my captors as she leaned in close, so her voice echoed in my ears and my ears alone.

"If you want to survive, you must trust me. You are no longer safe here."

5

Nate

It was getting on towards noon before we were on our way to the Harkanians and their headquarters out in the middle of nowhere several miles outside of Manchester. Stanhurst. A village where time stood still. I would swear down on my life the town had not changed one single iota since we had passed through it the months before. I had a pretty good memory for stuff like that, and it made me wonder if anyone actually lived there or if it was just some weird model village designed to look lived in. The only thing that *had* changed was the weather. Whereas before, the snow hadn't yet hit and autumn was still in the air, now it was a winter anti-wonderland. Slush and mush, a messy winter disaster waiting to happen.

But... we weren't interested in Stanhurst.

We were interested in the large office building, that wasn't really an office building, beyond the town and in the outskirts, just a mile or so down the road. A familiar feeling began to stir in my stomach as we made our way through the twisting back roads, passing field upon field of snow that had built up. Dread, anticipation, a tiny ounce of trepidation, and the burn of adrenaline. I was uneasy, I would admit that, but I couldn't deny the small element of excitement at the thrill of going into battle once more. Okay, so maybe not battle, but... it got boring sometimes. I guess, I just didn't realise how boring it got until Daniel and Charlie showed up in my life.

"So, what's the plan?" I asked, turning in my seat enough so I could face Daniel.

He focused on the way ahead, attempting to navigate the car through the snow laden roads. "We go in, we search their files, we get out."

"You make it sound so easy."And if it sounded easy, then it would never work. My luck wasn't good enough for that.

"It is," he said, but I sensed hesitation.

I waited a moment in silence for him to continue on, to explain. When he didn't, I raised an eyebrow and gave a roll of my hand to encourage him to go on. "But?"

"There's just one small problem," he finally admitted, and how I wish he had brought that up beforehand.

"Problem?" I questioned, taking a brief breath. "Which is?"

"We need to find a way in."

Right. Yes. I could see how that would be a problem. Not necessarily a small one. More like, a pretty big damn problem, considering the entire plan hinged on us being able to get into the building in the first place. Given the way it was locked down, we couldn't just crack open a window and climb on through. Last time we had used a security card to walk straight on through the entrance, no problems—small or big. Getting out had been what had caught us out.

"And why can't we just use your father's pass?" I asked, looking out at the road ahead. We were nearly there, and he was only just informing me we had a kink in the plan.

"They might have tagged it," he said, as if admitting something that he wasn't proud out. Yes, it was him who ate the last cookie. Yes, he had taken the money without permission. Yes, he had neglected to tell me about this ahead of time, when we could have come up with another plan in plenty of time.

"Tagged it?" I closed my eyes. "Which means *what* exactly?"

"When we used the pass before to get in, the system would have logged it. They knew who I was, and they would have checked the log to see if that was how we had gotten in. It would be a pretty huge oversight on their part if they didn't connect the dots."

"Maybe they're just not that smart," I offered up.

He looked less than convinced. "They probably deactivated the card as soon as they found out."

"And if they didn't?"

"Then, they tagged it."

"Which means?"

"If we try to use the card, it'll probably set off an alarm and they'll know we're in the building."

"Great..." I sat back in my seat, sinking into it and gazing out into the snow. "But I suppose you have a plan ready, right?"

Silence.

"Daniel?"

"You're the demonic criminal," he finally said after another long moment. "I was kind of hoping you would come up with something."

"That's your plan?" I asked, and when he didn't answer, I saw it was fit to repeat it. "That's your plan?! As far as plans go, that's a pretty damn shoddy one. Petty theft, a few picked pockets here and there, a little bit of murder every now and then... not breaking and entering."

"I was thinking more just entering, no breaking."

"That's worse!"

"You could, I don't know, possess someone? Get them to open the door then knock them out? That could work?"

"That *could* work? No. No way. That's not happening. I told you before—I don't do possessions. That sort of stuff—it makes you feel dirty. No. Nope. I draw the line there. If that's what you're wanting, then you either come up with another plan or you turn this car around and we get our asses out of here before we get caught."

In the next moment, Daniel was pulling the car over to the side of the road. When we had come to a stop, he pulled the handbrake up and into place and turned to look at me. "It could be the easiest and quickest way of getting in quietly and undetected."

"I don't know if you know this, Danny Boy, but possession?" I started. "Not easy."

He let go of a breath and I could tell, even before he spoke, that he wasn't giving up. "People get possessed all the time."

"Here's the thing about possession—you have to be susceptible to it. If you're not, then it could take years of whispering and shadows on your back for possession to actually work. Why do you think hunters train themselves so much to keep their minds strong? The stronger the mind, the stronger the will, the harder it is for them to get possessed."

"What about Coulby? He was a hunter. He was barely out of the room for less than a minute and he got possessed."

I rolled my eyes. "Coulby," I said, thinking back to the runaway hunter who had been more than just a little skittish when we had met him, "was a paranoid wreck."

Daniel went silent there, sullen almost. His gaze fell downward, away from me and toward his lap instead. I could see the cogs turning in his mind, but I didn't expect what he came out with. Perhaps I should have done, given the circumstances, but the kid had a gift for taking me by surprise.

"And my dad?" he asked, words bitter and hard on his tongue, each one forced out and seeping with barely concealed anger. "Was he a paranoid wreck too?"

I looked Daniel over and contemplated my answer, taking a breath before speaking. "I didn't say that."

He cast me a side glance. "But it's implied right?"

I shook my head, but he wasn't having it. He wasn't convinced.

"That's what you meant, right? When you said I might not like the answers I get? That's what you meant..." The anger died down and he worked his jaw, his knee bouncing from frustration. It made me think back to the last time we had faced the Harkanians. As soon as they had mentioned his father, his eyes had darkened. It was a sore subject for him, and I could see he felt a need not just to get justice for his father, but to prove his innocence—his strength. "They all think he was weak..."

"But you're going to prove them wrong," I said, part question, part statement. "That's why you're here—to find out what really happened and how it happened, right?"

"My dad was the strongest man I know." And I could tell he wanted to go on believing that.

"The demon that possessed him? He could have been at your father's back for months, or it could have been something else. If the Harkanians were involved in his possession and not just his death, then... then you don't know the real circumstances. You could be talking rituals, forced possession... That's dangerous stuff, and if you're outnumbered, it doesn't matter how strong your will is."

He gripped the steering wheel tighter and lowered his head against it, eyes closed from what I could see. "I'm not doing very well, am I? If my dad could see me now..." He let go of a long sigh, his grip tightening for a fraction before loosening again. "We've come all this way, *I've* come all this way, and I can't even think of a way to get inside."

"Actually, there's plenty of ways of getting in," I said, earning myself a raised eyebrow from the kid. "The problem is getting in without being caught."

"Which doesn't help us, at all..."

"Unless we plan for being caught."

He paused, eyebrows burrowing as he looked at me. "That doesn't make any sense."

"Let's just say they've tagged the pass but haven't deactivated it, how long will it take for them to track us down? I mean, it's a pretty big building and it's Christmas day. Even the Harkanians have to celebrate religious holidays, right? So that's an advantage... Less manpower."

"But we don't know what type of security system they have in place. We got lucky last time, and if they learned their lesson, we might not be as lucky this time."

I thought about that for a moment, but to me, a security system consisted of a few alarms and some cameras. How hard could it be? "Okay, so worst case scenario? What are we talking?"

"Security cameras, motion sensors, really loud alarms—and that's just from a human perspective. They could have demon traps and barriers built in, set to trigger if any alarms go off."

I nodded my head. "And how would they access all that?"

"The cameras and such? On site probably so they can get to it quickly, possibly through whatever network connections they have running throughout the place."

"And if somebody from outside wanted to delay their response... maybe set up a few false readings, would that be possible?"

He shrugged, frustration clear. "I don't know, maybe?"

"And if somebody really wanted to get inside, would they at least try?"

He let go of a breath. "Nate..."

"How much is it worth the risk?"

He chewed at his lip in contemplation but didn't answer right away. When he did, he adjusted himself back into a driving position and put the car back into gear, releasing the handbrake. "This isn't going to work," he said, but that meant he was willing to try it.

"All we need is time, right?"

"I hope you're right."

"Well, that makes two of us, Danny Boy."

*****

Turns out, they hadn't deactivated the security pass, which either meant, they were as dumb as I thought they were, or they were expecting us to come back and had left it open as a trap. The latter was the most likely option. We got into the building easy enough, no alarms blaring and deafening us. The next step was to find a computer connected to whatever network the security system was on. It was mostly above my head, so I let Daniel worry about all that. He was the one with the smarts for computers.

Unlike last time, there were security cameras dotted about here and there, covering the hallways and making it extremely difficult to move about unseen. That was where I came in. A little push of my demonic powers and those security cameras would be seeing nothing but snow. It was all about electrical interference. I had never bothered to truly learn the inner workings of it, but even demons were bound by rules of physics. Some of us were just better at controlling it and bending it to our will.

We made our way as quickly and as quietly as we could through the fluorescent lighted halls and toward one of the computer rooms. It was strange seeing the building more decorated than the month prior when they had been giving most of it a makeover of some kind. The rooms were no longer empty shells with plastic sheets covering the floors and ladders propped about here and there, and loose electrics and paint tins, the usual mess and dust you usually found at such a worksite. Now it actually looked like any other office building you would come across. That was just the surface of things. It was the floors below that held the real treasures of the Harkanians. I had only truly been privy to a library turned warehouse of mystical goods and treasures that the hunters had collected throughout the years. That had been where the Occultus was supposed to be, back before we discovered that *it* was a *they* and not just a magical amulet.

We entered the room and I shut the door behind us before also closing the blinds on the glass panelled window. He was already at the computer, booting it up and tapping his fingers on the desk impatiently as it seemed to take an eternity to click and tick and whir into life.

"If this doesn't work," he started, and I could see he was bouncing from the apprehension and adrenaline running through his system.

I didn't let him finish. "We run like hell."

He snorted, sparing me a glance but quickly returning his attention to the computer at hand. I had seen him work several times, quick and efficient, every move deliberate. He was certainly better with computers than he was at exorcising demons, both of which was a benefit to me. It left me wondering idly though, if he had improved any since his time in Scotland. Charlie, I had no doubt, was probably brushing up on as much as she could. She was new to our world. Daniel? He was more experienced... in that he had been here longer.

So far so good. No alarms. No flashing red lights strobing up and down the halls alerting the hunters to our presence. But that didn't mean they didn't know we were there. They could have just been biding their time. I moved to stand behind Daniel, looking over his shoulder at the computer screen. None of it made any sense to me.

"Well?" I asked.

His fingers worked deftly, and he continued clicking and pressing buttons, his eyes locked on the screen, even as he spoke to me. "The silent alarm tripped as soon as we opened the door. They know we're here."

"Ah..."

"They've got motion detectors all over the place and the cameras... It's crazy. They've gone security mad on the place."

"But?" I was really hoping there was a 'but'. I was praying for one.

"I've cut off the security cameras, so they're blind. They can't see us that way."

"And the motion detectors?"

"That one was a little trickier." He pulled back away from the computer and turned to look at me, the faintest of smirks sitting at the corner of his mouth.

"Was?"

"I set off a few false alarms. The corridor leading to the warehouse and the one leading to the file room. That'll be where they expect us to go."

"Yeah," I said, raising an eyebrow at him. "I was kinda expecting the same thing."

He motioned to the screen and what looked to be a very rough map. "I've knocked off all the sensors along here, the offices on the second floor. As long as we're careful not to get lost, we shouldn't trip any more alarms, and they'll hopefully be so busy chasing down the other two spots that by the time they realise, we should be gone."

"I just have one more question—what's on the second floor?"

"David Atkins." Okay, more of a who than an actual what, but I'd take it. "I recognised him when we were here before. He was mentioned in my dad's notes."

"And you want to interrogate him?" I asked cautiously, thinking back to the two hunters we met last time we snuck into the place. I wondered idly which one was Atkins. The exorcist or Mr Trigger Happy. The way Daniel's nose twisted up at the name, my guess was the exorcist. He managed to get right under the kid's skin.

"Not him. His computer."

Well, that made more sense.

I gave a nod. "Then lead the way."

And he did.

The corridors were pretty empty, and we only had to duck into a room once or twice to avoid the sound of oncoming voices. There was no panic in the air, which made me wonder what the Harkanians were up to. I wasn't ignorant or blind hopeful enough to believe they didn't know we were there. So, what were they playing out? By the time we reached the office, my paranoia had tripled at, and I was on edge, waiting for the walls to start closing in or something of the like. But none of that happened. In fact, I almost allowed myself to believe we were safe.

Almost.

"So, explain to me—why couldn't we check his stuff on the other computer, if all the stuff in here is linked on a network?" I clicked the lock into place on the door when I shut it this time. We didn't know how long we would be, and it would be best if we weren't suddenly disturbed by a surprise visit from Atkins.

"Not everything is shared over the network." He looked to me with impatient eyes. "Don't you know anything about computers?"

"I know how to switch them on."

He simply shook his head and took a seat behind the office desk, getting to work on the computer. I kept watch by the door. Mostly. I admit, I did find my eyes wandering every so often around the office and at the gadgets dotted about here and there. It was mostly ornamental, but there was also some pretty serious weaponry hidden beneath what looked like just pretty and fancy decorations.

"So, Atkins," I started, "he's the one Charlie shot in the leg, right?"

"Yeah," Daniel answered, distracted, but still attentive. "That's the one."

"And your father had notes on him?"

"He had pictures and notes on a few different ones—Atkins was one of them."

"And the other guy? Atkins' partner? Did your dad have notes on him too?"

Daniel shook his head. "Not that I had seen."

"Right..." I let go of a breath and looked around once more. Well, that confirmed my thoughts then. The exorcist, and not the kind you'd invite to your neighbourhood barbeque for a good old natter. All of the stuff in the room was meant to kill or maim demons in anyway shape or form, it wasn't just there for show. It made me shiver. Sure, demons are stronger than humans, but with the right weapon, you could pierce right through the shell and into the soul—and that, that hurt like hell.

"Nate," Daniel said, after another few minutes of quiet, "do me a favour..."

I looked to him and moved forward. "What do you need?"

"Look around the desk and the drawers for a USB stick or something."

"A what?"

He looked up at me and blinked, not once, but twice, then let go of a heavy sigh and began searching himself. "Never mind."

It took a few minutes of rummaging, but it seemed his search turned up successful and he was plugging something into the computer below the desk. I just watched with curiosity. My guess, the kid had found something.

"And now you're...?" I started, waiting for him to finish the statement for me.

"Transferring a few files onto the stick. Some of them are encrypted, and some are too big for me to look through them here thoroughly. I can get a better look at Aunt Suzie's." He pointed to the screen, so focused on it that he wasn't probably even aware I had joined him around that side of the desk. "There's a list here of names. I think they're hunters. My dad's name is on the list and then there's this other name... Felix Ravenwood. I know that name from somewhere."

"Huh...?" I pondered, looking at the names. "Felix Ravenwood."

I had to admit, the name sounded familiar to me also. Probably a stage magician with a name like that, but still, it scratched at the back of my mind like an impertinent itch. A memory began to stir, but it fell away again before I could grasp a hold of it fully. No. It was gone, and I was shaking my head.

Out in the hallway, the loud ring of an alarm started, and I narrowed my eyes at Daniel and the computer screen. "What did you do?"

He shook his head and pushed up from the seat a little, straining to see the window in the door. "Nothing... that's a fire alarm."

"A fire alarm..." I repeated, and now I could hear something else. Water. "Forgive me if I'm wrong, but doesn't there usually have to be a fire to set off sprinkler systems?"

I made my way toward the door and opened it up as Daniel finished at the computer. Great. Well, I guess that answered the question of whether or not the Harkanians knew we were there. "Holy water..." I breathed out.

There was no escaping that way. Not now. Daniel could, sure, but we both knew it wouldn't be a smart idea to split up. I cast a glance backwards toward the window on the other side of the room. It was probably breakable, but whilst I could no doubt get down from the second floor unscathed, Daniel wouldn't have the same luck.

Damn...

"You know when you said about planning for getting caught?" Daniel said, coming to stand beside me at the doorway. He knew it was holy water. He had worked it out too, without needing to see it burning through my skin. "This wasn't what I had in mind."

"Of mice and men," I muttered beneath my breath, my gaze searching for another solution. The door was out. The window was out. My eyes moved up toward the ceiling. It was the old-style panelled ceiling that a lot of office buildings had—made it easy to access wiring and such.

Daniel's mind, however, was on other things, his brow furrowed as he looked between the hall and the office. "How come there aren't any sprinklers in here?"

"Take a look around," I answered, half paying attention to him and half to my wandering thoughts about the panels in the ceiling. I climbed up onto the desk and tested the panel above it. "Half of this stuff has demonic properties. Throw on some holy water, they won't work as well anymore."

The panel was heavy, but after a few pushes, I managed to budge it and create a large enough gap to crawl through. With a heave, I pulled myself up enough to see how much crawl space we would have. It would be a tight fit for sure, and with all the wires here and there, it would be tricky, but if the panels remained sturdy enough, we could make our way out of Atkin's room at least and maybe closer to the stairs, providing the walls didn't block our way.

"You're not serious, are you?" Daniel questioned, joining me by the desk.

"Got any better ideas?" I waited for him to answer, and when he didn't, I pulled myself completely up into the dark of the crawl space. Some light made it through, making it so I could just to say see ahead and where to go.

"And once we're up there, where do you plan on—" But his words died away, and I felt my heart sink.

"Jayden's kid, right?" came a familiar voice from the doorway. Atkins.

I heard Daniel fumble, saw him reaching for his gun, but a gunshot from another gun had him stilling. I cursed beneath my breath.

"Play it smart, kid," Atkins said, and I imagined him to be aiming the gun at Daniel. "Where are the others?"

"There are no others. It's just me."

"You're a bad liar, kid. Who were you talking to?"

"Myself..."

A scoff, harsh and disbelieving. "Come on down," Atkins called out, "and I won't shoot the brat in the leg." He went on to add, a little lower, directed toward Daniel, "I owe you that much after what your girlfriend did."

There was no space for me to formulate any kind of attack from where I was, and if I couldn't see the hunter, I couldn't hurt him. I didn't have a choice but to play along. I lowered myself onto the desk, making sure to face the doorway. Atkins stood alone, gun in one hand trained on Daniel, radio in his other, and a sneer upon his face.

"Anyone else up there?" he asked, looking me over.

I offered up a dry smile. "Why don't you check for yourself?"

He gave a dry chuckle. "You're a comedian, huh? We could do with a good laugh. Gets a bit boring around here sometimes." He motioned to the ceiling with his gun, the threat clear. He would open fire. "Now, one last time—is there anyone else up there?"

"No," I answered tightly.

He didn't shoot, apparently accepting my answer. Instead, he lifted the radio to his mouth. "You can shut off the works. We've got two guests coming down for a chat."

Within the next moment, he swapped his gun for another one tucked into the waistband of his trousers, and the sprinklers out in the hallway slowed to a nerve-grating drip, drip, drip. It was in that moment I saw my opportunity to strike. I pushed out with my powers, aiming to send Atkins flying backwards with enough force to hopefully knock him out.

It didn't happen.

My face must have betrayed my attempt and lack of result because he was grinning and tapping the carpet covered floor with his foot. It had me wondering what lay beneath it, but at the back of mind, I already had an idea. A suppression circle. It couldn't trap a demon, but it could neutralize their powers.

I didn't even have time to react before he pulled the trigger of his gun. I was aware of immediate pain in my chest, a sharp sting followed by what felt like fire spreading out through my veins, and I was aware of Daniel immediately grabbing for me and of the world slowly beginning to fade away with a fizzle and a pop, my body growing heavy and numb. Then it was gone, and blackness took hold.

6

Daniel

My reactions weren't quick enough to stop Atkins from firing at Nate, nor were they quick enough to stop the bullet from hitting him. Except, once I turned to look at the damage, I realised it wasn't a bullet at all. No blood spread out across Nate's shirt, and Nate was going down too fast for a regular shot to the chest. Bullets hurt but didn't kill. A tranquiliser dart, though? Depending on the potency, that could put a human or demon out for the count real fast, and the quicker their blood was pumping, like say if adrenaline was rushing through their veins like wildfire spreading across a too dry forest, then the quicker the drug would work.

Nate was out before he hit the ground, which meant whatever was in that dart was strong. The one and only time I had ever been part of drugging a demon, it had taken almost twenty minutes to start working, and that had been enough drugs to knock out a large animal, like a bear or a lion. I went down with him; hands tightly gripping his arms in an attempt to slow his descent. It barely worked, and by the time I recovered enough to remember to fight back, Atkins was at my side, lashing out with the butt of his gun. The sharp pistol-whip to the head sent me down again, dazing me enough to slow my reactions even further.

"You should have stayed away, kid," Atkins taunted, lowering himself to his haunches and gripping me by the scruff of my neck.

I tried to fight back, tried to go for my gun, but before I could even reach for it, I felt the sharp sting of a needle in my neck. Combined with the sharp pain already growing at the side of my head, whatever drug Atkins had just injected into me was enough to put me on my back... but not completely out. It seemed that would be too kind. My vision blurred, my head swam, but I was still aware. I could still hear the movements around me, even if all I could make out were blurred shapes.

"Take them down to the visitor centre, we're going to have ourselves a good chat," Atkins said, his voice sounding both deafening and faraway all at once.

I tried to push up, but my body was numb and far heavier than I remembered it being. Firm hands gripped me, fingers digging in painfully to the muscles of my arms as I was hoisted upwards and dragged forward. I lifted my head enough to see them pulling Nate along too and was thankful for his sake that only his feet trailed along the floor soaked with holy water, his boots offering him protection from the stuff that would no doubt burn straight through his skin if he was exposed too long to it.

"It was a nice try," Atkins whispered beside me, and I blinked, turning my head to look at him, taking in the twisted sneer upon his face. With the drugs in my system, I swear his teeth were like razors, his smile spreading up to his ears and then outward further, his eyes a swirling darkness that tried to drown me. "But you shouldn't try to play with the big boys."

"Scr—ew you," I pushed out, the words barely louder than a breath. It drained me so much just saying those two simple words, so when he gripped my hair tight, yanking my head upwards, I barely even felt the pain.

"Manners, boy," he spat at me. "Manners. Didn't your coward of a father ever teach you that?"

Even the anger that boiled at my blood and caused my heart rate to spike wasn't enough to give me the strength to fight back. It made him laugh in such a harsh and bitter way to see me struggle, to see me attempt and fail to fight back.

"Don't mind them, Natty," whispered another voice, all calmness and tranquillity. It was like it spoke directly in my head, and as it spoke, my world waivered. We weren't in the hallway anymore but waiting in front of a lift. That was when I realised the drugs were really kicking in. I was fading in and out, and Atkins continued to grin at me like a manic crocodile.

"Remember what I told you?" the other voice continued, a hint of excitement in his words. *"About the time Father fought that dragon..."*

Another lapse of time, my own distorted reflection staring back at me from the metal of the lift doors as they closed and we began to descend.

"How he swung the axe again and again and again until he chopped off its head?"

The lift jerked and jolted, and I floated, stuck somewhere between reality and dream, fading faster and faster as the darkness blinkered in and out of existence.

"That's how he met Mother. Remember, Natty?"

By the time the doors opened again, I didn't have the strength to open my eyes let alone hold my head up anymore. All I knew was that we were moving again, footsteps echoing through empty corridors, my body heavy and growing heavier by the second.

"The dragon wanted to eat her, but Father, he was the only one who stood up against it." There was a smile on the voice, tainting each word, making them come to life inside my head. *"So don't mind them, Natty. You and I know the truth. Father was the bravest man in this whole village."*

And I was gone.

I couldn't have been sure how much time had passed before I was waking up again, but one thing I was sure of was that I was getting tired of people drugging me. Unlike my aunt, however, the Harkanians hadn't laid me on a couch in front of a fire with a blanket covering me to keep me warm and comfortable. No, they tied me to a chair in a cold, dark room, rope tight around my wrists and ankles.

I groaned and lifted my head, trying to take in what I could through the blurred vision and darkness. A light hung somewhere above on the high ceiling, but it was so dim that most of the room was still covered in shadows. The only other person I could see was Nate. He sat in a chair opposite me, bound to it like I was, a large circle painted in white on the floor beneath him, the patterns within it barely visible in the dim light. I squinted and focused a bit more, taking him in and looking more closely at the chair. It was actually nailed to the ground, offering him no movement. It made me take a look at my own chair which wobbled slightly when I tested it.

So that was how it was. This was a room designed for a single demonic occupant. An exorcism chamber if I was right. My dad had told me about them, but he had refused to show me. I was too young, he had said, and besides, it was something he never wanted me to see. It was a side to hunting he wished I would never witness. Well, unfortunately for him, his wish wasn't going to come true. They had brought in the extra chair, just for me. A front row seat. My stomach turned over at the thought, a cold shiver running over my skin.

"Nate," I whispered in the harsh type of whisper meant to be heard from some distance, but only by the intended target.

He didn't stir.

"Nate!" I tried again, louder this time.

Nothing.

"Nathaniel Godwin!"

He grunted and began to move, slowly at first, but he was waking.

"Come on, Nate," I continued. "Time to get up!"

He lifted his head and looked around, no doubt taking in his surroundings just as I had done. When his gaze turned to me, I could see the frown there and the wince of pain he tried to hide. "What did I miss?"

I snorted and shook my head. "Remember that plan?"

"And which plan would that be?"

"The one where we planned in advance for getting caught?"

A slow smile crossed his lips. "Oh yeah, that one..."

"Well, we got caught." I watched him as he slowly pulled himself around and back into reality. "And drugged."

"That explains the bad taste in my mouth and the fact my head feels like it's stuffed with fluff." He went to lift his hand to his head, then looked at it accusingly when it failed to move from the arm of the chair it was tied to. "Well, this sucks."

"You think?"

We didn't have a chance to continue our conversation, the door opening and spilling further light into the room. Two people entered, one large and bulky, the second shorter, who walked with the slightest of limps. I didn't need to see their faces to know it was Atkins and his partner. They closed the door behind them and moved closer, choosing to stand in such a position so both Nate and I could see their faces. Atkins held a book and wore a wicked grin, whilst his buddy loomed beside him, weapon concealed but there, of that I had no doubt.

"Going to interrogate us?" Nate asked with a cocky smile and an air to his tone. He relaxed in his chair, chilling there as if he wasn't tied down. "'Cause I gotta tell you, I don't know much. And the kid? He's a wet towel."

"Think of it more like returning the favour," Atkins answered, teeth on show like a predator waiting to strike. I could tell he meant the leg, and most probably the damage to their reputation also. That had probably taken a hit the previous month when we had broken in and managed to escape. "I figure we owe."

I could feel myself tensing up. I couldn't play it off like Nate could. I couldn't pretend it didn't get to me.

"And what better way," Atkins continued, patting his book as he spoke, "than by teaching Jayden's kid how to do an exorcism?"

So, I was right. This was an exorcism chamber.

"Oh, really?" Nate asked, and how the hell could he be so calm about it? They were going to exorcise him! They were going to send him back to Hell.

"It's about time the kid learned a few things from a real hunter," Atkins answered.

"And what?" I spat out, fighting against my restraints but all in vain. "You're going to teach me?"

"Somebody has to," the other hunter said, and he made me feel just as sick as Atkins did. "Running around with demons? After what happened to your father?" He shook his head. "And to think, you were supposed to be his legacy."

"I'm sure he would be proud of you," Atkins picked up where his partner left off. "You're just like him after all. He liked to play with demons too."

"Shut up," I forced out, gripping at the arms of the chair. "You don't know anything about my father."

Atkins snorted. "Who do you think performed the exorcism?"

My heart dropped, my entire body sagging for the briefest of moments. Then the fight began to stir in me again and I rocked back and forth in the chair, writhing at the ropes keeping me bound, desperate to be out and to be at him. "You son of a bitch!"

He looked to his partner and bobbed his head toward me, and the second hunter moved forward until he was behind me. I heard the scrape of metal then felt the cold bite of it trace the line of my jaw before coming to a stop at the skin of my neck just below my chin. I stilled instantly, the threat clear.

"First, we'll send your little pet back home, then when we're alone, we can really get down to business." Atkins straightened his back and turned his attention away from me and toward Nate instead. Again, my stomach clenched, and I found myself wanting to shake my head in denial but the blade at my throat was a sharp reminder that I was as helpless as I had ever been.

"Nate," I called out, and even I could hear the desperation in my voice, "do something."

He sat up straighter and stared the hunter down, giving a small flick of a smile. "What would you suggest, Danny Boy?"

"I don't know, fireball him or something..."

He closed his eyes and lowered his head a little. He already knew it was useless. When he opened his eyes again to look at me and then at the circle beneath him, I began to understand. "Would if I could... but as long as I'm in here, no superpowers to help me escape."

"You're a demon!" I all but screamed, feeling the bite of the blade cutting into my skin as my throat bobbed and tensed.

He just smiled at me.

Atkins chose that moment to start his little exorcism. As soon as the first stream of Latin words left his mouth, I could see Nate's face twisting up in pain. His jaw clenched, his eyes shut tightly as his head dropped forward. By the time the first verse was finished, he was panting heavily.

"Stop it," I said, voice hoarse and pained in my throat. "Please..."

The hunter behind me gripped my shoulder tightly, pressing the blade in closer, reminding me not to fight. But when the second verse started falling from Atkins' lips and Nate screamed out in pain, I felt myself hiss as I pushed forward, earning myself a slice across my throat.

"That the best you got?" Nate taunted when Atkins paused to turn the page of his book. He spat at the ground, and it wasn't until I noticed the red tinge across his lips that I realised it was blood. Still, he grinned at Atkins, awaiting his next moment of torture.

"Nate..." I breathed out, tugging at the ropes on my wrists. How could it have turned out like this? Where was Serena when we needed her? Damn it. Damn it. Damn it. I was screwing up left, right, and centre. This was all my fault, and unless I could do something, Nate would be gone... Because that was one of the things I had learned from my dad. When a demon got sent back to Hell, it could take them years or even centuries to find a way to crawl back out.

Atkins continued on and Nate was screaming again, back arching, muscles tightening, fists clenching. The Latin slipped from his lips so easily, each word another slash across Nate's soul. The pain was clear and Atkins just stood there, smiling as he read, as if he was listening to a babbling brook or crackling fire. As if it was the most serene song he had ever heard.

"Please," I called again, my stomach feeling like a ton weight had been dropped into it. Helpless. Guilty. If it wasn't for me… "Nate! Please, stop!"

But Atkins continued on. If anything, my cries and pleas only egged him on more. He made a sign of the cross in the air and moved closer to Nate, revelling in the pain he was causing. He paused a mere moment to allow a brief respite, as if offering up hope, knowing full well he would tear it away again.

"That it?" spat Nate. "What's the matter? Need to catch your breath? Must be your age."

"I was just thinking… I've never actually had a demon stupid enough to practically walk into an exorcism before."

"Guess I must be a masochi—" But Nate was cut short as Atkins began to close up with the last passage.

Another scream… Then nothing.

Silence.

The words were mere echoes now and Nate collapsed in the chair, lifeless. Nothing. He didn't move. Didn't writhe. Didn't speak or mock or groan. He just… stopped. An empty husk.

"No..." I breathed out. "That's not... It... No..."

Atkins moved forward until he was directly in front of Nate, lifting up his listless chin and forcing open his eyes. The whole time, Nate was motionless. Not even a flinch. When Atkins seemed happy with the result, that wicked grin returned to his face, and he turned his attention back to me.

"Really?" he said. "This is what you were using as protection? This pathetic excuse for a demon? I've seen more fight in a field mouse."

My jaw tightened as I regarded him. All the things I wished to say to him. All the names I wished to call him, all the threats I wished to spew. But I held it all back and leaned forward, allowing the blade to cut into me as I did so. "Why?"

"Why?" he asked, and when he did, he circled behind Nate, gripping a hold of his head on both sides. "You and your demon humiliated me. Your father, I could take it from—he may have been weak, but at least he was a hunter. You and your *pet*," he continued, pushing Nate's head forward and away from him as he spoke, "you need putting in your place."

The second hunter pulled at my head, grabbing my hair to yank it backwards, exposing more of my neck to the blade. "How do you want it? Quick and painless... or would you like the full works?"

"Screw you," I spat.

"Maybe you wanna go the same way as Daddy?" he leaned in closer so his breath was in my ear. "Screaming like a child."

Atkins chuckled, moving closer until he blocked my view of Nate. "You should have let your demon kill us when you had the chance."

"And what would have been the fun in that?"

Everything in the room froze then, including Atkins and his partner. The voice, the attitude. That was all Nate. Atkins slowly turned around to face the demon who now lounged in his chair, free of his ropes and most definitely in possession of his body. That was impossible to say the least.

"It didn't work?" the hunter behind me questioned, and I could feel the unease beginning to rise between him and Atkins.

Atkins clenched his jaw and unclenched it, adjusting himself. "Then we'll just have to try again."

Before he could begin reading though, the book flew from his hands, smashing against the wall somewhere in the darkness. Nate looked overly happy with himself at that and lifted his foot from the ground to reveal a newly scratched opening in the circle beneath him.

"Funny thing about magic circles," he said, and in the next breath, the hunter behind me was sent flying also, "they only work if they're whole."

"I don't need a book to send you back to Hell," Atkins spat out.

"Go ahead," Nate said, opening his arms out. "Try it."

The ropes around my wrists and ankles began to loosen, and Nate met my eyes briefly. As soon as they were loose enough for me to break free, I launched myself forward, tackling Atkins before he could begin the ritual again. His gun fell from the waistband of his trousers, skittering across the floor, and in the next moment, we were both chasing after it. I got there first, but only just, snatching up the gun and spinning on the spot quick enough to send a shot off and get him in the arm this time. He fell backwards in pain, shooting me a look of pure contempt.

Nate moved forward, coming to stand over Atkins. "Here's another funny thing—next time you try to exorcise a demon, make sure they don't own the body first. Exorcisms don't work if they do."

"That's impossible," Atkins hissed out, glaring at Nate with a hint of fear in his eyes.

"Just highly improbable," Nate answered with that smirk of his.

He swooped down and gripped Atkins by the arm, making sure to dig in around his newly formed bullet wound, and dragged him up from the ground. Atkins screeched and screamed, but he struggled to fight back, only able to writhe in Nate's grasp as Nate dragged him across the floor toward the chair he had escaped from. I didn't miss the wince of pain on Nate's face or the way he waivered only ever so slightly. He may have faked being exorcised, but the rest of it had been very real. I didn't mention it, not yet. That would be a conversation for later. So, for now, I pretended I didn't notice the exhaustion and the barely hidden agony showing in the tightness of his jaw.

"What are you doing?" I asked instead, pushing myself forward also, following him toward the chair. I cast a quick glance backward toward the other hunter, but he was out. He wouldn't be bothering us again anytime soon.

"Getting answers," Nate said, all but throwing Atkins into the chair and roughly tugging his arms into place. He wasn't careful in the way he wrapped the ropes around tightly, offering up a twisted and bitter grin when Atkins hissed in pain. "Oh, sorry," Nate said, feigning sympathy. "Was that a little too tight?"

Even as he asked the question, he pulled the rope tighter still, and continued to manhandle Atkins until he was bound to the chair just as Nate had been, and just as I had been bound to mine. Finally, he took a step back to admire his handy work.

"We should be getting out of here," I said, coming to stand beside him and looking toward the door. If someone heard us, we would be in even deeper trouble. I doubted we would be lucky enough to manage to escape a second time, which meant we had to take our chance there and then.

"You should listen to him," Atkins taunted, venomous tongue lashing out. "Because next time, we won't go so easy on you. You'll be screaming to be released from that body you've taken over."

Nate shook his head, and I took that as being directed at Atkins and me both. But it was Atkins he spoke to when he leaned forward, each hand on either side of the chair, gripping Atkins' arms and pushing them against the arms of the chair. "Do you really think you're the first hunter to try and exorcise me? The first one to threaten to do worse? You don't know what true pain is, so don't try to threaten me with your petty little words. They don't work on me."

For a moment, I could see Atkins' face paling. He fell still, very, very still, as if he was trying not to be seen by the predator in front of him. It was the cold calmness in Nate's demeanour that was the most terrifying. The way he leant just a little bit more on Atkins' injured arm. It was in moments like that that I remembered what he was. A demon. It was so easy to forget sometimes, when he moped around and acted childish and insolent, or when he was complaining about being bored, or when he offhandedly talked as if he cared then went on to deny it or act like he was just being curious and that was all. He could be so very human... but this, right here, was not one of those times.

"You're going to die," Atkins forced out against the pain and clenched jaw.

"We've all gotta go sometime," Nate answered, "and right now, it's not looking so good for you."

"Nate..." I tried to say, but my words went unheard. He was completely focused on Atkins, staring Atkins down and refusing to break eye contact.

"You were there," Nate said, more statement than question, and it took me a moment to click onto what he was talking about. "What happened to Alan Jayden?"

Atkins scoffed and tried to laugh, but the laughter quickly died, turning into yet another screech of pain as Nate dug his thumb into the bullet wound. The screech only died down when Nate pulled back just enough to give Atkins room to answer, but no more.

"I was just part of the clean-up crew," Atkins answered, and there was an air of smugness about him that made me sick. "By the time I got there, the worst had already been done."

"What happened?" Nate repeated, and I found myself no longer fighting for his attention and for us to leave quickly. I wanted to hear this. I wanted to know.

Atkins grinned and leaned forward. "I wouldn't know. All I know is the stupid son of a bitch got himself possessed and we had to put him down. You want the rest of it, you should speak to someone who was there before the bloodshed started."

Bloodshed? I felt my own blood run cold.

"Give us a name and we'll go speak to them," Nate continued.

Atkins considered us both for a moment, looking me up and down before doing the same with Nate. "I'll give you a name," he said, and the words were like grease, sly and dirty, sliding from his mouth too easily. "And when you find him, you can be sure to tell him hello from me."

"Who?"

"Francis Shay." Atkins grinned.

Shay. I repeated the name in my head. It couldn't be the same man we had met down in London, the one who ran the antique shop that wasn't really an antique shop, the one with a demon for a bodyguard, and the manners of a shark. It was just a coincidence. But, from the look in Atkins' eyes, I knew it wasn't. Shay had a certain effect on people, and I could see that he had certainly had an effect on Atkins.

"Why are you giving us his name so easily?" I asked, cautious.

"Slick bastard cost me a week in the hospital. Seems right I repay the favour." He ran his tongue over his teeth and let go of a dark chuckle. "Way I see it, if he kills you or if you kill him, it doesn't matter to me—either way I'm better off. Maybe I'll get lucky. Maybe you'll all kill each other."

"And maybe you'll die of blood loss first," Nate threw in, digging into the wound one last time for good measure before pushing away from Atkins and making his way toward the exit. We had what we had come here for, a piece to the puzzle. It wasn't much, but it was something. It almost made the whole ordeal worthwhile.

"One last thing, kid," Atkins called out. "Keep your pet on a short leash because one day, he'll turn on you, and when he does, you'll be begging me to put him down too, just like I did with your dad."

I stared at him a moment longer but held my tongue. I wouldn't rise to it. I wouldn't. So, I turned away and continued on after Nate instead. The sooner we got out of that place, the better.

7

Charlie

"Find the girl!" a strong voice called out.

Heavy footsteps followed the words. My body was numb, my mind completely at a loss. My captor dragged me further backwards and into the dark of the room beyond the doorway. When we were safely inside and the door was shut tight behind us, she removed her grip on me and looked me over. I was free to run away, free to escape, but I found I no longer wanted to. I stared at my captor instead. Myka, the woman from the library. She still wore that same imposing look, the dangerous one that made me shrink back into myself a little.

"We need to move," she said, turning away from me and walking toward the other end of the room.

It was then that I began to take in my surroundings, my eyes adjusting to the darkness and shadows. We ended up inside a random vestry, the room filled with an assortment of bits and pieces—books, scrolls, unused and broken crucifixes. The window was but a slit, too narrow for someone to crawl through, and even if it hadn't been, the height would have been enough to put someone off from escaping that way. We were trapped, and Aiden had just been murdered.

"No, this is wrong," I said, shaking my head, unable to stop myself looking backward toward the door. This was supposed to be sanctuary. We were supposed to be safe here. "The Occultus are meant to be the good guys."

"The Occultus are men," Myka answered, tone sounding as if she had little patience for my words. She stood by a cupboard several feet away, emptying it of the random bits and bobs stored inside the cramped space. If she expected me to hide in there, well—something told me it wouldn't work. "It is as capable of corruption as any other order."

"Corruption?" I questioned. "What do you mean, corruption?"

"I mean, *girl*," she said, without even looking at me, "they decided to sell you for their thirty pieces of silver."

She pushed against the boards inside the cupboard and tapped and knocked until finally something clicked, and I heard wood scrape against stone. She turned to face me then and held out her hand.

"If you wish to live, we must move now, unless that is, you wish to be found?"

I huffed but moved forward all the same, accepting her help with minimal gratitude. For all I knew, she wanted to kill me also. It seemed it was an effect I had on people. When we passed through the opened slot in the wall behind the cupboard, she pulled out a lighter and lit a torch on the wall, pulling it from its place before shutting the way behind us.

"I didn't know this was here," I said, referring to the secret passageway.

"Not many do," she answered, already leading the way ahead and down a set of steep steps that had no end in sight through the darkness.

"Then how come you do?"

"I spent a summer here when I was young, and my tutor was strict. When I was hiding from him one morning, I stumbled across an opening—one of many. It made me explore the church and I mapped out every last passageway and opening I could find." She came to a sudden stop and held her finger up to her lips, indicating for me to be silent.

I held my breath and strained my ears. I could hear faint noises through the walls and pressed my ear closer, the stone cold against my skin. The voices were muffled, but they were urgent. How many of them were there? How many brothers and sisters of the Occultus were looking for me?

When the voices and footsteps began to quieten, growing distant once more, Myka pushed on again. She held the torch out in front of her, the flame low but enough to lighten the walls. The steps ended, and we walked along an uneven dirt pathway instead, the gap so narrow we had to move sideways. Myka ran her fingers along the walls, and it was another minute or so before she came to a stop again, but this time she didn't quieten me. She held the torch close to the wall, illuminating the scratches that looked nothing like words to me but more like random squiggles. She seemed to understand them though and nodded.

"This is the one." She dipped the torch down, rolling it in the dirt covered floor until the flame went out. She took a breath, then pushed. Slow and cautious. A small amount of light broke through a gap in the wall, and she made sure to go first when the gap was large enough for us to pass through.

"Come," she said when it was safe, and I followed obediently.

She strode down the corridor with a purpose, stopping at each intersecting hallway to look around each corner before continuing on when it was determined to be clear. I found myself looking around constantly too, listening for even the slightest of noises. From what I could tell though, we were reasonably safe.

"I hope you do not have anything of value in your room as you will not be able to return," she said, still focusing on the way up ahead.

I thought about it, but the answer was no, I didn't. I hadn't had anything of value since my world had been turned upside down, when the police locked me up on the fourth floor of St. Matthews hospital when I had explained to them that I hadn't killed my boyfriend. It was a demon. After escaping, I had been on the run without a single item of my own to my name. I had my clothes, sure, but they were unimportant and replaceable. The only real things I kept with me was the letter from Daniel and the book still held tightly in my grasp, almost as if my hands were unwilling to give it up.

"Why are you helping me?" I questioned, deciding the subject needed to be broached before we went any further.

"I have no need for silver," she answered, no hesitation at all, "and all the need to stay true to what it means to be an honourable woman."

She held up her hand just outside the doorway that led to the kitchens. I could hear the voices inside, the words only just audible.

"Sister Lorelei, the girl? Has she been down this way today at all?" asked one voice, strained but trying to remain calm and offhanded, like the question was merely one of curiosity.

"Charlie?" Lorelei asked, tone as chipper and bright as ever. "Not since breakfast. Why? What's happening?"

"Nothing," the other voice said, a pang of aggravation hidden under that one word. "Perhaps you should retire for the day? There's an unrest about the place and it would be a shame for you to get caught up in it."

"Unrest?" she questioned, a light laugh there, but it quickly died, and when she spoke again, the words were dulled. "What have you done?"

"Nothing you need concern yourself with, Sister Lorelei."

"There's blood on your shirt..."

"Is that a problem?"

Silence for the briefest breath. "I suppose it's best I retire after all."

Shuffling followed the voices and Myka gripped me, pulling me away from the doorway and out of sight behind a cabinet, just in time as the door opened and Sister Lorelei emerged, a second shadow creeping across the hallway floor beside hers.

"I don't need an escort," she said.

"For your own safety, Sister."

She didn't argue and started at a slow pace down the hall and toward us and our hiding spot beside the cabinet. Another couple of steps and she and her escort would be able to see us. They didn't make it far before Lorelei was clucking her tongue and stopping in her steps.

"Oh drat... would you look at that? My shoelace came undone." She let go of a light breath and the shadows paused in their reaching. "Just give me a minute..."

I went to close my eyes and take a breath, but Myka's sudden movements had my eyes shooting open again, my gaze following her. She pulled something from her belt, a long tube-like thing, and put it to her lips as she darted out from the hiding spot and outward so she could see Lorelei and her escort. One quick blow followed by quick and silent steps, and she was moving again. I peeked around the corner of the cabinet to see the escort falling backwards, only to be caught by a fumbling Lorelei. Myka helped her lower him to the ground silently and she leaned forward.

"My keys are on the rack by the door," Lorelei whispered, the words only audible as I hurried closer to the pair—that was when I also saw the small dart sticking out of the escort's neck. "They're the ones with the rabbit's foot. You want the green Ford over the street— my little Toby. You'll know which one when you see it." She pushed up from the ground and turned to me, gripping my hand. "Be safe."

"You should leave before they know you helped us," Myka offered up, still as stoic as ever.

She shook her head. "I will not allow their betrayal to destroy the rest of us."

And then she was gone, off down the corridor, leaving us to our escape.

"They will be waiting," Myka said in hushed tones, her hand on the door to the kitchen ready. "Are you prepared?"

"I'd feel better with a gun," I answered honestly, because whilst I didn't revel in the idea of shooting someone else, I did like the idea of being able to defend myself.

"Let us hope you do not need one," she said in return. She bowed her head, motioning that now was the time to act.

She pushed the door open and entered first, her blowpipe at the ready. I followed with just enough time to see another man fall from a dart to the neck. That left two others in the room—the one with blood on his shirt and a second, somewhat squatter man. Both turned their attention to us and were moving instantly. There wasn't enough time or distance for Myka to use her blowpipe again, so she met the squat man with a left hook that sent him sprawling across the work surface. I didn't get to see what happened next, the one with the blood coming straight for me.

Aiden's killer. I knew in my heart I was right, and when I saw the knife still in his grasp, I felt anger bubbling up inside of me. My gaze flickered quickly between him and the door leading to the outside world as my mind tried to come up with a plan. Fight or flight. He held up his hands as he approached, then slowly placed the knife of the countertop well out of my reach but still within his own.

"This doesn't have to be difficult," he said, taking another step forward until he was barely a foot away.

"Of course not," I answered, eyeing him with caution. Daniel had taught me a few things, but I was by no means an excellent fighter. Capable maybe, but nothing more.

His hand shot out, gripping my wrist tightly and causing me to drop the book. He pulled me into him, forcing me around so my back was to him as he tried to push my hand up. I threw my head back and heard the satisfying crunch as my head made contact with his nose. I hoped it was broken. The shock had him letting go and I ducked down to grab the book. When I came back up, he was already recovering, blood beginning to seep from his nostrils, and I lashed out firmly with the book. It cracked him across the jaw, and I prayed it hurt him like a son of a bitch.

I didn't wait around to fight any further, launching myself forward instead. The door was waiting for me and freedom with it. I could hear him recovering, hear him quickly giving chase. By the time I reached the rack of keys and had spotted the right set, he was breathing down my neck, his hand reaching out to grab my hair to pull me back. His fingertips brushed against it, and I spun around in time to see him being dragged back by Myka. Then he was being thrown over a worktop to go crashing into a wall of plates.

"It's time we leave," Myka said, and I couldn't have agreed more.

I nodded and rived the door open, throwing myself out into the cold snow and forcing my feet to keep moving. Book in one hand, keys in the other. The way my heart pounded in my chest, it brought back memories of the months before. And to think we were supposed to be safe with the Occultus.

When we reached the car, I was out of breath, my chest tight and painful from the bite of the cold wind. Toby. It was the only green car there and the number plate kind of looked like it said Toby, so it had to be the right one. I leaned against the framework, allowing my head to fall forward onto the glass. Daniel had only been gone for a day. When he found out what happened, he was going to tell me I attracted bad luck—though more likely, that would be Nate's line. I felt a pang in my chest and found myself hoping they were safe.

"Girl," Myka said, gripping my shoulder to get my attention, "we cannot stop yet. We must leave before they can pursue us."

She held out her hands which I took to mean she wanted to drive. Part of me considered keeping the keys and climbing into the car alone to speed off somewhere safer, but she had just saved me. I wasn't entirely sure what she had saved me from yet, but she had saved me. My heart felt heavy in my chest, my mind going to Aiden.

My grip tightened on the keys, and I looked to Myka meeting her eyes. "You knew they were planning something," I said. "You could have helped Aiden. In the library, you could have told him what was coming."

"My presence had already aroused suspicion, speaking out could have caused more trouble," she answered, and it made me think of the other brothers from the library. The one whose behaviour had made me gather my things to leave and the other mysterious one who I had only heard and not seen.

I lowered my gaze, relenting, and offered up the car keys. She took them with ease and was inside the car and starting it up before I was able to shake myself from my thoughts. I didn't have a clue where we were going or what I was going to do next, so I clambered into the car and whacked the heating right up in preparation for the car warming up. There was no need for me to sit there freezing my ass off in indecision and uncertainty. I could do it quite well enough whilst warm.

"What now?" I asked, not even caring to look back at the church as Myka pulled away.

"Now we find somewhere safe to wait until we can come up with our next move."

"And I suppose you have somewhere in mind?"

"A traveller such as myself must always know the best places to rest."

8

Nate

As far as escapes went, it could have gone worse. I managed to make it all the way outside before I almost collapsed, and considering the holy water that still drenched the floors, I was thankful for that—my boots thick enough to keep my feet safe. We used Atkins' security pass to get out this time and we got lucky in the halls. As far as the other hunters knew, we were both tied up in the room downstairs and there was no escaping. They were in for a surprise when they opened up the door and found Atkins' a little tied up and his partner passed out, a crumpled heap against the far wall. It was about as much as they deserved.

Fresh air hit my face as we stumbled free of the building, and I made it one step further before my head began to swim a little too much and my knees gave out on me. Danny Boy didn't notice at first, too busy making sure we weren't followed, and if I had been able to catch myself, I could have passed it off and pretend it never happened. What he didn't know wouldn't hurt him. Too bad I never got the chance. I fell to the ground with a harsh thump, landing on all fours, the impact sending sharp jolts up through my body. Daniel was beside me in the next moment, one hand on my back and the other on my arm in an attempt to pull me up.

"Nate," he breathed out, all questioning and worry.

"I'm fine," I said, trying to brush it off. It might have worked if I hadn't needed his help getting back up. "I just tripped."

Over thin air...

"This is not fine," he said, pulling me upward and all but dragging me in the direction of the car. "You were coughing up blood and now you can barely walk."

"All part of the act," I lied.

He wasn't buying it. "That pain—that was real."

I tried to shrug, but I could barely even manage to lift my shoulder. "It was barely even a tickle. Seriously, I am fan-bloody-tastic. Haven't felt this good in..." But my head spun again, and I had to stop walking and close my eyes for a moment until it passed. "This is why the Vatican only uses exorcisms as a last resort."

An exorcism was the act of trying to pull away a soul from the body it resided in. In the case of demons, it was painful enough as they desperately clung onto each cell and atom in an attempt to remain where they were. The longer a soul was inside a body, the more the two began to fuse, and if the soul had been there since birth, the pain could be immense. If you tried to exorcise a soul that wasn't meant to be exorcised, it could create a tear in it. A dangerous thing to have in a soul.

Daniel was quiet for a moment, no doubt contemplating something. It was what the damn kid did best. When we started moving again though, I could tell he was getting ready to speak, but he held it in until we reached the car. "What happened back there?"

"He tried to exorcise me. He failed. End of story. Simple as."

"But it didn't work," he said, like it bore repeating. "Why didn't it work?"

I let go of a sheepish smile and shook my head, choosing then to climb into the car. "Funny thing that, right?"

"Nate," he reprimanded, climbing into the driver's side and then turning in his seat to stare at me. "What did you mean? You told him that exorcisms don't work when the demon owns the body. What does that even mean?"

"Long story short," I said, "I know a guy who knows a guy who knows a necromancer. And necromancers? They're pretty talented people. Did you know that back in the 1500s one necromancer alone almost wiped out an entire army? Now that's pretty powerful stuff."

But he just looked at me with a bored expression, unimpressed by my attempt at diverting the conversation. I coughed and lowered my head.

"What did he do? Evict the previous occupant and give you sole ownership?"

"*She* actually. And no."

"Then what? Demons don't own bodies. They just possess them."

I closed my eyes and thought about my answer and the number of ways he would take it the wrong way and call me sentimental or soft or any numerous amounts of insults. "Most demons were human once, Daniel. When they die, their soul leaves their empty husks behind and then on they go to their journey through Hell. I just chose to look mine up again when I finally resurfaced."

"So, your body... that's actually... You chose to possess yourself?" He looked at me with disbelief, and I could see his mouth working for a moment. "How is that possible?"

"With a great deal of difficulty," I answered, trying not to cringe at the spike of pain shooting through my chest. Having something try to tear your soul away from its body—painful to say the least. "Now, and I'm just wondering here, but are you actually planning on driving anytime soon? Or are we just going to sit here until they realise we're missing and come looking for us?"

It was his turn to look sheepish now and he turned his attention to the car and starting it up. I had the feeling he wasn't through with questioning me, but he chose to leave it for now and pulled away, so I took the opportunity to turn the conversation around, taking the spotlight away from myself and putting it on Daniel instead.

"How's your neck?" I asked, barely able to look at the red streaks marring the skin of his throat. The cuts weren't too deep that they were dangerous, but they looked painful and sore. Eventually they would heal, but they would leave scars, thin white strips marking his skin. My chest tightened painfully as I thought about how I could have prevented them if I had been quicker. Once over I would have been able to escape from being bound within a matter of minutes, but as with everything else, I had gotten lazy.

He touched the cuts carefully and winced, bringing his hand away and shaking his head. "I'll be fine."

"You sure, Danny Boy?"

"Barely even a tickle," he answered, mimicking my own words to him with the slightest of smirks.

I bobbed my head in appreciation. "Touché."

He swallowed whatever thick lump had been forming in his throat, his grip adjusting on the steering wheel. He was deep in thought again and trying to figure out a way to express those thoughts. I swear, the kid was going to be the death of me.

"What is it?" I asked, dry and bored, rolling my eyes and sinking into the seat some more.

"Shay," he said, and it was all he needed to say.

Shay. Francis Shay. It was a name I hadn't expected to hear again anytime soon, and I knew Daniel and I were both thinking the same thing. It wasn't a coincidence that the man we had met in London shared the same name as the man with answers regarding Daniel's father. That man gave me the creeps and I was a demon. But what I remembered most from our encounter was the hunger in his eyes, pure want and desire, and how those eyes had been so focused on Daniel. He wanted what Daniel had and he would quite happily use the kid to get at it. I wasn't prepared to let that happen. I had stopped one monster, so maybe I could at least hold back a few others for a while longer.

"Maybe we should focus on what you found on his computer," I suggested, attempting to keep myself in denial a little longer.

"That information could take days or weeks to decrypt and sift through, if it's even possible to decrypt it in the first place." He shook his head and glanced my way briefly. "And if we can decrypt it, for all we know it could be useless. Shay is a solid lead. And how do we know that whatever I find in all that data doesn't just lead us back to him anyway?"

"We don't even know if it's the same guy."

"He has a pet demon. He collects things with magical properties. He knew about Coulby. He's the guy. You know it, I know it."

"I just don't think it would be a smart idea to travel all that way and put ourselves in that sort of danger to turn up at his shop and go 'Hey, is your first name Francis by any chance?' only for him to turn around and say 'No, actually it's George—but whilst you're here, come enjoy a cup of coffee with my demon buddies and me.'"

"I can handle it, Nate," he said, earnest and true, and damn, was I really that easy to read? Was my worry for him that obvious?

"Charlie won't be with us this time, Danny Boy," I said in return. "She won't be there to tell us where their marks are."

He shrugged. "Well, we already know where Benji's is."

"That's one demon, out of countless others that Shay might be hiding. Not to mention Vassago—or did you forget that little detail? Never met him myself, but I hear he's a son of a bitch and then some. He's out of my league, that's for sure."

"Then what?" he asked. "We go back to my Aunt Suzie's and hideaway behind a computer screen? I need to do this. I need to know what happened to my dad."

I let go of a weary sigh, slumping forward in my seat and staring at my empty lap. "No," I relented, and I scrubbed a hand across my jaw, feeling the prickle of my stubble on my fingertips, "we go to London. But I still think it's a bad idea."

"How bad could it be? We ask him a few questions, we leave. What's the worst that could happen?"

"You really had to ask?" I said, sending him a sidelong glance, eyebrow raised. "Really?"

"What?" he asked, innocent and completely oblivious to the giant jinx he had just placed on us.

"I like your optimism, Danny Boy, but now you've gone and said that, the worst thing possible is going to happen. There'll be flying monkeys, maybe a hurricane or two—I wouldn't even be surprised if the earth itself opened up. You just can't go around saying stuff like that." I shook my head and relaxed back into my seat once more. "There isn't even any wood around to dispel the bad juju you just threw at us."

"You're just being superstitious," he tried to say, but even he was beginning to worry that he had just placed a massive curse on what could have been a simple mission.

"You're talking to a demon. One, who I might add, has had bad luck ever since meeting you and Charlie." I shrugged. "But you know, if you happen to hit a rabbit whilst driving, you might want to get out and cut off one of its feet—or maybe all four."

"I'm not going to cut off some poor rabbit's foot just because you feel unlucky," he said. "Go find yourself a four-leaf clover if that's how you feel."

"At this time of year?" I scoffed. "I'd be lucky to find a three-leafed one. No pun intended."

He shook his head and let go of a snort. "How bad can it be?"

But even as he said it, I could sense his doubt. He remembered what Shay had been like. It was a feeling more than anything. The way he made you feel dirty just by looking at you and the way his grin was akin to a crocodile, and his fingers like skeletal claws spread neatly out in welcome. He would eat you whole if you gave him half a chance. I didn't feel like giving him that chance. But Daniel was right, of course. He was our best lead, and I knew that out of everyone, Daniel would be the least enthusiastic to go back to that little antique shop on Haverstock Hill.

"He's only human," Daniel continued when I said nothing, the words forced out as if he was trying to convince himself of that truth.

Human Shay may have been, but he wasn't much of one. He may have still owned his own soul, but that didn't make him any less despicable or any less dangerous than someone who didn't.

"You think that'll stop him?" I asked.

Silence, for a long breath, then Daniel spoke. "No, not really."

"Just swear to me that if there's any trouble, you get out of there quickly." I watched him carefully. "Amon may be gone, but your gifts aren't. He wants to use you and you can't let yourself forget that."

"Nate," he started, and I sensed an argument on his tone and shook my head, cutting him off before he could go on.

"I mean it, Danny Boy—you leave. As soon as it starts, you leave."

He chewed his lip and cast me a glance before nodding his head in agreement.

"Okay," he said, "I swear."

And even in that moment, we both knew it was a lie.

*****

It was about a four-hour drive to London. Given the state we were both in and the fact we hadn't eaten since so early on in the day, it took us more like six—giving us a couple of extra hours to stop off somewhere and clean ourselves up, make it look like we hadn't just escaped from danger and that we weren't suffering because of it. For me, all I had to do was tidy myself up a little bit, straighten my clothes out here and there. All the little injuries healed themselves, some slower than others, but most of them were well on their way to disappearing before we were setting off again. Sure, I still felt weak and woozy from the attempted exorcism, but that too would pass in time. I just needed a good night's sleep, which would come soon enough—I hoped.

Daniel, however, well—that was the downside to being human. You didn't heal so quickly. Even after a bit of first aid on his most visible wounds, he still looked like he had just emerged from a fight. Every time I glanced his way, my eyes were drawn to the cuts across his neck. He didn't make a big deal of it, and he pretended he didn't see me looking, but we both knew Shay would take one look at him and eat it all up.

"Maybe we should rest first?" I suggested when we pulled up on Haverstock Hill, a short walk away from our favourite antique shop. With the time we had lost passed out under the Harkanian's watch and then the time spent travelling, it was nearing midnight and the prospect of visiting Shay so late at night wasn't one I looked forward to.

"We'd just be putting off the inevitable," Daniel answered. He didn't make any attempt to turn off the engine though, his eyes locked on the side mirror that reflected the faint image of Shay's shop.

"Who said that was a bad thing?"

"Nate..." A low, drawn-out warning.

I sighed in return and shook my head in defeat. "Fine. Let's just get this over with."

He nodded and turned off the engine, albeit with some hesitation. "That's my intention."

The cold winter air seemed to be even more biting when we clambered out of the car, and I pulled my coat around myself tighter. It did little to warm me, which probably meant it wasn't just the air sending a chill through my bones. Each crunch of a footstep closer to the shop was one footstep further away from safety. When we reached the door, that was when I knew there was no going back.

The lights were off inside, the sign on the door telling us the shop was closed, and you almost could have believed that no one was home. But looking closer, I could see a faint trickle of light at the very back of the shop, shadows moving across the floor. I placed my hand on the handle, fingers wrapping around it tightly before finally testing it. It opened with ease. The sign of a man who didn't fear thieves, or perhaps one who was expecting visitors. Maybe even both.

The bell above the doorway jingled as I opened the door further and we stepped on inside. It jingled again when I closed the door and by the time I turned around, Benji was there at the counter waiting to greet us. He stood tall and proud, ready to act and straight-faced as ever, but unmoving, not prepared to make a move without his master's say so.

"Please, show our guests the way back out," Shay's voice echoed through the shop from the small room at the back of the place, polite and in control, but distracted. "My meeting with Miss Undershaw is running on a little longer than I had thought."

Benji made to move forward but I held up a hand and stepped forward, speaking out before the demon could come any closer. "Then when would be a better time for us to return?"

There was no reply at first, just the sound of wood scraping across wood followed by footsteps. In the next moment, Shay appeared from the curtained off area with that wicked grin of his splitting his face. Just as I figured, he wasn't one to forget a voice, and he knew that with my voice, Daniel surely wouldn't be far behind.

"My boy!" he beamed, and those ice-cold eyes immediately locked on Daniel. He opened his arms out in welcoming and pushed forward. I resisted the temptation to step in front of Daniel and block Shay's view of him. Shay's interest in him could only work to our advantage, not to mention the small fact that Danny Boy would probably just get pissed at me anyway. "Would you believe that I found myself thinking about you and your gifts just this evening gone? Such a happy coincidence you find yourself at my door now."

"Mr Shay?" questioned a voice from the back, and a woman emerged with red bouncing curls for hair and piercing eyes that betrayed her age much more than the rest of her appearance. Those eyes found us for a mere moment before returning to Shay, her head held high, her lip curled in the corner impatiently. "Am I to take this to mean we have a deal?"

He turned away from us to address his guest, taking her hand and offering a half-hearted bow. "My dear, Miss Undershaw, given my sudden good mood, I will take your offer. If you give me a week, I will no doubt be able to procure the item you require. Until then, I believe we can call our meeting to a close?"

Her impatient smile grew satisfied and this time when she looked to me and Daniel it was with a shine in her eyes. By my guess, Shay's sudden interest in us—or rather Daniel—and his eagerness for her to be gone meant she had no doubt saved herself some money for whatever item she had been attempting to buy from Shay. "I do hope you don't leave me disappointed, Mr Shay." She took her hand back and gave her own little curtsey. "Until next week."

And with that, she was leaving.

She slipped by us like a breeze and was gone with only the briefest jingle of the bell. That meant Shay was all ours. The last time we had come here seeking information, we had learned very little, and in the pit of my stomach I wondered if this time would be any different.

"It is so good to see you again, my boy," Shay said, and he waved us inward, toward the curtained off area of the store.

I allowed Daniel to move ahead, following closely behind and keeping my eyes on Shay and Benji. As far as I could see, there were no other demons there, but that meant nothing. Just because you couldn't see them didn't mean they weren't haunting the shadows and hovering just out of sight. Some demons didn't possess humans, some preferred not to, and some preferred the freedom of moving from host to host. Given how the demon Shay had sent to keep an eye on Coulby had been, I wouldn't have put it past him to have a few more demons skirting around the shop like disembodied ghosts, keeping watch.

"Take a seat, take a seat," Shay ushered, busying himself immediately at the kitchenette area, just like the last time. "Your friend, Charlotte? Is she to join us later?"

I narrowed my eyes on him. He had been doing his research on us. Charlie hated her name, so there was no way he had learned it from us the last time we were in the shop. She was Charlie, not Charlotte. Blondie, sometimes, but mostly just Charlie. It made me wonder how much he knew about us now since we had last met.

"She didn't think it was worth her time," I said, offhanded, deciding it was probably best not to go into detail with a man like Shay.

"Shame," Shay said, but he didn't sound too let down. "Still, all the same—it truly is so good of you to come to see me once again. I gather this is not a social visit, which intrigues me. Either you have something you want to sell, or something you want to buy." He turned to look at us whilst the kettle boiled. "So, which is it?"

"Francis Shay," Daniel said, part question, part statement, the name thrown out there simply to see how Shay would react to it. He didn't disappoint, the corner of his mouth ticking upward, his head tilting ever so slightly to the side in intrigue. "You worked with the Harkanians."

Shay chuckled, and turned back to the kettle and cups, busying himself once more. "My dear, Daniel," he said, the name sounding sickly sweet on his tongue and used simply to say that he knew it, "you have it wrong. I didn't work with the Harkanians." When he faced us once more with the tray filled with goodies, his grin was ear to ear. "I *was* a Harkanian."

"Was...?" I repeated, narrowing my eyes on him.

He took his place at the table and motioned for us to sit too. Unlike the time before, neither of us argued, but Daniel made sure to keep plenty of distance from Shay. Benji took up his place by the doorway, arms folded over his chest like a bouncer outside some posh London club. I spied a copy of some Oscar Wilde novel on a counter near him and wondered if we had interrupted his reading session. The thought didn't linger though, as Shay began talking once more.

"I outgrew them," he said, preparing his cup of coffee and breathing it in. "It no longer benefited me to play along with their little games. Where I wished to advance, they remained stuck in their ways. Hypocrites."

"What do you know of a man called Alan Jayden?" Daniel asked, each word so carefully placed, his body stiff, his hand ready to go for his gun and his legs ready to push up should he need to.

"Your father?" Shay questioned, so bright and cheerful. He drank in the sight of Daniel before him, his eyes lingering on every last inch of him that he could see. "Yes, I remember Alan. You are so much like him, you know. I should have recognised you the moment I saw you." He bobbed his head. "He was a great man."

Daniel's hand tightened into a fist. It unnerved him, to hear Shay talk about his father. It probably ticked him off. But we had little choice. If we wanted answers, we had to listen. Shay took a sip of his coffee and closed his eyes, revelling in it. We waited. When he was done with that sip, he placed his cup on the table, unconcerned that neither of us had touched the two cups he had placed on the tray for us.

"You wish to know about the circumstances involving his death?"

Shay asked, all pleasant and forthcoming. Eager and knowing. If he really had researched us and had learned of who Daniel was, he had no doubt been expecting a visit from us eventually.

"And you're going to tell us?" I asked, drawing his attention off of Daniel, if only for a short while.

The smile on his lips irked me. Smarmy. "I will tell you anything you wish to know."

"But?" I questioned.

And there it was. The catch. It sat on his tongue, hidden behind his wolfish grin, all teeth. "I'm a businessman, Nathaniel Godwin. It would serve me no benefit to provide you with such information without getting something back in return. You, of all people, should understand that. You and I, we make deals. We offer up our services for something in return. It is how we survive in this world."

"And what is it you want from us?"

"Your services, nothing more."

"For what?" Daniel asked, and he looked like he wanted to be sick from simply asking the question.

"There is something I wish to procure. The owner does not wish to sell it and my demons are unable to get close to it. Try as I might, it remains out of my reach. If you could help me, then perhaps in return, I could help you."

9

Charlie

Back on the run again. I slumped in the passenger seat and stared out of the window at the passing scenery. Given the darkness that had set in, there wasn't much to see. Part of me was angry with Daniel for leaving me there with all that, and part of me wished he was here with me. A familiar face I could trust would have been good right about then. Myka came across as being trustworthy, and she had saved me from whatever that all was, but I didn't know a thing about her. For all I knew, she was taking me away from the frying pan and right toward the fire.

"Who were they working for?" I asked, without looking her way, my mind still thinking back to Aiden and the way he had sagged to the floor, like a discarded doll.

"I'm afraid I cannot answer that," Myka said, and it felt so cold. There was nothing about her that screamed rescuer. It was like she was completely devoid of emotions. Even Nate had shown his caring side, no matter how much the demon tried to hide it. Did that mean Myka flat out didn't care, or was she just better at hiding it?

"Can't answer?" I asked. "Or won't?"

I looked to her, studying her profile carefully as she focused on the road ahead. Nothing exterior betrayed her inner thoughts. Her muscles didn't tighten, her hands didn't clench at the steering wheel or relax, and her face remained so still that it was like looking at a photograph or statue, not an actual human being.

"There are things even I do not know," she simply said in return, and that made me snort. It implied a sense of all-knowing, as if she thought herself smarter than everybody else. Maybe she was, or maybe she was just as full of it as Nate was.

"Then what do you know?"

"I know they wished you harm," she said. "Your friends placed you in the protection of the Occultus for a reason and I intend to hold up the honour for which we stand. I cannot rightfully allow those who are easily corrupted by promises of silver and power to tarnish the name of the Occultus once more."

That got my attention. I narrowed my gaze on her. "What do you mean, once more?"

She glanced my way briefly, but quickly returned her attention toward the dimly lit road ahead as it took us past empty fields and overgrown hedgerows. "You have no doubt heard the legend of the Occultus, have you not?"

"Actually, no. Not really."

"The legend says a wise king once enlisted help from a group of magi to hide away his greatest treasure," she said, and maybe she did know a few things. "They created an amulet known as the Occultus, the Hidden, to hide this treasure from the evils of the world. Over time, the amulet was lost to the world, and the treasure remained hidden for years to come."

"But the amulet isn't real," I said, huffing out and sinking further in my seat. The amulet was just a hunk of metal with no special powers that the real Occultus wore, like Christians wore crosses and the Jewish wore the Star of David. It was a symbol.

"Neither are all legends. More often than not, they are mistruths and half facts. The truth is the Occultus existed long before the story. They went by many names over the years, and travelled through many places, but their mission remained the same. Their secrecy allowed them to pass by unnoticed by the majority, mere stories to be told by campfires. The less people who knew the truth of their existence, the better they could do their job."

"Which is keeping things hidden?"

"Exactly," she said.

"What does that have to do with tarnishing the good name of the Occultus?"

"An old king did indeed enlist the help of the Occultus to hide a treasure," she said. "His one and only daughter. His country was gripped by war and the kingdom around him was falling, but he desired to keep at least one part of it safe from his enemies. For five long years the Occultus kept his daughter hidden, and still the war waged on. His enemies attempted to bribe the order, but they stood strong. They gave up their own lives to protect hers, just as it should be. Until the fifth year."

"They took the bribe?" I asked, surprised at the interest lining my words. I didn't even realise how on the edge of my seat I had become, how tense my body was in reaction to her story.

"One man was all it took. They sold her whereabouts for land and a title, and the king's enemies moved in immediately. Many brothers died that night, and the young girl, a mere babe, was slaughtered in her sleep." Her head fell forward a fraction, eyes downcast. It was the first sign of emotion I had seen her wear. "The order was banished from the kingdom and their story became mere legend. Since then, many have sought to restore the name of the Occultus. But there are those who care more about restoring their power. Greed and pride can twist a person's heart into an ugly thing and make them do terrible things."

"Likes the ones back at the church?" I questioned.

"Precisely."

I sat there for a moment longer in silence before speaking again, barely even daring to look at Myka. "How did you know? About them coming for me, I mean."

"I keep my ear to the ground and know others who do the same. It pays to have connections."

"But how much does it cost?" I wondered idly, not really meaning to say the words aloud and certainly not expecting an answer in return. All the same, I got one.

"Sometimes nothing," she said, "and sometimes, far too much." She straightened in her seat, craning to see the end of the road up ahead, and then bobbed her head. "This is it. This is where we will spend the night."

"It is?" I questioned, squinting into the darkness outside the car. I couldn't see anything beyond what the headlights of the car hit. There were hedgerows and trees and then, the closer and closer we got, the more I could make out an opening up ahead, with a dirt road leading away from the typical tarmac road we were currently travelling on.

Myka turned onto that road, focusing on the dimly lit way ahead, and from there it didn't take long before I saw the iron gates left open and the large, gothic building that sat behind them. It looked like something out of a horror movie, disused and forgotten, no lights on inside, no warmth, just a looming cold shadow of disarray and loneliness. I wasn't the bravest person in the world, but I wasn't a coward either. That said, even I had my limits. I knew demons existed, and angels too, and with that in mind, who only knew what else lay out there in the world. Looking at the building in front of me, as Myka parked the car, I was beginning to think maybe ghosts existed too. If they did, there was no doubt that this building had a fair few of them.

"What is this place?" I asked, and nope, my voice did not quiver. Not in the slightest. Nope. No. Not my voice.

"It was once a hospital, but as with many, it fell into disuse when it no longer lived up to code."

"Did people die here?"

"More than likely."

"You say that like it means nothing."

I barely noticed her looking at me with a furrowed brow, I was too focused on the building and its overbearing gloominess. I swallowed the thick lump in my throat and looked to her, trying to school my features, but I was nowhere near as good at it as she was.

"Does death bother you, girl?" she questioned, as if she was almost surprised by the thought of it.

"Death, not so much," I answered, casting another nervous glance up at the building. Did I just see the shadows shifting in the upper windows? "Ghosts, though... they bother me."

"Ghosts are but shadows of lives once lived. The world is filled with them, and this place will be no different." She climbed out of the car and closed the door without another word, as if what she said was meant to comfort me in any way at all. It still didn't change the fact that the building we were about to enter looked about as haunted as old Victorian buildings came.

"There's no such thing as ghosts," I muttered under my breath, gathering myself together. I hugged the book to my chest and climbed from the car also, slowly, very slowly, trailing after Myka and up to the old building. "How long are we going to be here?"

"Until the morning," she called back, already at the large entrance, the double doors made of a dark wood that looked sturdy and old. "Then we shall move again before we can be tracked down."

"And that's the plan?" I asked, following her through the door she held open for me and into the large open space of the building. "To keep on running?"

"To keep you hidden," she said in return, closing the door with a thud and a clack. "*That* is the plan."

Her deep voice echoed around the emptiness of the large hall that looked about as tall as it was wide. It was barren, lacking furniture and furnishings. The light fixtures looked like they might have blown up if ever switched on, and the paper on the walls had all but peeled away, graffiti lining so many of the walls—a range of words and pictures drawn about the place in a wide range of different colours.

"This way," Myka said, drawing my attention away from our surroundings and back to her instead as she headed toward the back of the room.

I followed in silence, taking everything in, as we turned left into a stairwell and went up two levels before coming out on a long corridor that looked just as badly done to as the entrance of the old hospital. The wind whistled and howled through the empty spaces and every little skitter and scrape sounded like ghosts and ghouls, watching and waiting for us to drop our guards. An abandoned wheelchair down the corridor had me pausing for a moment as I considered the straps on the arms and legs. The sight of it held me in my place. It brought back memories of the hospital room I had been placed in the few months prior for that brief period of time.

"What type of hospital was this?" I questioned, tension rippling through my words.

"An old one," she answered, pausing only briefly to spare me and the wheelchair a glance. "I believe this floor was where they treated those ill of mind."

"Ill of mind," I repeated with disdain, hating how that sounded. "You mean the people they thought were crazy."

If I had lived in the times when this hospital was open, I would have found myself on this floor earlier that year, being subjected to whatever inhumane tortures the doctors believed would cure these people. I wasn't crazy and I doubted many of the people who had visited, and perhaps died on, this floor would have been either. People had strange and dangerous methods for dealing with things and people they didn't understand.

Myka continued on, ignoring my words and ignorant to my inner thoughts. She finally stopped outside one of the rooms and held the door open. "In here."

I took one look at the room and shook my head. "No."

"It is only for one night."

"That's not a room, that's a cell."

"There is no lock on the door, at least not on the outside."

I looked at the door in question, taking note of the lock. It struck me as strange, I had to admit, that the door would have a lock for the inside and not the outside. Surely it should have been the other way around, to stop people getting out, rather than in.

"It is a safe room, girl," Myka said, moving on in despite my refusal to enter it. She moved about inside as I watched from the doorway, pulling a mattress down from where it leaned against a wall to reveal a small hole which she reached into. When she pulled her hand back out, she was holding a bag. "The supplies will see us through until morning, then we will move onto another place."

"Supplies?" I had to admit, I was curious. I took a step forward, chewing on my lip, but I still couldn't enter the room.

"You can remain out there if you wish," she said, "but I assure you, you will be much safer and much more comfortable in here."

I was in no eager rush to go back into a room such as the one before me. The claustrophobia I could already feel, just from standing in the doorway, was almost paralyzing. I had faced demons, and here I was, afraid of ghosts... and a room.

"If it helps any," she said, and she sounded almost amused as she held up a small bar of something, "I have chocolate."

"Well then, that just makes everything else fade away," I answered, each word and syllable dripping with thick, acidic sarcasm. I was no fool that would turn down chocolate, but given the circumstances, the thought of it didn't exactly give me the extra push I needed to enter the room.

I imagined what Nate would say if he could see me now. He would mock me for sure, and Daniel, he would comfort me. He would find a way around it, so I wouldn't have to enter that room. He would put himself out so much that in the end, I would give in and cross the threshold. I closed my eyes and took a breath. It took me a moment, but I got there. I pushed my feet forward and I stepped into the room. I didn't feel any less claustrophobic, but the door was still open, which meant I wasn't trapped there.

Myka set up a place on the mattress, spreading a blanket there before dragging a large metal canister over to it from the nearby wall. "Make yourself at home," she said, waving her arm at the mattress and blanket, and she continued to dig about the bag until she had evidently found what she was looking for.

I moved over to the mattress, eyeing it with caution, but it didn't look as old as I thought it would, actually seeming kind of out of place in the old air of the building. When I took my place on it, Myka threw the chocolate bar to me then continued on with what she was doing. I didn't realise what that was until the fire started in the centre of canister, the warmth and light making the room feel much less daunting.

Until she went and closed the door, locking it.

I was up on my feet immediately. "What are you doing?"

"Relax, girl," she said, holding her arms out, attempting to placate me. "It is for our own good. Take a look around you, if the door is not closed, the circle is not complete, and we are at risk."

I did as she said and looked around the room. Just like downstairs, the walls were filled with graffiti, random words and markings painted here and there, even on the back of the door, and now that I looked, the floor and ceiling too. I narrowed my eyes on the markings. The styling of them reminded me of the marks demons bore, different but similar.

"And what are we at risk from?" I asked.

"A great many things," she answered, coming to sit near the fire too, but allowing me to keep the mattress and blanket to myself.

I slowly lowered myself back down, still looking around at the etchings on the walls. "And this, whatever this is, is meant to protect us?"

"From some things, yes."

"Like demons..."

"Yes."

"How?"

"All creatures must abide by certain laws, even demons."

I sorted. "People break laws all the time. Laws are fallible."

"Human laws," she said, as if correcting me. "But they are not the only laws in existence. Laws of nature are a different thing. Just as humans cannot fly without aid of machine because gravity keeps them grounded, there are rules that demons have no choice but to abide by."

I didn't fully understand it, but if I didn't think too hard on it, it kind of made sense. It also kind of made my head hurt. "And this room will keep them out."

"Demons, yes." She nodded. "The evil in the hearts of men is beyond what's written on the walls. For that, we have the lock." She actually smiled. A small, small smile that I almost missed, but a smile, nonetheless. She met my gaze. "You should rest, girl. Always sleep when you can because you do not know when you will get another chance."

I couldn't deny that I was tired. The day had been a long one and now that we were winding down, suddenly in one place and no longer on the move, all the adrenaline was leaving my body. I fought back on the yawns wanting to escape and stared into the flames of the fire. Despite the warmth, there was still a chill in the air, and I was soon wrapping the blanket around myself. I didn't think I would be able to sleep, not with everything that had happened, but sometimes you can surprise yourself. Sometimes you were just too drained to fight it anymore, and when it took you, you allowed it to.

10
Nate

Shay's offer was a bad idea if I had ever heard one. It felt wrong. If we went through with it, it would surely come back to bite us in the ass. Given my string of bad luck, I was pretty damn certain that bite would come sooner rather than later. But when you wanted something, sometimes you had to make deals with the devil. Strange how that was. I was supposed to be the demon, and yet it felt worse to be making a deal with Shay. At least with demons you knew what you were selling, I suppose, but with Shay, there was no guarantee that what sounded like a simple task would be just that.

"Okay, spill," I said, looking Shay over. "What is it and where is it?"

He pushed up from his seat and walked a little way until he came to a pile of folders at the other end of the room. When he had finished rummaging through them, he returned with a photo he placed on the table in front of us. "Her name is Maria," he said, almost caressing the name with his tongue.

I looked at the photo, my own tongue stilling for a moment whilst I struggled for the right words, but when the right ones failed to emerge, I just went with the ones that circled around my head. "She's a doll."

"A puppet," he corrected, and he pulled his fingers away very slowly from the photo as if letting it go was a difficult act. "A very old puppet."

"Old?" I raised an eyebrow. Old was an understatement. Maria the puppet was downright Victorian. It was hard to tell really with just the photo, but she appeared to be made of some form of ceramics, her large glass eyes vacant. The paint had begun to chip, her strings no doubt tangled in places, and her clothing was yellowed and worn. She was, in three words, ugly as hell. "You want us to steal... that?"

Daniel was quiet, but his eyes were on the photo and his mind no doubt wondering the same as mine. What did Shay want with a decrepit old puppet?

"Steal. Buy. Acquire. Whatever it takes." Shay's fingernails tapped gently against the tabletop, his gaze moving between Daniel and me. "But if you don't think you can handle it, then I guess I will keep my secrets to myself."

Daniel narrowed his gaze on Shay. "Why do you want it?"

Shay waved the question off. "Inconsequential. It doesn't matter to you. All you need to know is that I want her."

At that, Daniel gritted his teeth, his face twisting up in conflict. He wanted that information, but he would be damned if he would help Shay out in the process. It was a long moment before he spoke. With a shake of his head, he pushed the photo back along the table to Shay and stood. "No. I'll find another way to find out what happened to my dad. I don't need your help."

He was halfway toward turning to leave when Shay gripped his wrist. It stilled Daniel instantly and I imagined the touch to be clammy and dirty, like the touch of a long dead skeleton come back to haunt your dreams.

"I believe you should reconsider," Shay said, and his voice was honey dripping with poison. "I am the only one left living that knows the circumstances of your father's demise." He released his grip and leaned back in his seat. "Unless, that is, you don't much care to learn the truth.”

Daniel rubbed at his wrist but refused to look to Shay. He refused to admit that he wanted that information. He was a good kid, through and through. To compromise that goodness, it would be to compromise his identity, the very core of his being. He wouldn’t do it. He wouldn’t so carelessly give in to a man like Shay. That wasn’t who he was.

Good thing he had me with him.

I leaned back in my seat also, mimicking Shay and stretching out. “We’ll do it.”

Daniel’s head snapped around to look at me so quickly it could have given him whiplash. “Nate,” he said, the name drawn out and low, the minute shake of his head barely visible, a warning I ignored.

“Tell us where she is,” I said, focus solely on Shay and a smirk on my lips, “and we’ll get her.”

Shay sat forward, elbows resting on the tabletop as he brought his hands together like a prayer. He rested his chin on his interlocked fingers and looked me over, judging me. “You are a most unusual demon, Nathaniel Godwin. Perhaps when you are done with your task at hand, whatever the intricate details of that may be, you will consider entering my employ? I always have need for a good demon or two.”

“No such thing as a good demon,” I answered, my smirk growing ever more, but there was a disturbing twinkle in Shay’s eyes that had me feeling more than a little unsettled. “And I do believe we’re going off track.”

He smiled and bowed his head but kept his eyes locked with mine. “Indeed.”

“Nate,” Daniel said, still standing and making no effort to return to his seat, “we should leave.”

Again, I ignored him. Deals with devils was what I was good at.

“So, where is she?” I asked.

"She is a collector's piece in a rather unique museum." He pointed at the photo once again and this time I took note of the small logo and name I could see on what could have been a window or glass casing. In the next movement, he flipped the photo over and an address was scrawled in blue ink on the back of it. "If you can successfully acquire her and pass her on to me," and here his attention turned to Daniel, "I will tell you everything you want to know about your father. Trust me, you would be a fool to turn down my offer."

"Trust you?" I questioned, snapping up the photo and pushing it into the inside pocket of my jacket. I shook my head and stood up. "Never trust a trickster."

"You should know," was all Shay said in return.

"I know a great many things, but what I don't know is why we should believe you."

Shay let go of a light snort, his lips curling up into one of those devious smiles he liked to wear. "Then I'll offer you a name, one tiny speck of information that might just pique your interest."

"What name?" Daniel questioned.

"Felix Ravenwood."

Daniel's eyes met mine and I gave the briefest of nods. We both recognised that name from Atkins' computer and Shay was right. It was barely even a scrap but it was enough to let us know he had information and that was our cue to leave.

We did so without looking back. Daniel played it cool the whole way, until we were outside in the fresh air and Benji had locked the door of the shop behind us. We took two steps before Daniel came to a stop, his hands balled up into fists and his head bowed, gaze focused on the pavement. I stopped too, turning to look at him.

"Danie—" I tried to say, but he was having none of it, interrupting me before I could even get his name out.

"You shouldn't have done that." He wasn't angry, I could tell that much, but he was definitely concerned. "We don't know why he wants that thing or what he's going to do with it. If something happens, all because I want to find out about my dad..."

"Then it's on my head," I said. "I made the deal. Not you."

He shook his head. "That's not the point."

"Yes, it is." I turned away, shoving my hands into the pockets of my coat and starting the walk back to the car.

"He's dangerous."

"Well," I called back over my shoulder with a shrug, "so am I."

He groaned, no doubt at the inner conflict waging on inside his mind, but quickly caught me up. "It was never going to be easy, was it?"

"The only thing that separates him from the likes of me," I said, casting Daniel a side-glance, "is that he still owns his own soul. Probably a few more too. God only knows. In fact, he probably buys them on the Black Market and grinds them into that God-awful coffee he drinks."

He huffed out and chewed at his lip, which made me feel like smacking the back of his head to rid him of the habit.

"Relax, Danny Boy," I said instead, looking him over. He had held up well, considering the way Shay had been so fixated on him. "It'll work out in the end."

"I wish I could be that confident," he answered, coming to a stop at his car to fiddle with his keys until he managed to unlock it. We climbed on in and he sat in silence, unsure of himself and the situation.

"Well, what do you say?" I said, drawing his attention away from his thoughts and toward me instead.

"To what?" he asked.

I motioned our surroundings, the dimly lit streets, the shadows hulking in the alleys. "Perfect time for a robbery, wouldn't you say?"

We were both exhausted. It had been a long day, but tomorrow would be an even longer day if we waited until the night to go on our hunt for Maria the puppet. There was no way we could do it during the day. No, the best way would be under the cover of darkness, which meant there was no time like the present. We had to buck up and shut up and just get on with it. Once the deed was done, then we could rest. After all, how hard could it be to steal one little doll from one little museum?

"What's the address?" he asked, already shifting my legs out of the way so he could access the glove compartment.

I handed him the photo and he pulled out a map that I didn't even know had been in there. It made me curious as to what else was hidden in that compartment because something told me it wasn't gloves. Whilst Daniel looked at the map and the address on the photo, I dug around a little bit. Actual gloves. Who knew? A torch, that actually worked—probably one of the few things in the car that actually did. And a small plastic box. Now *that* was interesting. I pulled it out and it was only when I was opening it that I realised Daniel was staring at me with a bored glare.

"What are you doing?" he asked when my hands stilled.

"Exploring?"

He rolled his eyes and shoved the map back into the glove compartment and handed the photo back to me. "Well, when you're done *exploring*, we have a robbery to do."

I grinned and returned my attention to the plastic box in my hands, expecting some kind of treasure to be hidden within, only to find myself confronted with bits of metal when I opened it. "What the...?"

"Lock nuts," he answered, taking the box from me and returning it to the compartment.

"That is the most boring answer ever." I huffed out. "You could have at least made something up and kept me in suspense. Told me they were magical beans or something."

"And that would have made you happier?"

"It would have made it a little bit more exciting and interesting," I said, rolling my eyes and crossing my arms over my chest. "Instead of so... boring."

I barely caught the smile on his lips as he turned the key in the engine. "I thought you liked boring."

To that, I opened my mouth to disagree but found myself caught out. Once upon a time, or more like just several months ago, I thought I did. I lived a dull and uncomplicated life. I kept things simple. It was easier that way. It kept me alive. But now, now... boring wasn't always best.

*****

The idea of a toy museum sounded almost whimsical and innocent. I wasn't sure what I had been expecting, but given the nightmarish nature of Maria, I should have been more prepared by the time we arrived at the small toy museum a few miles east of Haverstock Hill. From the outside it didn't look too off-putting, if maybe just a little out of place in the modern street it sat in with its colourful panels and old-style letterings. It was only when we grew closer to the window displays that I realised what type of horror we were letting ourselves in for.

"Maybe doing this at night isn't the best idea," I muttered under my breath, taking in the several dolls displayed in the window and the rocking horse that was practically threadbare. With the faint lighting from the streetlights, I could just make out more of the same horrors awaiting us inside. Thousands upon thousands of eyes ready to follow our every move.

"They're only dolls," Daniel said, but even he had turned pale at the thought of entering the place. Creepy didn't even cover it.

"*Only* is a dangerous word," was my reply and I pushed back to take a breath. My eyes wandered up and down the street then up and down the three-storey building. "How are we going to do this then?"

"I was hoping you would have a plan."

"I did—my plan was for you to make the plan whilst I implement that plan."

"We could come back when it's open?"

I looked to him with a raised eyebrow. "And then what? Stuff the puppet up one of our shirts like a watermelon? Hate to break it to you, but I don't think anyone will buy the 'I'm just pregnant' line from us."

"Well, we can't do anything from here," he answered, and with that he was moving away from the front of the shop in search of an alleyway. It would be our best bet. Find the back door where no one could see us and sneak in that way.

I trailed behind him. "Don't suppose you know how to pick locks, do you?"

Silence.

"Nope... Didn't think so."

"Can't you use your powers or something?" he asked in return.

"To what?"

"Unlock the door."

"It wouldn't work."

"Why not?"

"I could never get the hang of it," I admitted in a low mumble.

"What?"

"Locks are tricky, okay? They're more complicated these days. Once over you just had to just a small push to nudge the latch of the hook, or fiddle a bit before you heard it click. But these days... It's complicated."

I could almost hear him rolling his eyes at me. "Maybe we'll get lucky."

"How?"

"I don't know. Maybe they left a window open? Left the key in the door? You never know." He turned down the alley and followed it until it came out across a bunch of small backyards.

It was easy enough to find the one that belonged to the toy museum. It was the yard that looked like it would eat anybody who dared enter and spit out only their bones once it was done. If we went in, we might never make it out again. I shook the thoughts from my head. Such things shouldn't have bothered me, but given that this was the location of the puppet, and that Shay wanted that puppet? I had my doubts about the innocence behind this little toy museum.

The gate was locked. Big surprise. But the wall was low enough to climb over. A good old run and jump and we could be over in a flash. I felt along the top though, where I couldn't quite see, just in case there were any nasty surprises waiting for us there, like glass or ragged edges. Nope. We were safe. Yet, I didn't feel much comfort in that.

I strode back a little bit and judged the distance and height. Easy. I could make it. A quick run, a push up from the ground, and I was gripping at the wall, pulling myself up. In another moment, I was sat at the top with a wide grin across my face as I stared back down at Daniel, waiting for him to join me. He eyed the wall with wariness, and I rolled my eyes, remembering the last time we had done something similar and he hadn't quite been as successful as me.

With a snort, I swung my legs over and into the yard and dropped down, calling back as quietly as I could, "I'll see if the gate opens from this side."

He was lucky, I could already see the bolt from where I landed. I started my way toward it but the sound of shuffling, or perhaps just the wind, had me stalling and I turned around to search the empty yard behind me. Nothing but shadows. I was losing it. Shaking my head, I attempted to shake off the chilling feeling and returned my attention to opening gate.

This time, my fingers were already wrapped around the bolt when I heard the noise again. I turned once more to search the darkness. It had to be a rat. There were rats and mice all over London, especially in areas like this. It was probably just hungry and I had intruded on its dinner—no doubt the corpse of the last person who had tried to break into the toy museum. That was—

CRASH!

The loud bang beside me had me all but jumping out of my skin and I turned around to glare at Daniel as he dusted himself off. Turned out the kid didn't need the gate opening after all. He had decided to try and make it over the wall and had not only succeeded in that but also succeeded in almost giving me a freaking heart attack.

"Jumpy much?" he said, looking me over, and I cursed him under my breath, sneering at him as he led the way up to the backdoor.

"Are you kidding? Have you seen this place?" I shivered at the thought of all those eyes inside waiting for us. "I've seen how these movies end, and it's never good."

"In your entire life as a demon," Daniel said, never sparing me a glance, "have you ever come across a living doll? Or any form of living toy for that matter?"

"That is not the point," I argued. "Until last year, Charlie didn't know demons existed, and hey presto—now she's forever wrapped up in this world. Just because you've never seen it, doesn't mean it doesn't exist. You ever seen Nessie?"

"Nessie is a myth," Daniel said, but he furrowed his brow all the same as if he was actually entertaining the thought.

"Only as far as you know. So, who's to say that dolls and creepy ass puppets don't actually come to life and attack people?"

He let go of a lengthy sigh and shook his head. "Just remember, you volunteered to come here."

And the kid had me there. It didn't matter how much I complained, we were going inside, so we might as well just get on with it. We just had to find a way in first.

"So," I started, drawing the word out as I considered the building in front of us, "what now?"

Daniel stood akimbo, looking over the house and the small yard. "There has to be something. A spare key, open window, something."

"Well, from here it looks like all the windows are shut, probably locked too, but you're welcome to climb on up and try a few if you want." I paced back and forth as Daniel began rummaging around the yard, turning over stones and empty flowerpots. "We could always break a window, but that would create noise and attract attention."

We had managed to break into the Harkanians' place, with all the security that held, and yet here we were in front of, or rather now behind, a building with minimal security and probably a dodgy alarm that didn't always work, and we were struggling to come up with ways to get inside. Granted, we *had* been caught by the Harkanians the second time and almost caught the first, but in the end, we had gotten in and gotten out. Breaking into an old toy museum should have been easy.

"Here we go," Daniel announced, joyous pride on his voice.

I turned around to face him with a narrowed gaze, taking in the silver key in his hand and the now open back door. "Are you kidding me?"

"It was in the flowerpot," he answered, pocketing the key and stepping on into the old museum. He fiddled with a small flashlight until it turned on, the beam not overly bright, but not so dim that we couldn't see anything.

"Why?" I asked, following him and closing the door behind us.

He shrugged. "Probably never thought someone would find it and use it."

"Or maybe they didn't care," I answered, taking one look around us and feeling that shiver return.

"What's that supposed to mean?" he asked. "Who wouldn't care about being broken into?"

"Someone with defences other than locks. Remember what Shay

said? Even his demons had trouble getting a hold of Maria. We can't let our guard down for a moment."

He nodded in understanding, then came to a stop, his shoulders slumping. "I... have no idea where to even start."

I had to agree with him there. Finding one puppet amongst everything else was going to be difficult and we didn't even know which room to start in. The room we were in looked to be a behind the scenes area, a small kitchen area turned workshop for the staff. Severed toy limbs sat here and there amongst dirty cups and jam jars filled with murky water and paintbrushes. All for restoration no doubt. Still, it didn't change things. They could paint all the toys up as much as they wanted, they were still creepy.

"It's a museum, right?" I asked. "So maybe if we make our way to the front of the place, they'll have a map by the entrance."

"It's as good a place to start as any."

So, we did just that. Through the door that led to the main museum and through the narrow rooms until we reached the even narrower hallway at the front where a table sat filled with leaflets. Daniel picked up one after another and I did the same, but they were mostly about other tourist attractions in London, until Daniel tapped the leaflet in his hand triumphantly. He held it open for me to see, showing off the photos, including one of an old Punch and Judy stand, complete with puppets, manic smiles and all.

"Right?" I said, unsure of how that helped us at all.

He tapped the picture again and urged me to look closer, holding the torch over the image. "There, in the background. Do you see it?"

"Maria."

He nodded and pulled the leaflet back, no doubt reading the description below the picture. "The classic show is on display on the second floor, along with a variety of other famous puppets and a collection of characters from around the world."

"Up we go then."

And up we went.

The whole while I felt on edge. Even when we found the stairs, there were still toys to be seen everywhere. I could feel their eyes and I swore I could even hear them moving. Wood and metal scraping, tiny feet thumping along the dark wooden floor. A row of a dozen toy soldiers on a shelf by the staircase had me pausing and I leaned in close. Each one stood in a slightly different stance, but they all held a rifle fixed with a bayonet, all except the small guy on the very end. His, I noted, had fallen from his grip and to the floor. Well, it could stay there. I wasn't making it any easier for those tiny devils to prick me to death.

"Nate?" Daniel question, several steps ahead of me.

I shook the paranoid thoughts from my head and looked to him. "I'm coming, I'm coming."

But even as I set off, I had to chance a look behind, just in case one of them had moved. They all stood as stock still as they had mere seconds ago. Still...

"Are they following us?" I questioned, trailing after Daniel but still sparing a glance at the toys around. There was a stuffed rabbit with one eye and a missing patch of fur on his stomach on the step beside me, looking very much like another stuffed rabbit I had seen when we had first started climbing the stairs.

"You're being ridiculous," Daniel answered with a huff and a shake of his head. "It's just a trick of the eye. You know, like in paintings, when the eyes follow you about? It's like that."

"Yeah, but that's the eyes, and there's a logical explanation for that. I'm starting to think that these toys are not just watching us but following us." I stopped beside another small shelf with toy soldiers lined up there too. Twelve to be exact, each with a rifle affixed with bayonet, all except the small guy on the very end. I nearly fell backwards from the shock of it. "Yeah—something here really isn't right. Either these toys are following us, or—"

"We're going around in circles," Daniel finished.

The strange part was that his voice didn't come from up ahead where it should have, but rather from several steps down from me. He hadn't doubled back on me, that much I knew for certain, which meant only one thing.

I glanced down at the floor below the shelf, spotting the small toy rifle that belonged to the soldier on the shelf. "Well, this explains a bit."

"Not really." Daniel shook his head. "Actually, it just confuses things. A lot."

"It's a loop, that's all."

"Really? That's all?" He wasn't impressed.

"They used to use them in labyrinths all the time. That whole keep going left thing to escape mazes? Not so easy if all you're doing is going around and around and around in an eternal loop."

"How does any of that information help us now?"

"Well," I said, with a smile on my lips, "I got stuck in a labyrinth once. Painful few days. No food, no water, just me and this never-ending loop." I took a step forward, placing both hands on the banister and tested the wooden frame. Pretty sturdy. Then I looked upward, through the gap created in the helix style staircase, toward the place we wanted to be. "Do you know what I learned?"

"No," Daniel said, sounding bored of my story already, "but I'm dying to find out."

"When people place these loops, they do it in a very straightforward manner, one foot at a time, one in front of the other. Very central. So, when you follow that path, you fall into the trap of the loop."

Daniel joined me by the banister, seeming a little less bored now and looked up at the flight of stairs also. "What you're saying is we need to get off that path?"

I looked to him and raised an eyebrow. "If no one told you that the rook could only move horizontally and vertically, you'd at least try and move them diagonally too, wouldn't you?"

He didn't need to say anything in reply. I knew he understood and by the small smile on his lips, I could tell we were in agreement. Carefully, I pushed up onto the banister before reaching across to the banister on the other side. If I fell, the fall wouldn't be too great, but it would still hurt, so I still had to be careful. Once I was fully across onto the opposite banister, I turned around to face the next task—climbing the one that led to the second-floor landing. By the time I had and was climbing over that part of the banister, Daniel was climbing also, not far behind me.

When my feet were firmly on the landing floor, I looked around and took in my surroundings. No stuffed rabbits, no shelves with toy soldiers, nothing that looked familiar. Daniel was by my side in moments. Hopefully he would be just as ready for the climb back down because as soon as we found the puppet, we couldn't risk falling into the loop again.

"See?" I said, clapping Danny Boy on the back. "Easy!"

"Now we just have to find Maria."

"Well, we didn't come all this way to leave without it."

From where we stood, I could see three rooms leading off of the landing, the doors open to each. None of them gave much away, the shadows too thick and secrets hidden too far into the rooms. I huffed out and considered each in turn. The one to the far left would no doubt have some light from the streetlights to help illuminate its treasures, even if only a little, and the centre one we could probably get away with turning the light on to help, which left the third room that seemed to look over the back alley. Using the light there could be safe, but if anyone from the other buildings happened to catch sight of it, it could lead to possible trouble, so torchlight would be our best bet there.

"I'll take the front room, you use your torch on the back one, and we'll meet in the middle," I said with a nod of my head, already setting off toward the front room.

Daniel didn't argue, just went on his way to search the back room, and I could see the light of his torch from the corner of my eye as he turned it on again. It was just an old toy museum with a few tricks up its sleeves. What harm would it do for us to split up? We would only be a shout away from each other. Nothing more.

The curtains were drawn in the front room, and I swiftly opened them, allowing the orange light to trickle in from the streetlights outside. It didn't help much, but I could see the bare bones of the place. Darkly lit stages for small wooden puppets, no doubt intricate in design, but in the shadows, I could only make out their basic shapes, and on one, a slumped puppet whose show had ended. A small wooden cradle sat in one corner next to a rocking chair which contained one of the ugliest and largest puppets I had ever seen, its misshapen head slumped forward.

Curiosity got the better of me and I wandered closer until I was directly in front of it, staring at the clay monstrosity with its threadbare hair and clown clothes. I shivered but reached out all the same until I could see the caricature face of the life size puppet, the paint worn and faded, revealing the brownish clay base beneath, along with the scratching of old letters on its head.

"Truth," I whispered, reading the old word out loud and tilting my own head to the side. Why did this all feel very familiar to me?

"Nate!" Daniel called, distracting me from the monstrosity and making me turn back toward the doorway. "I've found it!"

Thank go—

"Intruders," came a thick, clunking voice from behind. "Thieves."

I closed my eyes and tried to steady my breathing, listening closely to the scrapings that I knew belonged to the thing behind me that wasn't any ordinary puppet after all. Then in the next moment, I was being thrown from the room.

11

Daniel

As soon as I walked into the room, the light from my torch hit the stand of the old Punch and Judy show that had been in the picture on the leaflet. It brought back memories of watching the show during summer when I had been just a kid. The carnival would come to town, and what had once been a patch of green became filled with stalls and small rides, and a small booth that always seemed to be surrounded by kids. Punch and Judy. It was strange, looking at the empty puppets and their booth, to think that such misshapen things could be a symbol for childish innocence.

I pushed the thoughts from my head and continued onward, thinking about how the picture had looked in my mind's eye. Looking past the booth, I saw the display cabinet, and there, behind the glass, sat the puppet we were looking for. A grin slipped onto my face, and I pushed forward until I was right up against the glass and staring at the doll. She was just as ugly in person as she was in the picture, but she was what we were looking for.

"Nate!" I called out, feeling triumphant. "I've found it!"

Barely ten seconds later and there was a loud crash out in the hallway. My hand slipped behind my back, immediately grabbing for my gun... at least, what I was now using as my gun. Atkins had taken mine earlier that day and now I had taken his. It felt heavier in my hands than what I was used to, but it had a trigger and a barrel all the same which meant I could still shoot with it. My feet were moving of their own accord until I was out on the landing once more and staring confused at Nate as he leaned against the now broken banister.

"We might have a small problem," he said, casting me a quick glance before looking back at the room he had come from.

I followed his gaze to the hulking figure in the doorway. "Small? *Small*? That is not small."

"But it is a problem."

On that I couldn't disagree.

"Thieves," the thing called out as it lunged forward, each movement as heavy as the booming of its voice. "Intruders."

I threw myself to the right and Nate threw himself to the left, both narrowly managing to miss being caught by the thing that was... wearing a clown suit? Great. We were being attacked by a doll clown. Nate was right. The toys were alive. Who knew his paranoia and my ignorance of it could come and bite us in the ass?

"What is that?" I all but shouted, turning to face the creature and getting three shots off before it lunged at me again. The bullets just clipped it, doing no more damage to it than a feather would.

"I believe it's a golem," Nate called back, ducking out of the way as the thing swung its heavy arms at him. "Big clay creatures created to—" He ducked again. "Created to obey the creator's orders."

"Which would be to stop thieves," I muttered.

"And intruders," Nate added. "Don't forget intruders."

I dropped to the floor, narrowly avoiding getting hit by a lamp that the thing threw at me, all the while throwing Nate a glare of my own. "How could I?"

He attempted to set it on fire, but aside from its clothing going up in flames, it did little more but annoy the beast. I aimed my gun but cursed before taking a shot. It wouldn't do any good. I could shoot until the gun was empty and it would still keep attacking. We needed an actual plan.

"How do we stop a golem?" I called to Nate, ducking into one of the rooms to avoid another attack.

"There is a way," Nate said, barging at the golem and knocking it out of the way of the doorway, stopping it from pursing me. It crashed against something on the landing, but that would only slow it down.

"And that way is?"

"I'm thinking. They're not exactly common things these days, you know?"

He was sent flying again with an oomph and I cringed in sympathy. "Think harder, before this thing kills one of us."

"Easier said than done," he groaned.

I focused on the doorway, readying myself and listening to the steps of the monster. Taking a breath, I gathered my courage and charged, hitting the thing square in the chest as it entered the doorway once again. It stumbled backwards toward the banister, crashing into the same spot Nate had crashed into before. That gave me an idea, one that would probably give me a fair few more bruises, especially considering the ones I could already feel forming.

It dragged itself up from the floor, movements clunky and heavy, its clothing now ripped and burned away in several places to reveal the solid clay beneath, the rope like strips dangling uselessly from its limbs. I took one glance at Nate as he righted himself from the things last attack, and then turned my attention to the creature. Feet planted firmly, I judged it and the banister behind. I just hoped I had enough strength.

Once it started moving again, that was when I knew I had to just go for it, before I lost my chance. Putting all of my strength into my upper body, I leaned forward, right shoulder pushed forward, and charged. I collided into it with such force that the banister creaked for a moment before completely cracking and giving way. The creature, being large and clunky and thankfully slow, went with it, tumbling backwards with nothing to stop its descent. Down through the banister below, cracking and banging, until it had landed on the lower part of the staircase where we had been trapped in the loop.

Only problem was, I was perched on the edge of the landing where the banister had broken and was quickly losing my balance. My hand shot out to grip part of the remaining banister, but it fell away also, and I began to topple with it. My head spun with vertigo, my breath leaving me, as I could feel myself falling, and then— nothing. A sudden stop. A fist gripping at the cloth on the back of my jacket, stopping me from falling any further.

"I got you," Nate groaned from behind, tugging me backward onto the landing, his other hand gripping my shoulder to give him more of a hold.

I allowed myself to fall back until I had hit the ground, and there I stayed for a moment, seated on the carpeted landing, feeling very much out of breath and more than a little dizzy. Below us, the golem crashed and banged, all the while still shouting.

"Thieves! Intruders!"

Bang!

Crash!

Neither of us moved, both waiting and listening, barely even daring to glance toward the staircase in case that thing was somehow immune to the loop. After another moment, I pushed forward a little, slowly peering over the edge where the banister had been. There it was, disappearing around one corner only to appear again at the bottom.

"How long do these loop things last for?" I asked, cautious.

"Usually until it gets taken off by whoever put it there," Nate answered. "Usually…"

"Usually?"

"Well, it depends on the skill of whoever placed the charm."

"Maybe we should get the puppet and get out of here," I said, shaking myself and pushing up from the carpet, "before that thing breaks free or before anything else attacks us."

"Lead the way, Danny Boy," Nate answered, clapping me on the back.

I made my way toward the room at the back, all the while listening carefully to the golem below. As long as we could hear where it was, it couldn't suddenly surprise us. That said, there could be numerous other things lurking about that could. All the more reason to move quickly.

"Here she is." I waved my hand at the display case. It was one of those with the sliding doors that were locked shut. I tested the door and sighed. Yep. Locked. "We need the key."

"I've got a key for that," Nate said from behind me, and I could practically hear the smile in his voice. I turned to look at him and barely even had chance to take in the wooden chair in his grasp as he moved past me, swinging the chair and bringing it down against the glass. It shattered with such an explosion of sound that it drowned out the crashing of the golem for what was mere seconds but felt like much longer, the fragments of glass raining down onto the wooden floor beneath.

"That's not a key," was all I managed to say, staring at Nate and the now broken display case.

"It's open, isn't it?"

I nodded numbly in response, not sure what I was supposed to say to that. I supposed it didn't matter now, all the noise we'd already made thanks to the golem. If someone was going to overhear us, they would have done so already. Now, it was speed rather than discretion we were after.

Nate grabbed the puppet, his face turning up at it as he did so, and looked to me. "You ready for the climb back down?"

"Not really," I sighed, thinking of the golem below, "but do we have a choice?"

Nate just smirked and led the way out of the room. When he started the climb down, he made it look easy, moving deftly as I was left to watch after him. I closed my eyes for a moment and drew in a breath. When I opened them again, a sparkle of silver in the dim light caught my eye on the landing and I narrowed my gaze, moving over to investigate. It was next to one of the many broken pieces of furnishings that now littered the landing and when I picked it up, I recognised it instantly. A small silver lighter. It was Nate's. He toyed with it more than he ever actually used it. It was like a tick of his, like the one Charlie had developed where she was constantly rolling her eyes at me.

I slipped the lighter into my pocket and turned my attention back to the climb down. By the time I reached the banister again and began to clamber after Nate, he was already nearing the floor below and as I glanced down, I saw him duck out of the way as the golem tried to grab at him. That was what I was dreading. When its clunky clay fingers reached out over the banister as I made my way past also, I could feel them brush against me, but all it did was make me move quicker. By the time I joined Nate at the bottom of the stairwell, I was panting from both overexertion and panic.

From there, we followed our same path outward, into the backyard and then alley. I dropped the key back in the flowerpot along the way, figuring we wouldn't need it anymore. Not that the damage hadn't already been done inside. When we finally reached the car, that was when I began to feel like I could breathe again. One thing I knew for certain—I would never be able to look at a toy shop or museum in the same way again.

"Makes you wonder what's so important about Maria here," Nate said, holding up the puppet and turning it over in his hands, investigating it.

"Whatever it is," I said, thinking about Shay, "it can't be good."

"How about we find somewhere to rest up before we find out?"

Considering how much I ached, I was all up for that. I definitely needed the sleep before having to face Shay again. I nodded and was just about to climb into the car when Nate slapped his forehead with the heel of his palm.

"Of course!" he shouted, the noise making me jump.

"What?" I asked, wondering if we had missed something and looking back toward the toy museum.

"The letter!" He grinned at me as if that made all the sense in the world. It didn't.

"The... what?"

"The letter," he reiterated, bobbing his head at me. "Truth—that's what was written on the golem's head. Legend goes that if you erase the first letter of the word, it becomes death, and thus ends the golem's life."

I closed my eyes and took a breath. "*Now* you're remembering this?"

He shrugged and climbed into the car, throwing Maria onto the backseat and out of sight. "At least you know for next time."

I just hoped there wouldn't be a next time.

*****

As Nate suggested, we rested up in a small hotel a good half hour away from the scene of our crime. It would have been further if I had had the energy to drive that far. My eyes were already threatening to close even before I had parked. I hid the puppet in one of my bags and we made our way up to the room in almost silence, both so exhausted from the day's events. By the time my head hit the pillow, I was already gone.

The dreams were quick to come, sending my mind into a spin. Unlike before, I was no longer a scared child. I felt older, stronger, but no less terrified. Everything was muted, just as before, but there were no shapes that looked like buildings this time. Instead, everything was open, smudges of purple and red stretching across what could have been fields, for miles upon miles upon miles, but my eyes quickly turned downcast, focusing on the weight in my arms, and what a heavy weight it was.

"I'm sorry," I whispered, the words painful in my throat. "I'm sorry..."

The weight in my arms didn't move, but the longer I looked at it, the more I began to realise it was a person and the sight of that person made my heart ache. I pulled the person tighter and lowered my head onto their chest, but the lack of movement, the lack of breath, only served to worsen my suffering.

"Your tears cannot bring him back," came a soft and familiar voice from behind me, a gentle touch to the shoulder following it.

"Leave me," I ordered, harsh and stronger than I thought possible.

But they did not. She did not.

She moved into my vision, hand still on my shoulder, the brightness of her light almost blinding me, wings spread out majestically behind her, yet through it all, I could see the sorrow on her face. "I cannot."

"Leave me," I said once more, grit and dirt in my voice, my teeth ground together. "Unless you can bring him back and set things right, I have no need for angels here."

"You know I can't."

"Then leave."

A single tear fell from her eyes and a sad smile spread across her lips. "I can't do that either."

Her grip grew rough, her voice more masculine, until I realised the dream was fading and reality returning. I woke with a sharp intake of breath to see Nate's face looking concerned as he looked down at me. He pushed back once he saw I was awake and narrowed his eyes on me.

I threw an arm up and over my eyes and drew in a deep breath. "Why'd you wake me?"

"You looked like you were having a nightmare," he said, "that, and it's almost noon."

I sighed and turned over in the bed to see the small strips of sunlight breaking in past the darkened curtains. How had the night passed so quickly? I felt even worse than I had before, and certainly not as well rested as I should have done. The nightmares, they were becoming more persistent. I raised my arm enough to consider Nate as he milled about the room, grabbing his shirt from the other bed and getting ready to pull it on.

There were scars there that hadn't been before, one in particular that I certainly hadn't seen that first time he had chosen to be immodest in front of me. It ran the length of his side and made me think back to when he had helped me save Charlie from that hospital she had been locked up in. He had been bleeding then. That was ages ago, and yet somehow, despite being a demon, it had never healed. One of the many things he hid. It made me wonder what else he was hiding. My mind went to the small silver lighter that still remained tucked in the pocket of my jeans. I hadn't taken a closer look at it yet, but I had felt an engraving on the back. It meant something to him, even if Nate claimed he wasn't sentimental. The lighter meant something, which just served to prove even more that there was more to him than he let on—too busy playing the obnoxious, know-it-all, demon.

I swallowed the thick lump in my throat and pulled myself up on the bed. "Have you seen Serena recently?"

He huffed out as he fastened his shirt up, looking over his shoulder at me. "Yeah, about ten minutes before you turned up back in my life. Why?"

"Just curious," I answered, lowering my gaze. "Did you... did you know her before?"

"Before?" he questioned, turning to stare at me with a furrowed brow.

"Before," I repeated the word, before expanding, "when you were human..."

He shrugged and finished fastening his shirt "I don't really remember. Why the sudden interest?"

I shook my head. "No reason."

"No reason, huh?" He wasn't convinced, which didn't surprise me as I wasn't very convincing. So, I decided to change the subject and cleared my throat.

"I'm going to take a shower," I announced, dragging myself from the bed and trudging toward the bathroom without looking his way. The feeling from the nightmare clung to me like the blood that still stained my skin in places and the bruises that had no doubt formed overnight. The more the dreams went on, the more confused I became. The voice, the brightness, the wings—I had no doubt that had been Serena. If that was so, what did it mean?

"Don't take too long!" Nate called out, his voice travelling through the closed bathroom door, but the words got muddled somewhere in my brain.

He was an enigma, and the dreams? Somehow, after this latest one, I felt it was all linked to him.

"You hear me?" he called again, this time louder.

"Yeah, I hear you," I called back, half-hearted and tired.

By the time I was done, I was beginning to feel a little more put together, and by the time we had stopped for breakfast and were making our way back to Shay's shop, the dream was fading away, all anxieties from it replaced by the ones I got from Shay. The puppet sat on the back seat, completely immobile and seemingly harmless, but things were never quite as they seemed.

"Are you sure this is a good idea?" I asked, turning to face Nate.

He shook his head. "No."

"Then should we really be doing this?" I looked back toward the shop. "If he gets his hands on this puppet..."

"We don't know what will happen." He let go of a sigh and opened the car door. "Only one way to find out."

"I'm not sure I want to find out," I mumbled, climbing from the car also. I let him grab the doll, giving him the responsibility of handing it over.

The shop was open as usual and Benji sat up front by the counter, reading once more. He barely even lifted his gaze as we entered and didn't even flicker as we approached. Shay emerged shortly after from the back room with open arms and a wide grin that made me feel uneasy. If there was anyone else around, they didn't make themselves known. That didn't mean they weren't there though. Still, the feel of the gun in my waistband steadied me. Benji's mark was on his hand, so if there was any trouble from him, I at least had somewhere to aim. Shay, however, was more difficult. He may have been demonic in ways, but he was still human, and I wasn't sure I would be able to shoot him with confidence.

"Remember what I said," Nate whispered to me, a look of determination in his eyes.

It took me a moment to catch on, but I remembered. Run. He had told me to run if there was trouble. Easier said than done.

"Come on through," Shay beckoned, already leading the way through to the back room. The coffee sat on the table ready for us, though we both already knew we wouldn't be drinking it. He had biscuits there too this time, laid on a small plate in the centre of the tray, an assortment of all the usual favourites by the looks. Custard creams. Bourbons. Digestives. It all looked very normal, but who knew what was in those things, and given that I had already been drugged twice within twenty-four hours, I certainly wasn't willing to risk it.

"We have your doll," Nate said, raising the doll up briefly before clonking it down into one of the empty seats at the table.

"Puppet," Shay corrected, his eyes seeming to glaze over with joy at the sight of it. "Or even marionette if you will, given the strings." He moved closer, running a hand through the messy hair that sat atop her head, looking very much realistic. "She is magnificent, is she not? I hope it didn't cause you too much bother."

"Would it matter if it had?" Nate asked, dry and impatient. He made no attempt to sit at the table, folding his arms across his chest. Nothing about him said that he was planning on staying, and everything about him said that he intended this visit to be as short as possible. I felt the same way.

Shay merely smiled in reply, a half-smile that lit up his eyes in a dangerous manner. His lack of answer was answer enough to Nate's question. All the more reason for us to limit our time with him. "Please, take a seat—we have much to discuss."

"You wanted the doll, we brought it to you," I said, refusing to sit. I much preferred standing. It allowed me to react quicker. "Now it's time for you to hold up your end of the bargain."

"Then allow me to be a good host. You must be hungry at the very least."

"We've already eaten."

He snorted and shook his head a little in disappointment. "Shame. But still, you wished for information, and I will gladly supply you with all you need to know. I can hardly do that if you refuse to at least be seated."

"Quit playing games, Shay," Nate berated, rolling his eyes. "It's been a long few days and we don't particularly care to partake in your tea party. So, if you would tell us what you know, then we can be on our way."

"What I know is a great deal," Shay said, before shrugging and moving to circle us. He placed his hand on my shoulder and leaned in. "Such as how your father played an important role in something great—magnificent even." He moved away, leaving me feeling cold throughout, and went to circle Nate instead, picking at imaginary lint on the demon's coat. "You wouldn't want to disappoint him, would you?" he crooned in Nate's ear. "He's so eager to learn and it would be such a shame for him to leave here emptyhanded." He plucked at a stray hair of Nate's, causing the demon to flinch from the pain and grit his teeth as he all but growled at the man. "You do as he says, after all, right? Look out for his best interests?"

A snide snarl crept onto Nate's lips, and he shook his head. "You have your doll, so unless you're prepared to actually start giving us information, we're leaving."

"Then please, take a seat," Shay said, motioning to the chairs as he made his way back toward the doll. He began looking it over, inspecting it as he waited for us to do as he said. He would be waiting a while, that was for sure.

Nate looked to me but remained silent and I nodded, understanding the unspoken thought. We were leaving. We had the flash drive to look over still, and maybe we could get another lead from there, because the only way Shay was giving us anything was if we played along, and we were both through with playing. I was already turning to leave when Shay spoke again, this time more forceful, more confident.

"Nathaniel," he said, standing up to look at Nate and tilting his head to the side, "sit."

Nate immediately took the seat beside him, any trace of a smile falling from his face.

"Nate?" I questioned, feeling more than a little confused by the action.

His eyes met mine and I could see the panic beginning to seep in around the edges, but he kept calm. "Daniel," he breathed out, attempting to keep his words even and in control, "run."

12
Charlie

It was hardly surprising that I barely slept. Despite the fire and blankets, there was still a chill in the air to remind us it was winter, and that winter was harsh and cold. I didn't enjoy it one bit and was looking forward to the summer sun once again. Still, that was a long way off, and somehow, I had to survive until then. By the time the sun was really starting to rise, I was already awake, huddled near the fire with the blankets wrapped tightly around me, the book I had brought with me open on the floor in front of me.

A few of the pages had been bent, folds in them where there had been no folds before. By my guess, it was something to do with when the creep in the library had dropped the book. It made me curious once more as to what he had been looking at. If the book had somehow landed on one of the pages he had been reading, then maybe the folds and bends would give me a clue. So far, the only thing to draw my eye was a drawing of a green gemstone that looked familiar.

If I remembered correctly, Nate had been looking at that when he had been conspiring with Serena as to how to stop Amon. It couldn't be a coincidence, could it? It seemed to me that lately, things had a habit of happening for a reason, and perhaps this had meaning too.

"What's this got to do with you, Nate?" I asked, barely a whisper as I looked down at the page. I didn't expect any kind of answer in response.

"Nate?" Myka questioned, the sound of her voice shocking me. I hadn't even realised she was awake.

"He's..." I started to explain, but I stopped myself. A demon? I definitely couldn't say that. There was no knowing how Myka would react to that information. If she found out I was friends with a demon, I could lose her protection, and until I could figure out a way to get to Daniel, I needed all the protection I could get. It made me miss my fancy Smartphone from my old life. It made contacting people so much easier, and now here I was without it, completely lost. I sighed and looked back toward Myka, brushing the thoughts away for now. "It's complicated."

She pushed up from where she sat and came to join me by the fire, overlooking the book in my hands. "And your book? Is that complicated too?"

I turned my gaze toward the pages and remembered back to the night before. "I was going to show it to Aiden. In the library, one of the brothers had been looking at it. He dropped it when he saw me. I think there's something in here that's related to what they want from me."

"Such as your pretty little death stone there?" Myka questioned, and I could hear genuine curiosity in her tone, which almost made me not hear the actual words.

"I'm sorry, what?" I narrowed my gaze on her, head tilting a fraction.

She nodded toward the book. "Where I was born, we have a different name for it, but it roughly translates to death stone. The Stone of Death, if you wished."

There was no name written on the pages, and barely any information on the green gem, but one thing I had read was that whosoever touched the stone would die instantly. If that were the case, the name Myka gave it was fitting. "And it's real?"

She nodded. "There are many stories of stones of its kind. One is said to bring people back from the dead and turn lead into gold. But as with many things in life, there are often opposites to keep balance in the world. Such is true of the stone on that page."

"So, if the stone touches you, you die?" The thought horrified me a little bit, I had to admit. Even a bullet had to hit you just right for it to kill or maim you, so the thought that some green gem had the power to do that without such precision unnerved me.

She chuckled at me and shook her head. "The truth is always more complicated than the story. In reality, the stone is born of blood magic. As with any magic, there is a price, but with blood magic, that price is much greater. Your sacrifice may seem insignificant at the time, but down the road, the true implications may become clear."

I stared down at the page, contemplating all she had to say before speaking, slow and cautious when I did so. "I think Nate used the stone to get rid of the demon chasing us."

"And this Nate is your friend?"

I ignored the question, lifting my gaze once more to look at Myka. "Is that why they're after me? To use as bait to get to Nate?"

Did they want him to pay whatever price Myka was talking about? If he had used the stone and used blood magic, what did that mean? It made me even more eager to find him and Daniel both, I just didn't know where I was supposed to start.

"I do not know, girl," was all Myka said in reply, and she was pushing up again, moving to put out the fire. When she was done with that and with gathering the few bits and pieces, she turned to me, holding out her hand for me to take. It was time to move.

I reached out for her hand but paused, my eyes catching on something familiar in style upon her wrist. A circular tattoo with a pattern inside and name around the edge. A mark, as Nate called them. I hadn't noticed it before, in the darkness and panic of the situation at hand, but now that daylight was beginning to stream through, I could see it clearly—so clearly, I could also see the edges of shadows that danced across the skin where the mark branded. Eyes widening, I snatched my hand away and backed up.

"You're a demon?" I questioned, feeling myself starting to panic. The only place I had seen marks like that were on demons, the only reason I hadn't noticed it sooner on her was because she wasn't shrouded in shadows like all the others. I had trusted her. I had actually started to even like her.

She shook her head, looking down at the mark on her forearm by her wrist and turning it over in the light. "I can see why you would think that, but I can assure you, girl, I am as human as you are."

"Then how do you explain that?" I asked, pointing at the mark as I pulled myself up from the ground.

"I made a deal with a demon and they placed this on me to ensure no other demon could lay claim to my soul." She prodded at the mark as if to show how it wasn't the least bit dangerous, but that didn't make me feel any better.

"You sold your soul to a demon?" I asked. "Is that why you're helping me? Some kind of redemption?"

"It is not my soul that they asked of me. Souls are not the only thing that demons make bargains for."

"No," I said, more to myself than to her, unable to stop my thoughts, "some make deals for magical necklaces."

"You do not have to trust me, girl," Myka continued, "but you should trust that we are not safe here. We must keep moving. Many of these safe locations are known to those within the Occultus and if the wrong members come looking, I can only do so much to hold them off."

I nodded numbly, unsure of what else I could do. I didn't have the first clue where to start looking for Nate and Daniel, so my only real hope was that perhaps Serena would find me. She would know where they were, and she could direct me. The only problem was her visits had been less and less frequent. Her last had been just before Daniel had disappeared. Being a fugitive on the run from the authorities was a great way to restrict your freedom, and as it stood, I wasn't the only fugitive. Serena had gone against the other angels when she had helped us and there were bound to be repercussions to that.

"Just so you know," I said, allowing myself to move closer to Myka and picking up my book on the way, "if you are a demon, I know how to kill you. You wouldn't be the first one I've killed."

She merely chuckled. "It is good to see you have so much fire in your soul. This is good, you will need it. Now let us go before they have a chance to find our trail."

We did just that, stopping only a few times on the way. Once to buy petrol and few bits and pieces from the petrol station, from drinks to food, precious food, and the second stop to buy a few essential supplies—such as a thick winter coat. The fact I had no money did twist at my insides, but that Myka paid so willingly for it all also enhanced my suspicion of her. People weren't that nice. They weren't. Not unless they were a young fool named Daniel with a heart of pure gold. But it seemed Myka had money to spare, and I wasn't fool enough to not take advantage of that. That was how I differed from Daniel. I knew how to use people, though my time with him had me feeling a little more guilty about it now than I ever had done in the past.

"Where are we headed to now?" I asked, feeling a lot warmer inside a winter coat. It went a long way to quieten the guilt that my mind tried to push on me.

"You wish to find your friends," Myka said in return, more statement than question.

"But I don't know where they are," I answered, slinking down in the seat and feeling just a little bit more hopeless.

"Then perhaps it is time we asked for help."

I raised an eyebrow at her. "What we gonna do? Stop and ask for directions?"

"Essentially..."

I shook my head. "That makes zero sense."

"In days old, demons were not just nightmares in the night. There were some who worked with them, enlisted their help. They were once heralded as great teachers and philosophers." She looked to me briefly from the driver's seat. "It may be hard for you to understand, but not all demons are evil. Whilst some are born from it, some are driven to it, and others... they merely live by their own code."

"You're saying that we not only stop and ask for directions," I started, more than a little shocked, "but we ask a demon?"

"There is another safe house a few miles down the road, we can stop there and perform a," she paused, a foreign word slipping past her lips as if she was trying to think of the right phrasing, before continuing on when she seemed to find it, "ceremony of sorts. But you must be strong of will, because demons are tricksters beyond anything else." She looked straight ahead now, not waiting for me to question her further. "If you wish to find your friends, then perhaps it is time to ask for help from mine."

*****

I expected another abandoned hospital, or perhaps a shack in the middle of nowhere. Anything that looked decrepit and old and haunted. What I didn't expect was a cosy little bungalow in a cosy little cul-de-sac filled with twinkling Christmas lights to light up the gloomy looking day. Not an abandoned little cul-de-sac, but one with cars and neighbours, and honest to God cheer about the place. It was the scariest thing I had seen.

Myka pulled up in the driveway beside the cosy little bungalow and strolled up the path toward it with such confidence and ease that I began to believe she may have actually lived there. Even the interior,

I noted, when we entered, was cosy and warm and happy. It felt like a magic trick, like if I blinked, it would all fade. It even had a Christmas tree in the corner of the living room with unopened presents beneath it, and maybe that alone was enough to break the spell, because it was after Christmas now and no happy little cosy home would have unopened presents.

"And your *friend*," I said, unsure of the word friend and the way it sat in the sentence in relation to a demon, "they live here?"

"Foras," Myka said, strong and confident, "and be sure to remember their name for it will give you strength. Foras lives wherever they choose to reside. This house is not one of those places, but it will offer us the space and privacy needed to summon them."

"Summon...?" I had gone from being attacked by demons and running from them, to befriending one. And now? Now I was going to be part of summoning one? It did not sound like a good idea in the least.

"Remember, you must have confidence. Be sure of your strengths and do not waiver."

I closed my eyes and breathed in deep. What choice did I have?

"But be respectful also. Demons are proud beings; it is their greatest downfall."

I couldn't help snorting at that. Wasn't that the truth? It was certainly true of Nate. Him and his pride. I followed Myka as she led me through the bungalow and to a room at the back with wooden flooring. It was sparser than the other rooms, and somehow darker and colder too. I shivered as I watched Myka work, drawing a chalk outline on the empty floor and setting up several candles about the place. When all but one was lit, she turned to me and handed me the last candle.

"When you are ready, light the candle—but only when you are sure."

I could feel myself shaking, nervous at the thought, but I drew in a deep breath and stepped forward to light the candle with one of those already on the floor. When I had done so, Myka motioned for me to place it in the spare spot around the circle and began chanting in a language I had never heard before. I stepped back and stared at the circle, waiting.

It reminded me of the demon we had interrogated in London, but it was different all the same. We had captured that demon and placed them in a circle similar to the one on the floor before me now, only then the circle had belonged to Dantalion. This one claimed itself as belonging to Foras. Were names truly that powerful?

The candles flickered, threatening to go out, and there was a loud crack, like thunder, a split forming across the ceiling of the room as a thick grey smoke began to seep into the centre of the circle. It swirled and twisted, and I watched in fascination, barely even realising that Myka had stopped speaking, so entranced by the sparks of tiny lightening that flashed across the smoke, until the smoke began to take shape.

It moved and stretched, bulging together and moulding itself, looking more and more like a man. Then I started to see it's features more clearly, familiar features that I saw so often in my mind's eye. I wanted to look away but couldn't, unable to until finally the smoke stopped shifting and all that stood before us in the centre of the circle was a man.

"Marcus..." I breathed out, staring at the memory of my old life. Marcus, my boyfriend of five years with his tousled dark locks and olive tinted skin. He remained silent but reached out a hand to me, eyes pleading, begging me to move forward. When I didn't, his shape changed further, a reddened gaping hole forming in his throat, blood pouring from it down his shirt—the one he had worn when I had plunged those scissors into his throat. Except it hadn't been him. It hadn't. But God... here he stood now, and my heart ached, throat tightening as I could feel the tears stinging at my eyes. "I'm so sorry,

Marcus… I'm so sorry."

Myka stood silent beside me, still and strong. She offered no comfort or support, but her words rang through my mind, as loud as if she had just spoken them then. Demons are tricksters. I knew that. Even as my heart told me Marcus stood before me now, my mind knew it was a lie.

I closed my eyes and composed myself, taking in a deep breath. When I opened my eyes again, I looked closer and stood tall, attempting to be strong. "He had brown eyes," I said, "not blue. You're not Marcus."

"So, you know who I am not, but do you know who I am?" the demon in the circle questioned, and he began shifting shape again, until he looked like any other regular man—a regular man whose very skin breathed black smoke that continuously coiled around him like a snake.

"Foras," I said, strong. "Your name is Foras."

The demon snorted and turned their attention to Myka. "What is the meaning of this? I was meant to be in slumber. Why have you woken me?"

"We seek your help," Myka said, lowering her head in a respectful bow.

"You and your guardian seek my help?" The demon scoffed. "It offers me no benefit to help one who so willingly kills my kind. Her sight is an abomination that should not exist. I shall not help."

"Excuse me?" I asked, unable to help myself, and taking a strong step forward but being careful not to step past the candles and the circle. Demons weren't the only ones who were proud. A little too much at times. "Abomination? And exactly where do you get off saying things like that? Just because I can see what you are, you call my sight an abomination?"

"You are a killer of demons," Foras spat at me, turning his head away.

"And you're a spoilt brat."

"Girl," Myka warned from beside me. "You must treat him with respect."

I shook my head. "I respect those who respect me, and I can tell you right now—there is only one demon I respect, and you are not him. For a moment there, I was actually starting to buy this whole idea that not all demons are evil, but I guess I was wrong. Keep your secrets and spoutings of my sight being an abomination, I'll find another way."

I made to turn away and could see Myka's head falling forward in defeat, but before I could make it much further than a step, Foras spoke up.

"I cannot tell you where your friends are," he said, and his tone had turned solemn. "I know only that they are somewhere cloaked from my sight, which can only mean they are within another demon's."

I span around to face him, energy returning to me. "Which demon?"

"He goes by the name of Vassago."

Vassago. I nodded. I knew that name, recognised it. "Shay. They're with Shay."

"Guardian," Foras said, drawing my attention to him once more, "now I have given information to you, there is something I wish to ask in return."

I narrowed my eyes at him, unsure of how to respond.

"And what do you ask?" Myka questioned for me, standing tall once more.

"I wish to keep the form of your lover. I feel it suits me more than my current form."

I swallowed hard, head lowering. How was I supposed to answer that? Of course, the answer had to be no. Why would a demon ask such a thing? I began to shake my head. "It's not mine to give."

"But the memory is," he said, head tilting to the side, blue eyes of his current form turning brown. "If you grant me this wish, I will offer you one last thing in return."

"What?" I asked, cautious.

"A warning," he answered.

I chewed at my lip and glanced to Myka before looking back for Foras. "What's the warning?"

He shook his head at me. "First you must grant my wish, then I will give you my warning. It could very well save a life."

I drew in a breath and thought for a moment before reluctantly nodding. "This better be worth it."

"See with your heart, and not with your eyes. You will know the truth."

13

Nate

Of course, Danny Boy—ignorant as ever—did *not* run.

There I was, practically glued to the chair and glaring at the kid, and he stood there. Granted, he at least had the sense to pull out his gun and point it at Shay, but we all knew he wouldn't use it. Shay was human, and Daniel was good. Too good for his own good, and my own good.

"Please," Shay said, spreading his arms out and motioning toward one of the spare seats, "sit."

Daniel shook his head and looked between me and Shay. He knew what was going on. We both did. That doll. That ugly as hell puppet doll. Why was I even surprised a snake such as Shay had used us to create our own trap? It was like getting the fly to spin the web that would later ensnare it. This is what happened when you made deals with devils, even the human kind. I was left unable to move, despite every inch of my mind trying to fight against whatever spell the puppet had woven.

I should have known when the creep had plucked my hair that he was up to something beyond being creepy and intimidating. He wiped his finger on a napkin and I saw a small sliver of blood there. So that was how he had done it. My hair and his blood. Shay was in control. He was the puppeteer, and I was his brand-new marionette. This was not good. In fact, this was the very definition of not good.

"Nathaniel," Shay ushered, and I closed my eyes, already feeling the invisible strings pulling, "would you kindly escort Daniel to his seat?"

Against my will, my body rose and moved toward the kid. I could see it in his eyes, how his reflexes wanted him to turn his gun on me, the new threat approaching, but he couldn't do it. He couldn't point it at me. With his face twisted up and a curse beneath his breath, he put the gun away and approached the table without my help.

"Why aren't you running?" I asked him, angry that he had disobeyed me. He had sworn. I made him swear he would run. It didn't matter that I had known he would break his promise anyway, but it still aggravated me.

"I can hardly leave you like this, can I?" he shot back, glaring at me from the corner of his eye as if this was all my fault. In part, I guessed it was. He had argued that there would be a catch to retrieving the doll and I had insisted that it would be fine. What could possibly go wrong? Well, for starters, everything. Everything could go wrong, and everything *was* going wrong.

When we were both seated at the table, Shay spoke again, leaning on his steepled hands as he had done many a time before, looking us both over as if *we* were the things he had just collected and not the puppet doll in the seat beside him. "The first time we met, I knew you had to meet Vassago. He truly was so disappointed that I couldn't detain you. I knew then that next time we met, I had to find a way. Maria here was the key."

"Well thank you, Maria," I spat out, sarcasm coating my words thickly. I had never felt so much disdain toward an inanimate object before, and I'd had my run ins with a fair few bad inanimate objects. Maria was just the latest in a long line.

"You see, she has no effect on humans, so it would be impossible to have her work her magic on you, Daniel, my boy, but demons," Shay said, with such a dangerous twinkle in his eyes, "they're a completely different story. She has a curse placed upon her you see, and that gives me the ability to control demons, so long as I have something personal of theirs."

"So, what?" I asked, "You feed Maria some of my hair and some of your blood and all of a sudden you're a freaking magician? These strings won't last. I'm a free demon, me."

"Freedom is a mere concept, an illusion. There is no such thing as freedom. You should understand that better than anyone."

And I wished he would stop saying that. Talking as if he knew me. Lumping me in with all those other demons. He was impossible.

"What do you want from us?" Daniel asked, getting to the point, because Shay certainly wasn't.

"Presently? I just wish to talk. Vassago will no doubt be here soon enough, but until then… I believe I owe you some information."

We both remained silent. In that moment we were trapped, but until we could at least come up with some form of solution, at least we could maybe learn something.

Shay seemed entranced, his gaze searching Daniel. "Your eyes… I really should have recognised you sooner. You're so like him, you know."

"You have our attention, Shay," I interrupted, drawing his attention away from Danny Boy, even if it was only briefly. "Now spill. What happened to Alan Jayden?"

"He was part of something magnificent… Historic."

"Get to the part where you tell us what that was."

A half smile, and a shine in his eyes. I could tell he was reliving the event inside his mind, and he was loving it. I just wished he would start giving us some details so we could start trying to focus on getting out of there. If I could have moved, smashing that doll would have been my first move.

"To understand it, you have to know the Harkanians aren't just hunters. They're scientists. Philosophers. Your father was going to be part of something that would have brought us all into a whole new era. We were going to bring the Harkanians out of the dark ages and into the light."

I didn't like where this was going.

"My dad was a hunter. He killed demons. That was his job." Daniel shook his head and closed his eyes, no doubt trying to steady himself.

"Oh, my boy," Shay said, pushing up from his seat. "It was not just a job. It was his legacy, and yours. Before the Harkanians even formed, there were families who passed down their knowledge of demons, families who hunted them down. Your father never told you?"

"Told me what?" Daniel asked, reluctant and tight.

"Your family history, of course! Your father was not the first of your family to be a hunter. It's in your blood! You and he were born to be hunters."

Even if Daniel hadn't known, I had. A little anyway. I knew because Serena had told me. His gift, to see angels, had been mine when I was human. When Serena had taken it from me, she had passed it onto a hunter to keep it safe, until it eventually found its way to Daniel.

Shay moved away from the table and toward a bookcase on the opposite side of the room. "You can only hunt and kill for so long. The world has changed, and we must change with it. Why do demons have to be the enemy? They have so much to offer us. Knowledge. Power." He turned to look between us once more. "Protection."

"What are you saying?" Daniel asked.

"Did you know that there are ways to trap demons?" Shay started, distant, thoughtful. Movements paused. Body stilled. He shook it off and waved a hand toward us. "Aside from trivial tricks like what Maria is capable of."

I knew of many stories of way to trap demons. Some true. Some…

not so much. I even knew of someone who had tried to trap a demon in an old oil lamp more than a few hundred years ago. It didn't work out quite as well as they had hoped. Then… then there was the interesting case of a small green gemstone. It currently sat somewhere inside the earth, along with my worst nightmare, trapped.

Shay pulled out one of the books from the case and flipped through the pages until a piece of paper fell out and floated to the floor. He dipped down, rather spryly, and snatched it up before bringing it back over to us where he laid it out open on the table. It was instantly recognisable as a family tree. At the bottom, I could see a name circled several times. Alan Jayden.

"Imagine," Shay said, "what a demon could give you in return for its own freedom. Imagine if you knew of a way to release a demon that had been buried for centuries."

I thought of Amon and the gemstone. "I'd leave them well alone. Let them rot."

He grinned at me and stroked Maria's hair. "If young Daniel were to release you from this spell, what would you offer him in return?"

I grinned back. All teeth, no cheer. "I'd offer to wipe that smile off your face."

But Daniel wasn't to be distracted. We had come for answers. That was why we were in this mess to begin with. "What has this got to do with my dad?"

"Your father was descended from the hunter who had been responsible for trapping a very particular demon." Here Shay's grin grew. He was like a predator that had spotted a rather vulnerable and meaty piece of prey. He was a real piece of work, one who had Daniel under one spell and me under another. "To free him, I needed your father."

"No." The word was firm, and Daniel was shaking his head again. "My dad would never agree to something like that. Raising a demon? He knows what demons are capable of. He was dedicated to ridding the world of them"

"You forget," Shay said, enjoying himself far too much, "your father wasn't the only descendant." He leaned forward and seemed to breathe Daniel in, his eyes hungry as they took in every inch of him. "If your father refused… well, he loved you too much for that."

Daniel swallowed and his gaze fell. I could see the guilt lining his features, even though he had nothing to feel guilty about. That was just the kid's way. He would feel guilty if his breathing caused someone to catch a cold. So, to learn his father had done something against his nature in order to protect Daniel—yeah, that was bound to be a kicker.

"He tried to fight it. He thought he could stop it, but he was too late. Vassago rose once more."

Vassago.

Daniel went pale and I could feel breath being stolen as it clicked into place. Of all the demons, it would be Vassago that was responsible for his father's death.

Vassgo, who was meant to be turning up any time now.

"Daniel," I tried to say, but he was gone, his attention fully focused on Shay. He was finally getting answers, even if he wasn't liking them.

"Then what happened?" Fists clenched under the table, his face as composed as it could be.

Shay looked at Daniel almost with pity. "You must understand, Vassago had been trapped for such a long time. He was weak. He needed a host, and the only one he could possess was your father. That was the curse left behind by your ancestor, the price to pay." He took a breath and shook his head. "It was not Vassago's fault. He didn't want to harm your father—but the others, they got scared. It was too much for them and they tried to exorcise Vassago from your father. It was… messy. Their souls had already begun to entwine, but the Harkanians were so afraid of the beauty of it, all the possibilities.

They destroyed him."

"Daniel," I tried again, harder and more forceful.

He flickered only slightly but did not glance my way.

"Daniel, we need to leave."

I could see the conflict in his eyes. Vassago was coming. The demon responsible for his father's death. He wanted to stay and fight, take out both Vassago and Shay. Revenge was clouding his judgement.

"Danny Boy, not yet," I said, trying to reach the sensible part in his mind, the part that had grown so much. "You know we're not ready for this fight."

"He killed my dad."

"And how do you think it'll go down if we stay here?"

Nothing.

"Danny Boy?"

Still nothing, just a clenched jaw.

"Daniel!"

He snapped out of it a little. "Yes, I know. You're right."

It was time to leave, which meant it was time to do something about that doll.

"Then what are we going to do?" I asked.

I could see Daniel's shoulders moving as he worked to control his breathing. He bobbed his head, as if making a decision, his eyes never leaving Shay's. I was unprepared. But hey, the kid had always been fast. Within less than a breath, he shot forward over the table, to grab the puppet. He was quick, but Shay was just a second quicker. With a mere flick of Shay's head, I was lurching forward also, grabbing at Daniel against my will. My fingers dragged at his clothes, gripping him and pulling him back into his seat where my hands came to rest firmly on his shoulders, keeping him in place.

"I know what it is you mean to do," Shay said, picking Maria up and straightening her dirty dress, "but I'm afraid it won't work.

Destroying Maria will not break the curse."

My gaze levelled on Shay, but my words were aimed at the kid. "Daniel, you've got to run. Use your gun, I won't hold it against you."

Daniel shook his head. "I'm not leaving you here."

I could feel the distant crackling in the air, as if a thunderstorm was approaching. But this was no storm. There would be no lightning or thunder. Vassago was coming and there was no telling how much time we had left. "You don't have much choice."

"Daniel, my boy," Shay pleaded, "just speak to Vassago. Listen to what he has to offer. Name your price and he will give you the world."

"I don't need the world," was Daniel's answer.

Shay placed Maria on the table and held up his hands, and as he spoke, my grip relaxed on Daniel's shoulders. He didn't want to harm Daniel, that much I could sense about him. Harming Daniel would mean he couldn't use him. No, he wanted Daniel on his side—preferably of his own volition. "Break her. Burn her. Do whatever you wish. The spell won't break, but if you stay and talk to Vassago, I will release him."

"Daniel," I breathed out, a warning. My gaze flickered to the exit where Benji lounged against the doorway, book in hand. With Shay's control over me, he had very little need to take part in this 'discussion'. It was the perfect chance for Daniel to make a run for it. I silently begged that he would see the opportunity and take it.

He rolled his shoulders, as if testing my hold on him, then straightened up. "Why don't you release him now and then we'll talk about it?"

"I know you don't think me that stupid, Daniel," Shay answered, smiling from ear to ear.

Slowly, Daniel pushed himself up from the seat until he was standing, his movements deliberate. Either he was actually considering Shay's offer, or he had finally figured out that if we both couldn't get out of there, he needed to do so alone. If he wanted to be the knight in shining armour he could come back and save this damsel in distress another day. But the crackling in the air was getting stronger, and from the way I could see the hairs on the back of his neck standing on end, I knew he could feel it too.

"Nate," Daniel said, without looking to me, "I'm sorry."

I never had the chance to ask why, nor did Shay. Like I said, Danny Boy was quick. He pulled his gun from the waistband of his jeans and spun around to fire two shots into my thigh. The pain caught me off guard, and with the placement of the shots, my body was given no choice. I was sent crashing down, which gave Daniel his chance to dart toward the exit. Even as Shay commanded me to reach forward, my body disobeyed, my leg giving out again before I could even fully stand.

In that time, Daniel should have been out the door and away. Should have been. Benji's attention wasn't as absent as I thought it was. I could hear the chaos before I managed to lift myself up enough to see it. Another shot, some swearing on Daniel's part, and by the time I could see, Benji had hold of Daniel. He threw Daniel toward the table, causing it to shake beneath my grip, and I could see a gash on Daniel's forehead where it had collided with the edge.

"Not so rough, Benjamin," Shay chided, shaking his head and moving to kneel before where Daniel now sat on the floor. He gripped the kid's chin and turned his head from side to side, examining the cut, tutting as he did so. "Head wounds always bleed more, but you should be fine. I just wish you wouldn't fight me, Daniel. I only want what's best for you."

He stood and moved toward the sink, grabbing a cloth along the way. Did he actually plan on performing minimal first aid on the kid?

Now that the brief scuffle had died down, I could see Benji was returning to the doorway, book discarded and bloody. It was then that

I also saw he was bleeding from his hand. My head fell forward. "You shot the wrong hand, Danny Boy. His right hand has the mark… not the left."

The mark that was a demon's weak spot. The one that could kill us.

"I know," was all Daniel answered, dragging himself up from the ground. He reached into his pocket and pulled out an all too familiar knife, flicking it open in one smooth motion. The blessed blade I had given to him. He was going to go for round two and correct his mistake, the only problem was Benji was already readying himself for the fight.

Except… I could make out the smirk on Daniel's lips. Instead of lurching forward, the turned the blade on himself—or rather, on his shirt. It wasn't until he had used the knife to cut away a piece of the cloth that I saw the blood staining it. He held up a hand to his head before pulling it away to stare at his own blood. Then the kid did something so incredibly stupid that I had to admit, I was impressed.

He combined the blood, and in the next moment he was shoving the cloth into Maria's mouth.

"Benji," Daniel commanded, clear and in control, despite the way he swayed on his feet a little, "sit."

And Benji did just that.

I guess I had been wrong. He hadn't planned on making a run for it after all. Damn kid was smarter than I gave him credit for sometimes.

"Very clever," Shay mused, damp cloth now discarded by the sink. "You're a natural."

Daniel attempted to stand tall. "Release Nate."

"Can't you feel it?" Shay asked, "What good it would do you? Vassago is almost here."

"Daniel, now is your chance to run—I mean it this time," I tried, but he did what he was good at and ignored me.

"Benji," he said, "go to Vassago and stop him from coming here."

Benji obeyed. The demon left the body it possessed to crumple to the ground like an empty husk and went in search of it's true master.

"He won't be able to stop Vassago," Shay pointed out. "Vassago is not as weak as he once was. He is almost at full strength again, and a demon like Benjamin… he doesn't stand a chance."

"But he can delay him until you do as I say and release Nate."

Shay cocked his head to the side and looked Daniel over. "Perhaps I made the wrong choice before. I should have bypassed your father and come straight to you. You're barely a man and you already show so much more promise."

Daniel said nothing. Just swallowed hard.

Moving toward Maria, Shay held out his hand to Daniel. "The knife," he commanded.

Daniel made no attempt to hand it over. Instead, he gripped it tighter.

"You want me to release him, don't you?" Shay questioned. "Then I need blood."

"Wait…" I said, looking between the two. "This—no. Don't trust him, Daniel. Why would he break the spell now?"

"Because I can see that it's too soon. You're not ready to meet with Vassago." He motioned for the knife once more before simply taking it from Daniel's now slackened grip. "But I can tell the next time we meet, I won't need Maria. You'll want to see Vassago, and you'll be ready to make a deal with him."

"That will never happen," Daniel managed to say, shaking himself of the shock of Shay's actions.

"You think there is no price for your soul?" Shay questioned, yanking a hair harshly from my head. "There is always a price."

By the time he was done, gathering his own blood and my hair into a small piece of cloth and burning them, I could feel myself able to move of my own free will again. I felt the strings being cut. I should have felt lighter, but Shay's words rang inside my ears, and I could feel a deep weight settling in. Daniel had already shown what he was capable of when a friend was in danger. He had already shown the lengths he was willing to go to, putting himself at risk, all for the sake of a demon… So, what would he do down the line, when he was left with no other way?

14

Daniel

Our pace never slowed, even once we were out of the shop and onto the street once more. Sure, the gunshot wounds in Nate's leg hindered him, causing him to limp and hobble, but we kept our determined pace almost all the way to the car. That is, until we passed by a small alleyway. Nate ducked into the alley and dragged me in after him, pushing me up against the cold brickwork, his right hand curled tight in the cloth of my shirt as he stared hard at me.

"What the hell was that?" he demanded, his eyes hard and jaw tight.

I tried to hold his gaze, but I couldn't, my eyes drifting away and to the side, head falling forward a fraction. Swallowing at the hard lump in my throat, I wasn't sure what he wanted me to say. "Nate…"

His grip tightened a moment before he let go of a breath and his hand completely fell away. "When someone has you in their sights, you don't wait around to be shot. Not everything is worth dying for."

"Shay and Vassago don't want me dead." Of that I was certain.

"And there are also worse fates than death." Nate shook his head and took a step back. "Don't throw away your chance to see another day for a demon, Danny Boy. It's not worth it."

The 'I'm not worth it' went unsaid, but I could see it in his eyes and in the slump of his shoulders. I opened my mouth to contradict him or say something further on the subject, but the words caught in my throat. Ever since meeting Nate, everything I had learned about demons went out the window. Everything I thought I'd known barely even scratched the surface. My black and white view of the world and of what good and evil truly meant, it had disappeared, turning into a canvas full of shades of grey.

He cleared his throat before I could voice any of my thoughts and turned his attention back to the street. "We should get out of here. Maybe find somewhere we can use the USB drive we got from our friendly hunters. I'm sure there'll be a library somewhere."

I pushed away from the wall and made to follow him, but my eyes caught sight of a pawn shop over the road. It wasn't very big, and it probably wouldn't have what we needed, but it gave me an idea. "I've got a better suggestion… if you maybe feel like putting your pickpocketing skills to good use."

He looked over his shoulder and narrowed his eyes on me, a slight hitch of a smile tugging at the corner of his mouth. "Are you asking me to steal?"

"I'm just saying, we need money, and I don't have an endless supply. That kind of happens when you're on the run and don't actually have a paying job."

"Is that a yes?"

I opened my mouth to argue with him, but the look he gave me told me he wasn't going to let up until I agreed. Letting out a breath in defeat, I pushed past him and out onto the street. "Yes, okay? Yes…"

From there, the sullen Nate with a shadow hanging over him melted away for now, replaced by the mischievous demon who could not wait to make me his accomplice. Granted, we had already stolen Maria, but that was related to the supernatural realm of things. What I was suggesting now affected everyday folk, and that made me squirm initially.

But all ill thoughts quickly disappeared when we were back in our hotel room with a second-hand laptop in our possession. It had taken a couple of attempts to find a pawn shop with the right equipment, and then some bartering that Nate seemed to relish in. By the end of it, we left the pawn shop with a laptop and two cheap smartphones thrown into the deal. There was even enough left over in the wallet Nate had stolen to buy ourselves some food for the hotel room.

The room wasn't anything special. Two beds with relatively clean sheets, a bathroom with off-white towels, and a television that looked at least a decade out of date. It was dank and gloomy, and the dark colours of browns and beige mixed with the gloomy winter weather outside did not help matters. But it was a shelter. It was a place to rest, and it certainly beat sleeping in the backseat of a car, which was something I had grown accustomed to.

Since I had left Aunt Suzie the year before, I had to save what money I had where I could, and sometimes that meant sleeping in the back of the car. When my father died, I had the money he left me. The money he put aside, saving it up year after year, always knowing that with his job, one day, he wouldn't be coming back home. I had never really understood, because he was my dad, he was indestructible, until he wasn't. Until they came to the door with the letter in hand.

The Harkanians.

The way they stood, the way they spoke… it was so official and automated, like the words had been programmed into empty shells. Two of them, with suits and long, dark coats. Their words were wrapped up in secrecy, giving just enough information whilst ensuring they didn't say too much, and providing little comfort with their rigid language.

We regret to inform you that your father was involved in a recent incident where, unfortunately, loss of life could not be avoided.

It was only through his funeral I found out more. It was a small funeral, and the Harkanians were so regretful of my father's loss that they didn't even show up. Or rather, one of them did. An old colleague of my dad's that I recognised from my visits to their headquarters. She didn't say much, but she implored me not to join the Harkanians. She told me enough to know that his death was due to an exorcism gone wrong, and that he had been the possessed.

Two weeks later, I found out she also suffered a 'loss of life'.

This organisation that I had looked up to as a child, it was nothing like the dream I had painted in my mind. And now, I was closer than ever to getting answers. To finding out the truth.

My fingers worked at the keyboard, the flash drive sitting in the one and only working USB slot of the laptop, and I searched and searched for the software I would need to access the files I had copied over. It should have been impossible, and perhaps it would have been, if not for one thing. I had grown up with their computer system, and whilst I might not have been all that great at being a hunter, I was good with computers.

Nate sprawled out on the same bed he had taken the night before, munching away on a bacon cheeseburger as I focused on the laptop I had set up on the small desk near the window of the room. I picked idly at the fries beside me, but it wasn't until Nate spoke that I realised how far into a computer haze I had fallen.

"So, remind me," he said, and I turned to face him as he picked up one of the phones from the nightstand between the beds, "why do we have these?"

"Because I've been missing from the Occultus for days now, and Charlie is going to be worried." I thought about her, up there in Scotland, and pictured her cursing me as she paced the floor of the small room we had been given. I hated leaving her there, but after our run in with Shay earlier, I tried to convince myself I had made the right choice. She already had a target on her back, she didn't need another one because of my thirst for answers.

"One small problem, this… *thing*," he said the word with distaste and waved the phone between two fingers as if it was going to bite him, his nose scrunched up, "is here, and Charlie isn't."

"That's why I'm going to set it up and send it to her."

"Or you could just send her a letter?"

I let go of a sigh and pushed up from my chair to head over to him, snatching the phone from his grip and plugging it back in to charge. "Yeah, I'll go pick up a few postcards the next time we're out, shall I?"

He held up his hands in defeat. "I'm just saying, letters work."

"Welcome to the twenty-first century, Nate."

Huffing out, he rolled his eyes before motioning his head toward the laptop. My gaze followed as he spoke. "And how goes the laptop and wiffy?"

"It's Wi-Fi," I breathed out, turning back to glare at him only to find a smirk planted firmly on his face. My lips thinned and I toyed with the idea of cursing him but decided it would be more beneficial to return to the laptop. "It's slow, the laptop and the 'wiffy', but I think I've found something that'll let me access the files. I've just got to get it downloaded and installed."

"And in the meantime?"

"I guess we wait."

*****

By the time the program was running, busy in its attempt to decrypt the files we had stolen from Atkins' computer, I was exhausted. The sky had grown even darker, and my body finally gave out, my eyes stinging from straining at the laptop, and heavy like the rest of me. I barely even remembered climbing onto the bed or laying my head on the pillow, sleep coming to claim me so quickly.

It didn't take me long to realise I was inside that ever familiar the dream, the one where I wasn't me. The weight in my arms was as heavy as the dark shadows surrounding me, pushing in on me, until her light came once more and chased them all away. By the time the light dimmed enough for me to see her face, I was standing and everything but her, and her light, had faded away.

There we stood, face to face, on a white landscape that stretched out wide in every direction. No trees, no mountains, no buildings or people. Just white. Never-ending white. She looked to me with a sad smile on her face and raised her hand to touch my cheek. It did little to comfort the knot in my chest, but nor did I have the strength to pull away.

"I'm sorry, Nathaniel," she said, her words thick with guilt and sorrow. "I am so sorry."

"He's gone," was all I could say in reply, my gaze lowering to my empty arms and the weight no longer there. The grief gripped my heart, the tears wetting my cheeks. The intensity of it all, the anger, the sadness, the shame, it threatened to bury me alive.

She moved in closer, her eyes locking on mine, unwavering but oh so very sad. "It's not your fault."

I was about to answer, about to argue with her, but the sharp bite of steel to my gut stopped me. Confusion swept over me, my brow furrowing as her eyes closed and the tears slipped free through her lashes. I looked down and toward the blade buried in my abdomen, her hand wrapped tight around the hilt. My hand moved toward it, fingers pressing against the red already seeping out.

"I…" I tried to say, but I was weak, my knees giving out on me.

She followed me down to the ground, kneeling in front of me and finally giving up her hold on the blade to cradle my face instead, pressing her forehead against mine. "I am so sorry, Nathaniel. I'm sorry… I never wanted it to be this way."

I woke with a gasp, sitting upright on the bed and staring straight ahead. The only light came from the still working laptop, not enough to illuminate the entire room, but enough to remind me of where I was. Of who I was. My hand moved to my chest, my heart hammering hard inside of it as I struggled to get my breathing under control. For a moment, fear spiked throughout me, and I swung my legs over the side of the bed to turn the nearby lamp on. From there, I quickly pulled up my shirt, checking for any signs of blood, even though I knew I wouldn't find any. But I had felt it. I had felt the blade and the pain and the suffocation of death closing in on me. Except none of it had been mine.

Once my mind had settled enough to accept I wasn't dying, my eyes found the sleeping form of Nate. I swallowed the thick lump, considering the self-proclaimed lazy demon. Was it really possible? The dreams… it couldn't be. And yet my heart knew I was right.

Reaching into the pocket of my jeans, I pulled the lighter free. Nate's lighter. I couldn't explain fully why I still held onto it instead of simply passing it back to him, but perhaps it was because curiosity got the better of me. This demon, this being that kept confusing and surprising me, there was so much he kept hidden. Was it any surprise I wanted answers?

My thumb caressed the lighter and the scratchings on the back. He claimed he wasn't sentimental, but the lighter meant something to him, and as I turned it over in the light to look down at the inscription, I knew I was right.

To Natty,
With all my love,
J.

Natty. I had heard that nickname before, in my dreams, and whilst I doubted the person in my dream and the mysterious J were the same person, they did have one person in common. Nate.

Casting a brief glance toward the laptop, I breathed out and came to a decision. It wasn't long before I had thrown my jacket on and was outside in the dark London streets, staring up at the sky above.

"Serena!" I shouted, glaring at the air around me. She always appeared when I least expected it. She always seemed to know where I was. So, she had to be watching, right? She had to be nearby.

I looked up into the dark beyond the streetlights, ignoring the puddles beneath my feet that had already begun to soak through my shoes. The snow seemed like a long-forgotten memory now, the typical English rain washing it away. Apart from the odd random carrot here and there, the only reminder of where snowmen had once stood, it was as if it had never been. Such was life, and such was death.

"Serena!" I called again, and this time I earned a few glances from passing strangers who deliberately crossed the road out of my path. But I ignored them and focused on the empty air around me.

There was no shining light, no buzz of energy in the air. Nothing to say that Serena was answering my calls. I cursed her and took a breath, continuing to search the streets, until I saw what looked to be the steeple of a church just down the road. Shoving my hands into the pockets of my hoodie, I pushed on toward the church, bowing my head against the drizzle of rain starting up once more.

The gate to the graveyard was chained, but there was enough of a gap for me to slip through and even though the church doors were locked, I hoped it would be enough. I found some shelter under a large tree and prayed. I closed my eyes tight and prayed and prayed and prayed. Then finally, the soft glow began to illuminate the dark and I opened up my eyes to see her standing there in all her glory, shrouded in light and beauty.

"Daniel?" Serena questioned, confusion colouring her voice. "What are you doing here? Where's Nate?"

She looked around as she spoke, eyes narrowed and searching before looking back to me, her head tilted. Well, that answered one question. She had known I followed her trail to Nate. In fact, it wouldn't surprise me if she had deliberately made her path obvious for me. She always seemed to be a step or two ahead of everyone else, aware of our actions well before even we were. Adrenaline still pumped through my system, setting me on edge and I moved from one foot to the other, considering my words and what I would say to her.

"He's sleeping," I finally answered, biting my tongue as I waited for her reaction.

She seemed to calm a little at that, but only a little. "You should be with him. It's not safe for you to be out by yourself. The angels, they're still licking their wounds after their fight with Amon's demons, but if they so much as catch your scent, they won't even hesitate."

"Because of my gift…" I pondered lightly, looking down to the dirt ground as I tried to fit all the pieces together. "Because of my sight."

When I looked up to meet her gaze, she was nodding.

"Is that what happened to the others?"

She stilled. "Others?"

"The guardians. The ones who came before me, before Charlie."

A silence formed between us, and in the time I had known Serena, I had never seen her so hesitant or lost, so unsure of what to say. But finally, she spoke, and her words were slow and filled with sorrow. "Inevitably, yes. Death is the price a guardian too often pays." She cleared her throat and shook her head, as if shaking away the memories that had momentarily dulled her amber eyes. "But this time it's different."

"You say that," I said, "but I've been having these dreams."

"Dreams?"

I bobbed my head and took a step away from her, feeling the weight inside my chest. One hand reached out, finding the rough feel of a gravestone, to steady me, as I looked down at the other—the one that looked so different to the hand in my dream. "I feel like I'm someone else, like I'm remembering their life."

She let go of a breath and I imagined her nodding as she moved closer, coming to stand behind me. "It has been known. A gift, such as the one you have, can carry memories. Given everything you have been through, and how close you've been to…" But she cut herself off, clearing her throat, her next words falling away into the shadows. Still, I didn't need to hear them to know what she had been about to say.

"To Nate," I finished for her, and I waited a moment before turning to face her once more, locking eyes with her so I could see the truth in them.

She nodded.

"He was a guardian, before me."

"He was."

I chewed at my lip, my hand forming a fist at my side. "Does he know?"

"About being a guardian? He knows now."

"No," I answered, shaking my head and feeling my chest tightening. "Does he know about the part where you killed him?"

For a moment, I thought she was about to deny it, opening her mouth to speak. But once more, her words fell away and she simply shook her head.

"He trusted you. I trusted you!"

"I am not perfect, Daniel," she answered, "and it was not a decision I made lightly."

"You stuck a knife in his gut and watched him die. You could have saved him."

"By then, it was already too late. If I had not done what I did, Amon would have possession of the gift. And what do you think would have become of Nate then?"

I opened my mouth, tears stinging at my eyes. My mind and body remembered the pain, physical and emotional. It was intertwined with my own. "That doesn't make it right."

"No, it doesn't." She bowed her head, her shoulders and back straightening. "But sometimes there is no right and wrong, there is only what must be done and the consequences that follow either way."

15
Nate

It was the annoying beep-beep from somewhere in the darkness of the room that woke me. I groaned and pulled the pillow over my head for a moment before rolling over onto my back to glare up at the ceiling in frustration. Wiping away the drool from my chin, I let go of another grumble before forcing myself up in the aim of telling Daniel to keep it down. Except, Daniel was nowhere to be seen.

The sheets of his bed were creased and twisted, but empty—just like the chair in front of the desk and laptop. I pushed up and moved toward the open door of the bathroom, flicking the light on to find it too was vacant. No Daniel.

"'The hell you playing at, kid?" I questioned the empty air, eyes narrowed as I looked back and forth across the small expanse of the room, as if Daniel would magically reappear from nothingness. But it was no surprise that he did not.

What did come as a surprise, however, was the faint shout from somewhere outside. A familiar voice, and a familiar name. I moved to the window and pulled the dark curtain aside to look down at the street below. It didn't take long to spot Daniel; he was the one shouting into nothingness before setting off down the street with determination behind each step. There was frustration there too, frustration I knew well because it was a specific frustration brought on by a specific person. Or rather, specific angel.

Serena.

Rain ran down the glass of the window, growing heavier the longer I stood there, and I cursed both Daniel and Serena. We had a perfectly warm and dry hotel room, and now I had to go outside and get wet in order to go chasing Danny Boy down. I grabbed my coat and pulled it on, taking in the laptop screen and the flashing *'100%'* as I did so. It looked like it was finished with whatever task Daniel had set away. Still, none of it mattered if the idiot got himself killed by being reckless now.

By the time I reached street level, he was nowhere to be seen. Good thing I didn't need to rely on just sight. Despite his hatred of the Harkanians and his lack of skills at hunting, he still had the smell of one of them. It had grown fainter since I had spent more time with him, but still, it lingered. Old books and iron. I followed it a little way down the road, until I spotted the church up ahead and a smile crept onto my face.

"Bingo."

Daniel was calling out for an angel, and where better to find one then at a church?

The rain was coming down fast and heavy, and I swiped a hand across my brow to slow its descent into my eyes before shoving my hands into my pockets and cursing the glorious British weather. I was going to kill the pair of them for dragging me out in this.

The closer I drew, the more I could hear raised voices—or rather, just Daniel's. Serena's voice was as calm as ever. Though I couldn't make out the words, it didn't take a genius to realise Daniel was pissed. If it hadn't been for the rain pelting down and drenching me through, I would have hung back to listen, but a warm hotel room with something akin to heating was calling out to me, and whatever the pair were arguing about could wait until we were back there.

I squeezed through the gate and into the churchyard, clocking the pair by a large tree that offered some shelter, though not enough judging by the way Daniel's hair was now flat against his head.

Clearing my throat as I approached, I watched them, curiosity slowing my step only ever so slightly. Neither responded, so I cleared my throat again and decided to speak, putting on a gruff voice as I did.

"You shouldn't be in here," I said, unable to stop the smile when Daniel jumped as he spun around. Serena, however, was slightly more composed, but I could tell she had been caught off guard. Something had slipped into her hand at the sound of my voice, only disappearing when her eyes found me.

A blade of some kind? It made sense. After the dirty trick of leading the angels to a fight with demons, they were bound to be hunting her. That didn't explain the way she seemed to avoid meeting my eyes though. A frown tugged at my lips, and I narrowed my eyes on the pair of them, feeling very much like I was missing something. Maybe I should have hung back another second or two, just to try and make out their conversation.

"Nate, you're awake," Daniel said, his tongue snaking out to dampen his lips, and his eyes roaming over me a moment before falling away.

"Yeah," I answered, almost cautious, "your laptop thing woke me up. It was beeping at me."

He lifted his gaze then, meeting my eyes. It was as if whatever else had been on his mind fell away, his thoughts quickly distracted by this new information. "It's found something?"

I shrugged. "I don't know. You're the computer genius." I held out a hand, catching the rain in my palm and pulling a face of disgust and discomfort as I did so. "Either way, I think we should get out of this rain. Don't you?"

He nodded, casting a momentary side-glance toward Serena before moving forward and toward the exit. He said nothing to the angel, and I swore, I saw Serena's shoulders loosen and fall. What the hell had I walked in on?

"After you," I said to Serena, holding my arm to the side and allowing her to pass before I followed behind them. "I mean, that is, assuming you're sticking around for a while?"

"Sure," she answered, her voice even quieter than normal. "It couldn't hurt to see what you've found."

I rolled my eyes and grumbled, shoving my hands into the pockets of my coat. The air was as awkward as it was cold, and whilst I was used to being ignored or dismissed, this was different. Serena was distracted, more so than I had seen her in a long time.

"You knew, didn't you?" I asked, coming to walk by her side but continuing to keep my eyes on Daniel up ahead, each step and stride of his purposeful and determined.

"Huh?" she answered, if you could call it an answer, and when she looked to me, I swore I saw something akin to panic in her eyes.

"That Danny Boy would follow you," I explained. "When you came to see me, you knew he'd follow."

She nodded, but that was the only response she gave me.

I scoffed. "You put too much faith in me. What would you have done if I turned him away?"

"You wouldn't have done that," she answered.

"You don't know that."

Her hand gripped my arm as she brought us both to a stop, forcing me to face her as she looked up into my face. "You are a good man, Nathaniel. Of that I'm certain."

"You seem to be forgetting something," I began, once I had regained the ability to speak, so stunned by the look in her eyes and the earnest in her voice. "I'm not a man at all."

At that her hand moved up to the side of my face and pain twisted at the creases in her own face. "But you were, and I can still see him in you. After all this time, I still see him."

"Pffft," I pushed out from my lips, pulling away from her and setting off once more after Daniel. "If I didn't know any better, I'd say you'd been drinking. But then I'd have to ask, can angels even get drunk? And if they can, how much would they need to drink in order to get even a little bit tipsy? Do your bodies even allow it, or does alcohol just evaporate before it even reaches your bloodstream?"

Of course, she didn't answer. She didn't need to. We both knew I wasn't really asking. I was deflecting. There was only so much awkwardness I could take in one go, and the tension between her and Danny Boy was certainly more than awkward enough for that cold and rainy evening. So, distract and redirect the conversation toward anything but me and my humanity and perceived goodness. Once we had gotten back into the hotel room though, there was no need for any fake distractions. The laptop and what we were about to discover was certainly enough to put anything else from our minds.

Daniel was already shuffling the chair closer to the desk and laptop when we entered the room, his fingers working deftly at the keyboard. I swear, the kid didn't even blink as the screen filled up with various windows opening. I came to stand behind him, looking over his shoulder as he moved between each window in turn. Documents with thick black lines of redacted information, images that weren't the best quality but clear enough to see, as well as a list of what looked like video and audio files.

"Possible candidates?" I questioned, reading the file currently on display. It reminded of the list of names we had found before, except this one was more detailed. Ravenwood's name was there again, but unlike the others, his was highlighted in green and he was marked as the source of some kind of blood spell. Which meant the other names, they had to be relatives or descendants of some kind. That explained the family tree Shay had shown us before.

"Jacqueline Francis—deceased. Henry March—deceased. Peter Wills—deceased," Daniel read out, going down the list name by name. "Deceased, deceased, deceased."

"Margaret Hawthorne—location unknown," I continued, leaning closer and pointing at the screen as he continued scrolling. It was the same for the majority of the names on the list. Either location unknown or deceased. All except for three. "Susanna Jayden—confirmed, no relation."

"Aunt Suzie," Daniel answered, clearing his throat as he nodded.

"No relation?"

"She had a different dad, from my gran's second marriage."

"Which leaves…" I started, returning my attention back to the screen and the only other two names listed.

"Alan Jayden and Daniel Jayden, location known. Lineage confirmed. Match confirmed," Serena finished for me. "This wasn't just some random ritual. This was a blood ritual."

"What does that mean?" Daniel asked, already moving onto the next open window which appeared to be another document.

"More than likely, they weren't just conjuring some random demon. They were lifting a blood curse." Serena joined us at the laptop now, standing on the other side of Daniel as her brow furrowed, gaze focusing on the screen. "There is certain magic where only the blood of the caster can break binds of a spell."

"Like Maria," Daniel answered, no doubt thinking of how we had needed Shay to shed his blood to break his hold over me. "But when the caster is dead…"

"In some instances, if you can find a familial match, it is possible to break the spell. It might not always be as effective, but if the match is high enough, it can work."

"Felix Ravenwood," I breathed out, tasting the name on my tongue. Even now, it sounded so familiar. Somewhere, buried deep within my memories, I could feel it scratching at the walls of my mind. Felix Ravenwood. A hunter, no doubt, and I'd certainly come across my fair share of them over the years. But what made him so special? What made his blood and lineage so special?

"Jayden?" came a tinny voice from the laptop, the sudden sound drawing my attention away from my thoughts and toward the video now displayed on the screen. The image kept breaking up, lines zigzagging across the screen and static interfering with the display of the already unsteady camerawork. But despite that, it was still possible to make out most of the darkened image that now filled the screen.

There was nothing particularly special about the location, just another random cemetery filled with random graves and gravestones. Old, by the looks of it, no longer as well kept as more modern ones were, overgrown grass and weeds covering the ground, except for a wide circular patch where everything inside it appeared dead—even the man that lay on the floor.

"Jayden, I am ordering you to respond," the voice continued again, and someone passed in front of the camera to come to stand at the edge of the circle of dead grass. There were others there too, each one of them refusing the pass over the edge, as if they knew that to do so would be dangerous.

"Can you make it brighter?" I asked, squinting my eyes at the image and leaning in a little closer.

Daniel didn't respond at first, and I turned to look at his wide eyes and pale features. Only then did it click what must have been going through the kid's mind. That was his dad on the screen, in the patch of dead, and he was either already dead himself, or wasn't far from becoming so.

I cleared the lump in my throat and softened my voice a little. "Daniel? The brightness?"

He nodded numbly and tapped at some buttons on the keyboard. It didn't improve the image greatly, but it did lighten it enough to show the markings in the grass. A binding circle, made to trap and bind demons. Much like the ones the Harkanians had used on me earlier. As for the people around the circle, I counted at least five but there were no doubt others beyond the reach of the camera lens. Anything less for dealing with a demon like Vassago would have been suicide.

"Subject unresponsive. Project Revival, test one—unsuccessful." There was disappointment on the person's tone, and when they spoke again, it was dismissive. *"Porter—deal with the body."*

"Sir?" somebody else questioned, toeing the edge of the binding circle, reluctant to cross it.

"You heard me. Deal with it, Porter."

The reluctant man passed over the threshold, moving toward the body in the centre, and again, the image flickered, static disturbing it, though the voice of the person in charge remained clear as he spoke again. It was lower, no doubt talking to someone nearby, and it sounded almost bored, as if the owner hadn't just taken part in the murder of one of their own.

"Contact the elders. Let them know what happened, tell them we're moving to stage two."

"Stage two?"

"Yes, Michaels. Stage two."

"But he's just a boy."

"Are you disobeying my orders?"

A fraction of silence, a momentary pause. *"No, Sir."*

"Then do as I sa—"

But the man in charge was cut off by a sudden laughter from behind, a maniacal and mad kind of laughter. Porter, the Harkanian who had moved close to Jayden's body now stood still. He attempted to take a step back, attempting to spin on the spot as he did so, but he wasn't quick enough. His neck twisted, all the way around, but his body remained still. The sudden crack was chilling and audible in the silence that had fallen.

"Daniel," I said, unable to tear my eyes away from the image of the kid's father pulling himself up from the ground, "I don't think you should watch this."

Beneath Jayden's feet, the ground was cracked, the lines of the circle broken, making it useless, especially against a demon such as Vassago. The man raised his hand, looking down at his fingers and studying them before ripping something free of them and throwing it aside with something akin to malice.

"Jayden, stand down," the man in charge ordered, and it was the first time I had heard true emotion in his voice. It quivered with it, tightly wound with fear.

Behind Jayden, others moved into position, books at the ready, and one in particular holding a cross as if it was the most powerful weapon in the world. A second later, and he was screaming as the metal of the cross melted over his hand. It was when I saw the first sign of blood that I pushed out with my powers, the laptop dying instantly, the screen going black.

Serena looked to me, but Daniel was too busy tapping at the keyboard and hitting the side of the screen to see that I was moving away.

"No, no… It can't stop working now," he said, shirking away Serena's hand as she attempted to place it on his shoulder.

"Daniel," I tried, but he shook his head, hunched over the laptop in a vain attempt to get it to turn back on. "Daniel!"

Finally, he stopped and turned in his seat to look at me. His features were ashen, and I wondered if his heart was pounding as quickly as mine was. "I need to know."

"No," I answered, shaking my head. "You already know what happens next. That's not something you want to see."

His brow furrowed a moment, eyes dropping before raising once more to meet mine, suddenly realising I was the reason the laptop had gone off. He pushed up immediately, striding toward me. "Turn it back on."

"Daniel," Serena tried, but he simply swung to glare at her, and she was silenced immediately.

"Nate—I need to see."

Again, I shook my head. "No, Daniel."

"Turn it back on!"

"That man, that wasn't your father. By that point, your dad was already gone."

"No…" He turned away for a moment, looking back toward the laptop before focusing on me once more. "Nate, I swear, if you don't turn it back on…"

"Why?"

He paused, almost taken aback by the question. "What?"

"Why? What exactly do you need to see?" I moved closer to him, closing the gap. "You know who your father is, you know the kind of man he was. You don't need to have that image of him tarnished because of them."

He opened his mouth to argue, but I could see it in his eyes, the hurt and confusion, his confidence and determination wavering. "But we still don't have any answers…"

"Yes, we do." We had all the answers we wanted, including the ones we didn't even know we needed.

Alan Jayden was the subject of one of the Harkanian's experiments. It might not have had the results they desired, but it had worked. They had broken the blood curse placed on Vassago by Felix Ravenwood. The blood curse that had been placed in the very same cemetery years before. The blood curse that had gripped hold of Vassago and dragged him down into the earth.

How did I know? Because I remembered now. I remembered why the name sounded so familiar. I had seen him do it. I had seen Ravenwood banish Vassago to the depths of the ground. I remembered the curse, the words, the ring that Vassago had pulled from Jayden's finger. And I knew it was a ring, a beautiful ring with a deadly curse and a stunning green gem. I knew because it was the same ring I had placed on Amon's finger to place the same curse on him. Which meant there was also one other thing I knew…

"Serena," I said, turning to her with urgency, "you have to get to Scotland. Get to Charlie. If Cathal knows about the ring, she's in danger."

16

Charlie

"And you are sure about this?" Myka questioned from beside me.

I cleared my throat and attempted to shake away the thoughts that had consumed me since meeting Foras. His words still played heavily on my mind. See with my heart? What did that even mean? What truth was I meant to see? My head span at the thought, my chest tightening. The warning made little sense to me, but when combined with everything else Foras had said, I knew one thing for sure—I had to get to Daniel.

"Charlie," Myka spoke again, a little more forcefully this time, pulling my attention back toward her.

"Yes, sorry," I answered. "I'm sure. They're in London."

My gaze rose up and toward the large display ahead of us, watching as the names and letters and numbers flashed and changed. The train times and their platforms displayed, along with their destinations. We had ditched the car shortly after our meeting with Foras. It sat by itself in some random side-street in the middle of Newcastle, whilst Myka and I had made our way to the train station further into the main part of the city.

In theory, we would reach London sooner travelling by train rather than by car, and if the traitors who had turned on their brothers in the Occultus were still looking for us, then changing transport would give us an edge. Or so we hoped. But so far, the train was delayed, and the station was full of people, which did nothing to settle my nerves. In such a wide, open area and with such a tall ceiling, it should have felt anything but claustrophobic. But then, judging by the amount of people moving about, we had chosen one of the busiest times to travel.

I pulled one arm in tight against my body, my free hand rubbing at my bicep and teeth chewing at the inside of my cheek. Each person that passed us by a little too closely or looked our way a little too long, they made my skin crawl. Demon? Traitor? Or someone who paid a little too much attention the news? The list of people that wanted my head was far too long and being there, out in the open like I was, it made me nervous.

"Here," Myka said, thrusting something cold toward my hand. "Take this."

I accepted the item with narrowed eyes, looking down at the metal charm Myka had passed to me, a thick, black, leather cord tied to it. The charm itself was silver and worn, but the pattern was still clear—a Celtic knot of some kind. The pad of my thumb brushed against it, attempting to follow the pattern along with my eyes, round and round the charm.

"It is a Dara knot," Myka explained. "A symbol of inner strength. It was a gift from my mentor, but I think you need it more than I do."

"What does it do?" I questioned, still entranced by the symbol, my mind wandering to the book that now sat in the cloth bag slung over my shoulder, thinking of all the things inside that I had only just begun to scratch the surface of.

"For some, it is a reminder of what is already there. Then there are those who believe it gifts the wearer with something special. For others, however... It makes a good distraction from worrisome thoughts."

I let go of a light chuckle and I swear I saw her smile. I hadn't even realised how much the tension had left my body, my shoulders loosening and heart no longer thudding in my chest. All from such a simple act, from such a simple item.

It was just a shame it couldn't last.

She gripped hold of her wrist and the mark etched into her flesh, letting go of a sharp intake of breath, at about the same time the voice from behind spoke up. The words were sickly sweet, the Irish lilt colouring each one, but the beauty of it did nothing to cover up the cold, harsh malice set deep within the owner's tone.

"A trinket for tourists and nothing more," the voice said, and I spun on the spot to face the newcomer. He grinned at me; the shadows so thick around him they almost clouded his curly, red hair. "Evening, Miss McCray. Were you really planning on leaving without saying goodbye?"

Cathal. I remembered him well from our last meeting. Or rather, from the time he kidnapped me and held a knife to my throat. From the look in his eyes, he clearly remembered our encounter as well, rubbing at the right of his jaw with his thumb. Demons weren't hurt as easily as humans, but they were vain and they were proud, and to be attacked by a human, whether it hurt or not, whether it left a mark or not, I could see it all too clearly that he was pissed.

I stumbled back a step, but he caught hold of my arm before I could go any further. His nails seemed to almost sharpen the more he tightened his grip, digging into my skin and refusing to let go. A quick glance around told me he wasn't alone either. There were others in the crowd, blocking exits and possible escape routes.

"He isn't here," I spat out, forcing a grin onto my face and staring hard at him. "In fact, I don't even know where he is."

Cathal tilted his head to the side and let go of a chuckle. "I'm not here for Nathaniel, or your little lost puppy-dog. I'm here for you, Charlie."

"You're the one responsible for the attack on the order?" Myka spoke up, letting go of her wrist and letting it fall to her side, but I could still see the tension that remained, as if she was in pain.

Cathal looked to her with an upturned lip, as if her presence left a bad taste in his mouth. "And you're the rat that slipped through the cracks and stole my prize. You're good, keeping yourselves off the radar, making sure we couldn't pick up your scent… but you forgot one thing." He reached into his pocket and pulled out a card. It was golden in colour, shiny and bright, very much like the credit card Myka had used to purchase the train tickets for London. "We live in a new age, and there's always more than one way to flay a human until they beg for death. You should have just used cash. It's not as easy to track."

She cursed under her breath, at least I assumed the unfamiliar word was a curse. The sentiment behind it clear. But beyond that, she held herself tall, unwavering. "I will remember that for next time."

I wasn't sure when it happened, but at some point whilst my attention had been on Cathal, Myka reached into her pocket for something. I saw a cork drop to the ground, and in the next moment, she was throwing the contents of the glass vial into Cathal's face. He recoiled and hissed loudly at the pain, giving me the opportunity to pull free.

I sprinted away before I even knew where I was heading, my feet carrying me away from Cathal, pounding hard against the concrete floor, as I pushed through the crowd. Myka was beside me at first, until she slipped in front to lead the way. There were angry shouts and groans around us, some from the people we rushed past and others from the demons closing in.

"This way," Myka commanded, grabbing my wrist and leading me down a random platform and toward a random train. She climbed on at the first set of open doors and squeezed her way down the centre aisle, muttering the occasional small 'excuse me' every so often. It was only when we reached the second carriage that she let go of me, but she continued onward, despite the grumbling passengers, and I followed, obedient.

Chancing a look behind, I saw others moving down the aisle after us. The thick shadows that oozed from their souls almost darkening the previous carriages, blocking out the lights. The lights in our own carriage flickered before completely going out, and that was when I looked up ahead, toward the doorway leading to the last. It was blocked by a grinning demon who looked far too pleased with himself.

But before he could make his move, Myka pulled me from the train and out onto the platform once more. I fell forward, tripping over my feet but managed to right myself before swinging around to watch Myka as she faced the train doors. The words she said next sounded old to my ears, like a language that hadn't been spoken in years, and as she slammed her hands together, the doors slammed shut. Another few words, and another hand movement, and the train was moving, the demons still on board.

"How did you do that?" I questioned, staring at her in awe.

"I have picked up a few tricks in my years of this life," she said, turning away and already making to move off. "It isn't much, but it should buy us some time."

I was still too stunned, my gaze following the train as it left the station. "Can anyone do that? Myka?"

She didn't respond, and I turned around to face her, all set on chasing after her, but what I saw stopped me cold in my tracks. Myka held a hand to her throat, and it was only when she pulled it away that I saw why. A large slit spread across her neck and blood poured free. She didn't even have chance to speak before she fell to her knees and continued forward in her descent. Behind her stood the culprit, with his red hair and thick shadows, knife firm in his grasp.

Unlike the other demons, Cathal hadn't attempted to get on the train. He had seen through Myka's plan, and now we stood face to face. He wiped the blade on his jeans before looking down to admire it.

"I'm beginning to think that stubbornness runs in the family," Cathal said, finally looking up from the blade to meet my eye. "Stupidity too."

The words washed over me, meaning little, my mind suddenly empty as my heart sank in my chest. Hopelessness ebbed in, and for the first time since I had been locked up in that hospital wing, I felt truly alone. No Daniel, no Nate, no Serena, or Myka. No one but myself. "I take it this is the part where you kill me?"

"It should be," Cathal answered, and his words were tight, "but thanks to a certain spanner in the works, plans change."

"What does that mean?"

"It means you get to live a little longer. You should be happy."

But that didn't sound like a good thing. The sly little twinkle in his eyes and the way his lip curled up, none of it seemed like a good thing. The only reason he would allow me to live was if he had something else in mind for me. The fact that Myka lay dead at our feet was proof this demon would never change who or what he was.

When he reached out for me, I had no intention of making it easy for him. The cuts and bruises and bumps, none of it mattered, as I scratched and fought and clung to my freedom for as long as I could, until the inevitable came. I tried to run, tried to push back, but he brought me to the ground. Even then, I tried to fight. But his fingers weaved into what remained of my hair, and he grabbed hold tight, raising my head enough to send it crashing down to the ground. Once, twice, and then on the last, everything faded to black.

17

Daniel

Serena was gone from the room within moments, leaving Nate to pace the floor whilst I could only stare at him, still trying to figure things out inside my head but feeling too overwhelmed to fully understand.

"I don't get it," I finally said. "Why is Charlie in danger?"

Nate sighed and came to a stop, his shoulders slumping. "The curse your ancestor put on Vassago, it's the same one I used on Amon. And Charlie… when I was human, I had a brother. I never had anyone to carry on my legacy, but when he died, his wife was pregnant. She might not be a direct ancestor, but she's the closest thing to a blood relative that I have, which puts her in danger."

"But even if that's true, you're still alive. Felix was long gone, but you're not."

"True," Nate answered with a nod, "but even if I didn't know Cathal was one of Amon's, I do know Cathal, better than I'd like to admit. Charlie is strong, and she gives as good as she gets, but out of the two of us, she's the easier target. You know it, I know it, and Cathal knows it. And Cathal, he'll go for easy every time."

"But she's with the Occultus…" Even as I said the words though, I felt worry creeping in. We barely knew anything about the small brotherhood, just stories passed down through the years. They seemed like good people, for the most part, but that didn't mean they were. In a world where even angels weren't necessarily good, it would be impossible for an order comprised of humans to be entirely infallible. And I had left Charlie there, alone.

Nate raised an eyebrow at me, offering up a half-hearted shrug. He didn't argue. He didn't need to. I could tell he could already see the doubt in my eyes. He huffed out and sank down onto the edge of one of the beds, head falling forward. "I never should have left you both there."

I swallowed hard, the blatant honesty in his words catching me off guard. "I didn't know you cared," I both lied and joked, trying for a smile as I dropped onto the edge of the other bed. The lump in my pocket pressed against my leg, reminding me of the lighter, my mind once more thinking about the inscription on the back of it. For a demon that wasn't supposed to care, wasn't supposed to give a damn, Nate was really bad at it.

Reaching into my pocket, I pulled the lighter free and looked down at it, toying with it for a moment before holding it out to him. He looked puzzled at first, which only deepened when he took it from me and turned it over, his head tilting and free hand moving to check his own pockets.

"Where did y—" he started, and I couldn't help but notice the tightness in his voice, the slight widening of his eyes as he grasped hold of the lighter in his fist, as if afraid of letting it go.

"You dropped it, back at the toy museum." I chewed at my lip a moment before clearing my throat. "Who is J?"

"No one," he tried to lie, but the way the words caught in his throat betrayed him.

"She loved you, that doesn't sound like no one to me."

"*He,*" he corrected after a moment. "Joseph Griffin. And he was a damned fool."

"You loved him too…" I breathed out, without truly meaning to, the realisation washing over me as I watched Nate with the lighter.

But rather than answer me, his jaw tightened, and he swallowed thickly, shoving the lighter away and pushing up from the bed to move toward the laptop. He cleared his throat, his next words clearly a sign that the discussion was over. "We should pack up, prepare for the worst. Serena won't take long if she can help it."

I opened my mouth to say something further on the Joseph subject, but I thought better of it and simply nodded instead. My bag was already packed, and I was sliding the phones into the front pocket of my main backpack when Serena arrived back. I didn't see the blood at first, her dark clothes hiding most of it, but when she turned her hands over to reveal bloodstained palms, I started to take note of the flecks here and there, bright against her olive skin.

My body froze, a cold chill running through it, fear gripping hold as my stomach dropped. Looking at Serena, taking her in, I felt like the floor beneath me had disappeared, my head spinning and lungs refusing to work properly. The thoughts ran rampant around my mind and my knees very nearly buckled as my mind turned to Charlie. Once again, I felt guilt slithering in, churning my stomach, my own thoughts echoing Nate's earlier words. I never should have left her alone.

"What happened?" Nate demanded, moving forward immediately.

Serena lifted her gaze from the blood soaking her hands and met Nate's eyes. "The Occultus, they were attacked. Betrayed by their own. Aiden is dead, and at least a half dozen more."

"And Charlie?"

"She got out."

"So, she's okay, right?" I questioned, but by the way neither of them turned to look at me, I feared the answer. "She's okay…"

"Serena," Nate pushed on, "where is she?"

Serena shook her head. "I don't know. I tried to find her, tried to track her down, but I couldn't. One of the sisters said she escaped with a member from another faction."

"So, either this other member is really good at concealing, or Cathal already has her."

My hand tightened into a fist at my side, nails digging into my palm as I looked at Nate, my back straight and shoulders set. "You said prepare for the worst, right? So, say Cathal has her—he needs her alive, like the Harkanians needed my dad. If they're trying to bring Amon back, they need to do what the Harkanians did, so where would they go? What do they need?"

Nate nodded, as if coming to a conclusion. "The shack in the woods. That's where I performed the ritual, so that's where they'll have to undo it."

I pulled the bag onto my shoulder and reached for my car keys. "Then that's where we'll go."

*****

I felt like I was racing against the night itself, the darkened skies giving way bit by bit to the colours of dawn, my foot pressed down on the throttle, driving as fast as I could. On the plus side, there was no longer any snow to slow us down, but that just meant the roads were covered with water instead, and the rain that kept falling only made matters worse. Driving in the dark and wet, with the heavy weight on my mind, it wasn't the safest journey I had ever made.

By the time the city roads and motorways had turned to country roads, the sky had turned to a mixture of orange and pink, the sun rising somewhere beyond the treeline that surrounded us. We were almost there. Despite how different the way looked without the deep snowbanks at the side of the road and slush along the centre, I knew each turning. It was a gift I had. My father had always said so. I only ever had to visit somewhere once and I would know the way. He always used to say that if nothing else, I would never get lost. And yet, I felt so lost in that moment.

"Charlie is strong," Serena said from the backseat, but the words did little to fill the hollow in my chest. They were meant as comfort, but all they served to do was make me snort in disregard.

My father was strong. He was strong in body and mind and will, and all of that had meant nothing. He had still fallen victim to the ritual and been possessed by Vassago, and he had done so to protect me. Now Charlie was potentially moments away from the same fate, and it was my fault once more. I should have been there for her, but my own pride and my desire for revenge had led me away, left her vulnerable.

"And what happens," I started, "if we don't get there in time? What happens if Charlie isn't Charlie anymore? It wasn't Vassago that killed my father, it was the exorcism that followed."

"We'll make it," Nate said, and there was a quiet determination in his words. "Charlie is going to be okay."

"But you don't know that." I shook my head, grip tightening on the steering wheel.

"I do. Charlie is going to be fine, and once she's safe, she can tell you where to aim." Nate looked to me, and I could feel his eyes, feel his strange calmness that seemed to fill the car. "You still have your gun, right?"

"Of course."

I spared him a glance, narrowing my eyes at him before returning my attention to the road. I understood what he was telling me, understood the words on the surface. Charlie could see the marks on the demons and those marks were their weak spots. Just as I could see the crack in an angel's light, as I could see where the right blow could snuff out that light, Charlie could do the same with a demon's shadows.

"If Amon breaks through, he'll be weak. That's why he needs a body," Nate continued. "He'll be vulnerable. Charlie will know what to do."

"What are you saying?" I questioned, looking him over a second too long and almost driving off road and straight towards a tree, only managing to swerve at the last second. The car thudded and bumped, groaning at the movement, tyres taking a moment to straighten up on the wet road, but I didn't slow down, not until I saw the turning up ahead that would lead us straight toward the shack.

"I'm saying we're not going to lose Charlie. I didn't go through all the trouble of saving you both to have one of you die on me now." He stretched out as much as he could in the small confines of the car, rolling his shoulders and cracking his neck. Letting go of a sigh, he nodded at an empty patch of grass next the road ahead. "This should be close enough. If they're already there, we don't want to give them the advantage of hearing us coming."

I had to agree with him on that. As much as I wanted to get there as soon as possible, going in quietly and fully prepared was the best plan. It was about the only plan we had. When I pulled up, Nate pulled himself free of his long cloth jacket and folded it up neatly, placing it on the front seat. He rolled the sleeves of his shirt up to his elbows as I moved to grab my gun and the blessed blade from the back of the car, and Serena tied her hair back and out of the way.

It was so quiet in amongst the trees, the only noise coming from the early chorus of birds and the crunching of sticks and squelching of dirt beneath our feet. For a moment, it would have been easy to think that we were the only people in that forest. Until a scream pierced the air and shook me through to my core, birds flying up and out of the trees from the sudden disturbance.

"Charlie," I whispered, and in the next moment, we were running.

18

Charlie

The floor was cold against my skin, my eyelids fluttering open to take in my blank surroundings. My head thudded and I raised my hand to run my fingers along the bump that had formed and the caked-on blood that stuck to my skin and matted my hair. A wave of sickness had me doubling over, a combination of my pounding head and the memories washing over me.

Myka. I could still see her face in my mind's eye, see the blood pouring from the wound across her neck. She hadn't stood a chance. Neither of us did. Which made me wonder—why wasn't I dead? After all, hadn't that been the demon's endgame? Kill me and steal Daniel's gift so they could use it against the angels? Yet, there I was, in some random empty room with a wooden floor and wooden walls, not quite intact but certainly alive.

"Well, good mornin', princess," came the familiar sound of Cathal.

I pushed up from the floor and onto my knees, looking up toward the demon as he leaned against the doorframe. Arms folded across his chest, he tilted his head and smiled at me in such a wicked way that it made me wonder if I would wish I was dead by the end of it all. He may have been the only demon in view, but there were shadows tracing paths along the floor and out into the corridor beyond that assured me, he was not alone.

"You gonna use me as bait?" I bit out, each word as sharp as the last as I used the wall beside me to push up so I was standing. If I was going to die, I knew I would rather be on my feet.

He scoffed and looked me over. "I don't need to."

"And what's that supposed to mean?"

"It means," he said, moving into the room and taking a few steps toward me, "that for this part, you'll do."

Before I could comprehend what he meant, another demon appeared behind Cathal, meeker in appearance, and certainly more submissive when compared to Cathal and his domineering presence. This demon cleared her throat and only spoke when Cathal turned away from me to look toward them instead.

"It's ready."

Cathal inclined his head in response and the other demon scarpered off, leaving Cathal alone with me once more. He turned back to me with the sickliest of smiles on his face, and a glint in his eyes that made my stomach churn. As he took a step forward, I took a step back out of pure instinct. But the room was small, and the only exit was the doorway beyond Cathal. If I just had a gun, or something sharp… but there was nothing. Nothing but myself, the demon before me, and the inevitable that awaited me.

"As much as I would love to stay and chat and torment you, it's time," Cathal said, and he didn't delay any further, marching across the room to grip me by my arm.

I tried to struggle against his grip, but he slammed me up against the wall and held me there. When he spoke again, his breath was hot and sticky against ear, and my skin crawled.

"Now, do try and behave. We wouldn't want to hurt that pretty packaging, would we? I'd rather have you intact for what we have planned, but I'm sure Amon won't mind a few scrapes here and there, maybe a missing finger or two."

"Amon is gone," I breathed out, feeling suddenly cold, my body going numb. "Nate, he—"

"Nathaniel may have temporarily displaced him, but actions have consequences, and it just so happens that your current fate is a result of those consequences." He let go of a short and dark laugh that seemed to hold no true humour, only spite. "Your blood will set Amon free, but don't worry, sweetheart, most of it doesn't even have to leave your body. You have Great Uncle *Nate* to thank for that."

When he pulled me away from the wall, I barely resisted, too stunned to do so, my body sluggish but easily led. It was only when we reached the outside, the cold morning air hitting my face, that my senses returned to me. There was a circle scorched into the ground, through the grass and dirt, symbols and lines inside of it, that looked so much like other patterns I had seen before, and yet different.

"I can promise you this, Charlotte McCray," Cathal went on to say as he dragged me into the centre of the circle and bound me to the ropes that had been driven into the ground, "you will feel everything."

Jaw clenching, I looked him up and down before allowing a tight smile to tug at one corner of my mouth. As I spoke, my eyes flickered down to his left side, where I could see the tiniest glint of his mark, the thick shadows that moved over him concealing most of it. "Whatever you're planning, you better make sure that I don't get out, because I can see your weak spot and I will kill you."

"Don't worry, there's no escaping what's coming for you." He tightened the rope around my wrist with a sharp tug, the movement causing my skin to burn and ache. When he straightened up, he held his hand out behind him and another demon handed him a knife. Cathal held it up between us for a moment before gripping my arm and dragging the blade across my skin. His grip tightened, forcing the blood to overflow from the gash, and he handed the blade back to the demon as strange and foreign words dripped from his lips.

It was only when the first few drops of blood hit the ground that he let go of my arm and began to walk backwards, all the while repeating those strange words of his, over and over, as the blood oozed down my arm and hand, dripping from my fingertips to the dirt beneath. I pulled at the ropes, but it had little effect, unable to move my arms much higher than my waist. That was when the ground seemed to shift beneath me.

At first, it was just unsteady, but the longer Cathal continued his words, the worse the trembles became. It continued, the ground cracking and splitting beneath my feet. I could only watch as the thick black and red shadows shaped like smoke began to push free of the cracks. It pushed upward, sparking with energy, like a storm cloud above an inferno, and began to wrap itself around my legs, moving further and further up.

I tried to shake it off, but my movements had little effect on it, and it continued to coil itself around my body and arms, winding around my neck, prickling at my skin. I swore, I saw a pair of red eyes, but they disappeared as the whispering started, like scratchings inside my mind. When that thick smoke had me completely in its hold, that was when it began to constrict, growing tighter and tighter, the pressure becoming increasingly intense. It burned at me and I screamed, darkness edging in around my vision.

But it continued on, ignoring my protests, pushing in on me, as if it was trying to push inside of me through my very skin. I looked down at my arm and at the shadows seeping in and out of focus, weaving into the very fabric of what made me me. My heart thudded from the panic, my limbs feeling heavy.

"There's a good girl," someone whispered in my head, and it felt like a dagger being driven into my skull.

My body betrayed me, and as I fought for breath, I looked forward, out toward Cathal as the demon simply grinned. The shadows seeped across my vision, and for a moment, in the treeline, I thought I saw hope, thought I saw a familiar face, but before I could look again, everything faded away, and I fell forward, deep into the shadows that gripped me tight.

19

Nate

Every tree and sticking out root earned a curse as we sped through the forest, past each roughened trunk and low-hanging branch until we could finally start to make out the clearing ahead. It was the voices we noticed first, and at the sound of Cathal, I quickened my pace. I could see his outline clearly as I broke free of the last couple of trees and threw myself forward and into him.

We both tumbled forward, and though my body ached from the impact, the fact he was now silent felt like a small win. His grinning face, however, as he looked up at me, had my stomach dropping as I wondered if we were too late. I kept him pinned to the ground, but it didn't matter how much strength I used to keep him where he was—he wasn't struggling either way.

A deep breath, and I forced my gaze upward, toward Daniel and Serena. The two demons that had been closest to the forest boundary had been sent back to Hell by the blade in Serena's hands, and the others by the shack kept their distance. Death may not have awaited them at the end of that blade, but sometimes Hell was worse, and they knew better than to try their luck without say-so from the one in charge. The one currently pinned beneath me.

Daniel made sure to keep them in his sights as he moved forward, crossing over the edge of the circle that had been carved into the ground. His gun was ready, and the blessed blade was tucked into the waistband of his jeans. But still, I felt uneasy as he neared Charlie. She had yet to move since falling to the ground as we had broken into the clearing.

"Daniel, be careful," I warned, and Cathal laughed beneath me, a cruel and vicious laugh.

"Charlie, it's me. I'm here," Daniel said, his tone hushed and gentle, concern dripping over each word as he edged closer and closer to her. But she didn't respond. She didn't speak up or turn her head. She remained perfectly still, lying there on the ground.

At first, Daniel kept a hold of his gun, using his spare hand to try and rouse Charlie. But when that didn't work, he laid the weapon down beside him and rolled her over to check her. I swear, I could hear him holding his own breath as he waited to hear hers. It was only when he let his out and began untying the ropes around her wrists that I knew she must have still been breathing.

But the scene before me, looking over at Daniel and Charlie, inside that circle. It felt all too familiar. For a moment, I felt like I was back in the hotel room, staring at the static-filled video playing out on the laptop. Charlie's eyelids fluttered and she let go of a gentle groan, looking up to Daniel with big doe eyes. Except, it wasn't right. The soft smile on her face as he stilled and looked to her. It wasn't Charlie, and Daniel knew it too.

I could see the moment he realised, see him attempting to scarper backwards, but not-Charlie shot her arm out and wrapped her hand around his throat. As she rose from the ground, she brought Daniel with her. Her smile turned twisted, and her head tilted to the side.

"Char—lie," he tried to choke out, trying and failing to pull her fingers away, "please. This isn't you."

"You're right there," not-Charlie responded, and as her gaze moved toward me, her eyes locking with mine, I could see it ever so clearly. I could see exactly who was in control. "I'm not Charlie."

"Amon," I spat out, and I begrudgingly pushed up from the

ground to stare him down. "Let them go."

"Why? So, you can send me back down into that pit?" Amon shook his head. "You won't do that, not if I'm going to take her with me."

"I swear to—" I started, but Amon whipped his spare hand outward, his power forcing me off my feet and sending me backward. The movement and surprise of it gave Cathal a chance to fully break free. I never even had time to react, able to only watch as everything began spinning out of control, everything falling apart at once.

"You could always try exorcising me," Amon mocked, splaying Charlie's arms out, Daniel still tightly in his grip. "But then, I've got my hooks in real deep with this one."

He formed a fist with his spare hand and as if to prove a point, the skin along Charlie's arms began to bleed as if invisible hooks were penetrating her and yanking at her. Daniel fought against him, of course, but I could see his reluctance. The gun was too far away to reach, but the blessed blade was right there. He just didn't want to use it. Not against Charlie. Even as Amon pulled him close, so they were face to face, he hesitated.

"Let her go," Daniel spat at him, defiant and indignant.

"Why would I do a thing like that?" Amon crooned, breathing Daniel in before looking outwards towards me once more. "I do wonder though, how deeply her demonic sight must be intertwined with her soul. If I dig down deep enough, maybe I can see what she can."

Serena started forward, adjusting her grip on her blade, but Cathal was on her before I could so much as push up from the ground. He buried a knife deep within the angel's side, catching her off-guard. He dragged the knife with him as he dodged her blade, gutting her quicker than she could heal. When I made to surge forward, he moved deftly out the way, releasing his grip on the knife and pushing Serena toward me. I caught her before she could hit the ground, gripping her tight and helping to lessen the descent.

"I'll be fine," she forced out, but she was struggling to stand back up, the grip on her own weapon not as strong as it normally would be. "I just need time to heal."

"We don't exactly have time," I answered, my attention moving toward Amon and Daniel.

The upper-class demon had the advantage, and he knew it. We were out of time, and we were out of options. But then, I already knew it would turn out this way. That was the way my luck went.

I took a breath and looked down at my palm, clenching it tight to stop the tremble. There was one more trick up my sleeve, and I had hoped I wouldn't have to use it. In all honesty though, we were never going to make it in time. That wasn't how things went for me.

But I hadn't lied.

When I told Daniel that Charlie would be fine, that we would save her, I had told the truth. I just neglected to tell him how and what the cost would be. I didn't have to do it of course. I could have walked away. From all of them. But as I felt Serena breathing against me, fighting with everything she had, I knew it was impossible. She was right, and I was useless as a demon.

Swallowing down the doubt, I took the blade from her and pushed to my feet. I placed the tip against my forearm and took a breath before forcing it to break my skin. The first symbol was the hardest, but by the time I reached the fourth and final symbol closer to my wrist, the blood seeping out, I held my head high, filled with determination.

"Hey, Amon!" I shouted, holding my arm out and meeting his eyes, forcing a smirk onto my face. "It's my blood you need, right?"

He looked to me and snorted, narrowing his eyes at my bloody arm. "You wouldn't."

"What's the matter? Afraid you're not strong enough?"

He laughed, and it sounded so strange and wrong, coming from

Charlie's lips. "I always knew you were stupid, but this goes well beyond that, Nathaniel."

"I guess we'll find out," I quipped, before reaching into my mind for old words I had heard and read a long, long time ago. Old words that only fools and the damned would utter. Well, I guess I was both. The words tumbled over my lips, strong and determined. But to finish it off, I decided to add in my own little twist onto the end of the passage. "I invoke you, Amon, Grand Marquis of Hell."

There was a sly smile on Charlie's face, before her body jolted, falling suddenly limp, and a burst of what seemed like steam seemed to pass through the air. It shot across the small clearing and slammed into me, turning my vision black and leaving me with the sensation of falling. At first, I felt nothing. Then a thousand voices seemed to scream inside my head as every single part of me suddenly felt like it was both on fire and being frozen all at once. Nails digging through my flesh and into my very soul, going deeper and deeper, fighting for control.

The ritual that had dragged Amon down into the earth had weakened him greatly, but with a heart full of spite like his, it was enough to give anyone power. I could feel him, feel what amounted as his soul, twisting its way into my body alongside my own. If Charlie was quick, and Daniel was quicker—perhaps they could end it before he gained too much strength. Our one possible shot at ending Amon.

I could feel the smile on my face, or perhaps I merely imagined it, as a small sense of peace washed over me. If this was how I died, then I could at least take him with me.

20

Charlie

"Nate! No!"

The words echoed around the air, as if shouted from afar, but as I took my next big breath, feeling as if I was suddenly pushing free from a surface of water, the sound of them became louder. I sucked in the air around me, desperate for how clean and fresh it was, and raised my head to look toward the scene in front of me.

Daniel stood half a foot away, grip tight on the gun in his hand and attention toward the mass of black shadows that hung by the treeline. Except, the longer I looked, the more I realised that the hulking shadowy figure that seemed to spark with red lightning, was not a shadow at all.

"Nate…" I breathed out, and I pushed up from the ground, already moving to take a step forward. Daniel gripped my arm though, halting me, and I could feel his fear. My body ran cold. The voice inside my head, the harsh one with sharp teeth and claws, it was gone, as was the cloud that had smothered me, pushing me down, and as I looked out toward Nate, I knew exactly where it had gone.

"That's not Nate," Daniel warned from beside me, and I heard him curse under his breath before going on to add, "the stupid prat, what was he thinking?"

"What did he do?" I questioned, my voice barely louder than a whisper, my mind too preoccupied and stunned with the vision of

Nate. He stood there, arms loose by his side, head hanging forward, shoulders slumped. If it wasn't for the movement of the shadows around him, I would have thought he had been turned to stone.

"He invoked Amon. Son of a bitch… I should have…" Daniel adjusted his grip on his gun, letting go of the grip he had on me once he realised I wasn't fighting him. "He practically said as much. Why didn't I push him on it?"

"What? What did he say?"

"He said Amon will be vulnerable, that you would know what to do."

"What?" My brow pulled down and I shook my head. "Why would I—"

"He meant you'd see his mark, so we could…"

"So, we could what?" I demanded, but in my mind, I already knew, my hand moving up to my chest to sit just over my heart, mimicking where I knew Nate's mark to be. My gaze moved back toward him, as he lifted his head, eyes staring deep into mine. Beside him, I could see Serena moving for the first time, grappling for the blade that had fallen to the ground.

Her movements were slow and clunky, face twisted up in a wince of pain, but I could see her intention and I knew she didn't need my sight to know where to aim. She had known him far longer than we had, so there was no doubt in my mind that she knew exactly where his mark was. Right over his heart.

"No," I breathed out, voice small at first, but then I felt determination grip me and I shook my head, racing forward before Serena could get her feet beneath her. I knew what I was seeing with my eyes, I knew that Amon was there, inside of Nate, but it didn't feel right.

I wrapped my arms around him, covering his chest just as Serena was about to strike, taking her chance. The blade swept at my hair, the sudden adjustment had Serena falling once more, but my attention was on Nate. His eyes looked empty, dulled, as if neither he nor Amon was in control.

"Charlie," Serena berated, already attempting to push up again from the ground and wincing as she did so, "we have to strike now, before Amon takes over."

I shook my head, holding my ground. The words I had heard from Foras echoed around my head, and as my heart felt heavy and uncertain in my chest, I wondered if this was what he had meant. See with your heart, and not your eyes. "No, Nate's a demon. He can fight this."

"You should listen to her, Charlie," Cathal taunted from somewhere behind, and I swung my head to glare at him. "No one can win against a true demon like Amon. But then, what do I know?"

Daniel raised the gun to aim at Cathal as he took a step closer, but it made little difference to the demon's mockery and cockiness. He merely raised his hands up but continued forward. I lowered my eyes to his mark and the shadows oozing outward from it, my jaw tight and threat clear in my eyes. It was then that he came to a halt, smile still ticking at his lips and head tilting to the side.

I was about to open my mouth and tell Daniel where to aim, but another voice silenced me with what sounded like a command, foreign and deep, the words unfamiliar to me. A spark of flames spread out between Cathal and us, keeping him and his other demon pals back. A sneer slipped onto his lips, and he looked past me, my own attention suddenly drawn toward the newcomer also.

Instead of hope, I felt myself filled with dread. Two figures moved forward, and I recognised them instantly. Shay and his pet demon. As he moved closer, another demon skirted around the edges, one I had seen with Cathal before. At first, I thought he was about to attack, but as Shay tossed something small and shiny toward him, the demon simply bowed his head and backed away.

"Everyone has a price," Shay said as he drew closer, "even if it means working for another demon."

His eyes found Serena and he tilted his head to the side, looking her over as she dragged herself up from the ground. The wound along her abdomen seemed to be healing, though it was slow and still bloody. Not that it stopped her from adjusting her grip on her own weapon, ready to fight if need be.

"I don't believe we've met," Shay said, holding out his hand. "You must be the angel. I have heard a great many things about you."

It was no surprise that Serena didn't take his hand. But what did surprise me was the look of pure distrust on her face. Then again, you didn't need to be able to see demons to know that this man was tainted so thickly by them. Shay let go of a light scoff and lowered his head, but in truth, he didn't seem bothered by the lack of a warm welcome. After all, I imagined sharks would rarely be offended by the fish that swam away from them.

"What are you doing here?" Daniel questioned, and his voice was tight.

"I come in peace," Shay answered, and he looked to me, holding out his hand in a fist. He loosened it enough for a familiar charm to fall free, dangling from a familiar worn cord. "And to bring a gift."

I didn't take the charm immediately, but when he moved it closer to my hands, I found my body reacting without thinking. There was no doubt in my mind that this charm, this silver Celtic knot stained at the very edge with dark brown that looked a little too much like blood, was the same one Myka had given me at the train station. I hadn't thought about it or it's whereabouts since Cathal had appeared, but seeing it there, it caused my stomach to churn and chest to tighten.

"Is this some kind of a joke?" I asked, anger darkening my words.

"Oh, the necklace may not be much," he drawled, "but the charm I've placed on it is not to be scoffed at. Just a little something that may help your friend to lock away his inner demons... for now, at least."

My gaze was drawn to Nate once more, his hazel eyes darkening more and more the longer Amon was inside him. I was reminded of how suffocating those few moments had been when Amon had wormed his way into my body, taking control and pushing me under. In the darkness, I could see snippets, hear brief moments of what was going on around, but no matter how much I fought, no matter how much I tried, I couldn't break free.

"Why?" I questioned, only able to look at Shay from the corner of my eye, unwilling to fully meet his gaze. "Why help us? What do you want in return?"

"Nothing, at the moment." His words were so sly and dripping with ickiness that it made my skin crawl. "Consider it a gesture of a good will, a hope that in the future, we may eventually come to some sort of agreement."

"I don't believe you," Daniel spoke up, and I could feel his presence lingering just behind me, but I couldn't bring myself to look his way. If I did, he would surely see the hesitation on my face, my reluctance to fight and my willingness to not so much trust Shay, but not completely dismiss him either.

"Then perhaps you would like to offer something up in return." The smile on Shay's lips was clear in his tone. He held all the cards, and he knew it. "But I must impress on you that your demon's time is running out."

"And what do you want this time?" Daniel spat out at him. "Another errand where you try and trap us?"

Shay grabbed my hand and turned it over, revealing the ring on my finger and the bright green gem that sat in the centre of it. I hadn't even noticed it, too preoccupied with everything else, but now that I had seen it, it felt heavy and wrong, and I fought the temptation to pull it free there and then.

"Pierre de la mort," he whispered, staring longingly at the stone, greed hitching up the corner of his mouth to reveal his canine. "If you insist on paying me for my kindness, then I will gladly take this ring off of your hands."

"Charlie," Serena spoke up, her tone pleading and gentle, a warning laced beneath that one word.

But in the end, it wasn't me she should have been warning.

"Done," Daniel said, and a quick glance toward him told me that the word tasted bitter in his mouth, the weight of future complications already hanging heavily on his shoulders.

I followed his lead and allowed Shay to slip the ring free before returning my attention to Nate and placing the cord necklace around his neck. At first, there was no reaction, but then something seemed to change in his features, the dimness in his eyes disappearing, as if he was waking up from a deep sleep.

He drew in a deep breath and looked to be about to crumble to the ground before finding my hands steadying him. There was a brief moment of clarity before a look of pain creased his brow and twisted his cheeks, a sharp hiss slipping out through his lips as he clasped his right hand over the marks on his left arm. They were fresh and red with blood, but what struck me the most was the way the thick demonic shadow seemed to play across the symbols etched into his skin.

"Damn it," he cursed, before regaining himself and swallowing hard as he looked to each of us in turn, his gaze lingering longer on me, as if checking to make sure Amon hadn't left any nasty surprises. His back straightened when his gaze found Shay, his body turning rigid as he forced himself to push away any signs of weakness and pain. "What did you do?"

It was an accusation more than a question, spoken with venom and distrust. I couldn't blame him.

"I could always take back the necklace if you'd rather," Shay said in return, the condescending tone thick and taunting. "After all, it would be interesting to see, from a scientific standpoint. How long do you think a lower-level demon such as yourself would last against a demon like Amon? Should we place bets?"

Nate's hand moved up to the charm, grasping it tightly. "And is that what this is? Like Vassago and Alan Jayden? An experiment?"

Shay let go of a snort. "Vassago sees potential, and it would be such a shame to let good potential go to waste before we had the chance to utilise it. This is merely a chance for you to survive a little longer. The rest, my dear demon, is up to you." He rubbed his hands together and looked around. "Now, I believe this is the part where I take my leave. I hope to see you all again very soon."

There was emphasis on the 'very' and to say it made me uncomfortable was an understatement to say the least. That man had a gift for making you feel dirty, even with such simple phrasing. As he disappeared again, heading back to the treeline he had come from, the other demons that had been skirting about the area started to vanish too. I expected it from Benji, he was Shay's bodyguard after all, but the others, the ones that had come with Cathal, they didn't seem like the retreating type.

"Where are they going?" I questioned, not truly expecting an answer.

"They won't go against Vassago," Serena answered, and she came to stand beside Nate, pushing her blade away, the action reinforcing her statement, showing she no longer felt the need to fight. "He's shown his interest in you all, and with Amon currently locked away, they won't risk going up against him. At least not yet."

"Why do you say that?"

"Some demons are loyalists," Nate answered, and I couldn't help but notice his gaze was focused somewhere beyond. I turned to look and thought I saw a flash of red hair disappearing into the brush. "For them, the demon they follow is their cause, and even if that demon falls, they'll continue to follow what they stood for."

"And Cathal is one of those demons?"

"I never thought he was, but now… I'm beginning to think he's exactly one of those demons."

21

Nate

An angel and a demon in the backseat of a hunter's car… Correction, an angel and two demons. One locked inside the other, clawing at their insides and scratching at their soul. Amon. No matter how much I tried to push it from my mind, I could feel him. It was a persistent itch, setting me on edge, making me feel uncomfortable in my own skin. The symbols I had carved into my arm were healing, at least in the sense that they were no longer open wounds. The scars left behind would remain much longer, if they ever even faded at all.

Despite my warmth, I kept the sleeve of my shirt rolled down, covering up the most obvious reminder of what I had done. In truth, I had never expected to survive it. Whilst I was not truly eager to die, I had been sure that would be the consequence of invoking Amon. But for some reason, I was still there. For some reason, fate had taken pity on me. At least, I called it fate, because what else could it be?

Between Daniel and Charlie, Serena and Amon, and now Shay with his demonic connection to Vassago… I was being kept alive, over and over again. After all, Shay's words had not gone completely over my head. He could have spoken entirely on Vassago's behalf, but his words were deliberate. Vassago may have had plans for us, but so did Shay, and after the incident with the doll, I wasn't overly keen to discover what other plans he had.

"What happens now?" Charlie asked from up ahead in the

passenger seat.

We hadn't really discussed it. Once Shay had made his departure, the last of Amon's demons quickly following, we decided we needed to get out of there as well, but beyond that, we hadn't truly decided. So, for now, we were driving aimlessly, unsure of what was coming next for any of us.

I had never really had much of a plan before. That was how I lived my life, endlessly roaming from one moment to the next, no destination in mind, and that had worked for me. At the time, it felt right. No worries, no cares, just me and a few whiskeys for the road. But now, I found myself feeling somewhat lost and disconnected from that old reality. The thought of going back to that made me feel empty. Whatever came next, there was one thing I was beginning to learn—fate was determined to keep dragging me back to Daniel and Charlie. A guardian to the guardians. But it was more than that.

"Well, I think splitting up might be out of the question," Daniel answered, his words making me question if he had been thinking something along the same lines as me, that whatever path each of us went down, they were connected. Splitting up, fighting that, would be useless. "And I think the Occultus is out of the question."

Charlie seemed to sink in her seat at the mention of the brotherhood, and really, I couldn't blame her. She had been present during the attack. She had been there and had been witness to the death and bloodshed.

"Aiden died because of me," she said, voice barely above a whisper. "Myka too."

"They died because of who killed them," I answered, "but if you really want someone to blame, then it's me. They only came after you because of me."

"Can we not do this?" Daniel asked, and he sounded tired.

"Do what?"

"The whole blame and guilt thing. Bad people did bad things, not us."

"Technically, they weren't all people…"

"Nate…" It came out as a sharp reprimand, the warning following it silent. It didn't need to be spoken, that one short name was all it took.

I held my hands up, refusing to push the subject. "But still, the question stands. What happens now? It's not like we have anywhere to go. So what? We keep roaming about until Shay turns up wanting to cash in his chips, or until the pretty little charm on this necklace wears off?" I tugged at the charm for emphasis before allowing it to fall back against my shirt.

"Wherever we go, it needs to be safe," Serena offered up, to which I scoffed. That much was obvious, but what was safe these days?

"The Occultus have safe houses…" Charlie started, "But I don't know how safe they would be now."

"If only we had a loving family member that could take us in and shelter us…" I mused from my seat in the back, my eyes boring into the back of Daniel's skull.

"No," he said with a firm shake of his head, "absolutely not."

"What are we talking about?" Serena questioned, but Daniel ignored her.

"I am not bringing Aunt Suzie into this," he said instead, addressing me and meeting my eyes through the rear-view mirror.

"She's not as helpless as you think she is, you know," I argued. There was a strength to her, the same strength I saw in Daniel. "Or would you rather hole up in some random hotel or abandoned house?"

"The Harkanians know where she lives."

"Then it's a good thing we're not hiding from them. Not yet anyway."

"That's not exactly comforting."

"I'm sorry, I thought we were past the part where we lied to each other to make everyone feel better."

His jaw tightened and I'm sure I heard a low growl come from him, but beyond that, he said nothing.

"You know I'm right."

"No…"

"Danny Boy, she literally has a building on her property that demons cannot get to. You know how hard those are to come by these days?"

"Fine," he bit out, "we'll go. But the first sign of trouble and we're out of there."

"Trouble? Us?" I blew a sarcastic breath of air out. "As if."

There were no further arguments, just questions, mostly from Charlie, as we made our way toward the small home of Aunt Suzie. It was late afternoon by the time we drew closer. The snow had melted, leaving wet mulch on the forest floor surrounding the small cabin at the edge of the woods. As we wandered up the way toward her front door, I half wondered if she had put a charm on the place since we left, one that would keep me out. But nothing hit me, nothing slowed my pace or brought me to halt, and I figured either she just plain didn't know how to, or she hadn't thought it pertinent.

She was at the door before we even reached it, yanking it open and flying out to wrap her arms around Daniel. Once she finally let go, she looked him over, turning his chin this way and that, her eyes lingering on the newly formed scars and bruises. He tried to brush her off, even before she could voice her concerns, but there was no doubt that she was planning to take a good look at his wounds later.

"Aunt Suzie," Daniel pleaded, pulling back and moving aside to reveal Charlie and Serena, no doubt in an attempt to distract her. "These are my friends. We were hoping we could stay here for a little while, figure things out."

She looked them over in silence before nodding, accepting them, but then her gaze moved to me and I felt myself shift beneath it, my eyes falling, unable to meet hers. My hand moved to cover the scars on my left arm, and even though I knew she couldn't see them through my sleeve, I couldn't help but wonder if she could sense them, sense the darkness they held. But she said nothing of it.

"I guess I better stick the kettle on," she finally spoke, breaking the silence, "warm you all up."

*****

Aunt Suzie made herself a good host. While we cleaned ourselves up, she set to making warm food and drinks before heading up the stairs to sort out some space in the bedrooms. Daniel filled her in with snippets of information but didn't go into details—such as how he got the mark across his neck or how his demon companion was now home to an even bigger and badder demon. The less she knew, the less she would have to worry about. In theory anyway.

It was when she had sat him down at the kitchen table to clean the wounds that she could see that I excused myself. Or rather, that was when I silently removed myself, edging away until I was outside in the cool air. I leaned back against the wall of the shack and closed my eyes, breathing out. It was an action meant to ease me, to help soothe my mind, but it did little to help.

It took me a moment to realise I wasn't alone. I hadn't noticed her at first, too focused on escaping my own thoughts. But as I opened my eyes, I could see Charlie half watching me from the corner of her eye as she leaned against the wall on the opposite side of the door. Turns out I wasn't the only one in need of fresh air. She fiddled with the phone in her hand, the one Daniel had given her earlier, and whilst she kept glancing my way, I couldn't help but notice that she couldn't quite look at me directly.

"Is it really that bad?" I asked, watching her, wondering what her sight now saw when it came to me, what shadows she could see crawling over my skin and sinking in.

She shifted from foot to foot before finally meeting my eyes. "It's darker than before."

I nodded, knowing that was down to Amon's influence. "Figures."

It was another moment or two before she found her voice again. "What happens to the people demons possess?"

A sympathetic smile tugged at the corner of my lips as I thought about her brief possession. At the first possible chance upon arriving, she claimed the shower and had stayed in there until she was finally called out for food. To say she looked uncomfortable in her own skin was an understatement and the shadows she saw crawling over me now were a reminder of what she had endured with Amon.

"At first, they get pushed down, broken and bent out of shape, then little by little, their soul is consumed by the demon possessing them. After that, I don't know what happens to them. I guess you could say they die, or just cease to exist. Some take longer, years, decades… but in the end, the result is the same. It's just a matter of time."

"Is that what happened to the person you possess?"

I let go of a snort, a wry smile twisting at my lips. I did consider lying, turning myself into the villain. After all, it would make it easier in the long run, when Amon took control. If she could see me as the bad guy, then it would make it easier for her when the time came. But looking at her, looking into those blue eyes of her that reminded me of what I once had, long ago, when I had been human, I found I couldn't.

"No," I answered. "I got this body with the help of a necromancer. But there were others… before I found my body."

She swallowed and seemed to consider my answer a moment before going on to question me further. "How many?"

I shook my head. "I honestly don't remember."

Anger creased the lines of her face and she turned to face me fully. "How can you not remember?"

At that, I tilted my head. "It was long time ago. I bet you can't remember the name and face of everyone you've done wrong by. How many people you scowled at for jumping in front of you in the queue? How many people you cursed because you were having a bad day?"

She let the words sink in and as they did, the anger seemed to fade somewhat. I took her silence as an opportunity to redirect the conversation and nodded toward the phone still gripped in her hand.

"What are you doing?"

"I was searching the news," she admitted.

"Oh yeah? Anything interesting? Is that crazy chick that killed her boyfriend still on the loose?"

"Very funny," she huffed out, scowling at me, but then she turned serious, and her face turned thoughtful. "It's just… No, it's stupid."

"What?"

"The amulet, the one Shay gave me for you… it's the same one Myka gave me. I mean, it can't be, but it is."

"And why can't it be?"

"Because Myka died saving me. Cathal slit her throat. I saw the blood and I watched her die in the middle of a train station. Except, I can't find anything in the news. There's nothing about an attack, or a fight. Nothing about a dead body. Either someone is covering it up, or…"

"She's still alive," I finished for her.

"But she can't be."

"Stranger things have happened."

She shoved the phone away into her pocket and looked out into the trees. "Maybe, but it still doesn't explain Shay."

"I'm not sure anything will explain Shay," I mused out loud, going on to chew at the pad of my thumb as I allowed my thoughts to linger a little longer on that man.

I had come across a wide variety of people and beings in my time and that included men like Shay. Men who sought power and control, men with silver tongues and deep pockets, men with souls so dark you could easily mistake them for something other, something a little more like me. But usually, I could figure them out. It had always been my job after all. In order to bargain for a person's soul, you needed to be able to read them, to know exactly what they wanted. But Shay, his motives and desires were still hidden from me for the most part.

Maybe I was losing my touch, or maybe it was simply that I didn't want to look too deeply into the mouth of a wicked wolf, poised and ready to bite, and who could blame me?

"Nate…" Charlie spoke again, and it was strange to hear her voice so timid, so unsure.

"Huh?" I looked to her, waiting for her to continue.

"Cathal, he said something, about you… about my blood."

"And you want to know if he was telling the truth…"

She didn't answer at first, but after a moment, she gave a light nod.

"For the record," I started, "I didn't know. Not until we were saying our goodbyes the last time. But you have his eyes, so I guess it's true. Sorry to disappoint you."

"I'm not disappointed." She straightened her back and looked out towards the trees. "When my parents died, I had no one. Once all the legal stuff was out the way, my family didn't even want to know me. It wasn't until Marcus that I felt like I didn't have to be alone." Her head fell a little, her voice tightening, and I wondered if she was attempting to hide her tears from me. "That night, when he wasn't him anymore… that wasn't the first time. I've seen the shadows for most my life. That was just the first time they took notice of me too."

"And now you're here, stuck with boy wonder in there, a shiny angel who's more trouble than she's worth, and me."

"I want to know more," she said suddenly, and she spun on the spot to stare at me, determination lighting up her face. "There is so much about all of this that I still don't understand. This, this is where I belong, and whatever you want to call it, family, fate, destiny… I want to know it all. Demons, angels, and whatever else there is."

"That could take some time…"

"The way I see it, I'm not going anywhere. Are you?"

I scoffed and cast a glance back toward the shack. "No, I don't suppose I am."

22

Daniel

There was something so surreal about standing in a room that was once yours, looking over items from your past, covered in a thin layer of dust. The memory I had of packing my bags and sneaking out, it couldn't have been any more than a year old, and yet it felt like an eternity ago. I had deliberately avoided the room when Aunt Suzie had forced me and Nate to rest before, but now we had returned with the intention of hiding out for a while, there was no escaping the memories it held.

Technically, it was a guestroom, but over the years, for as long as I could remember, I was the only guest that Aunt Suzie ever had stay over. So as time passed, it became mine a little more each time I stayed. Until my father died and I came to live there permanently. She had given me a home when I was left without one, and even after I had run away, she had kept the space relatively untouched, apart from a couple of storage boxes balanced in the corner.

It was in that small room, at the small desk by the bed, that I had made my plan. That I decided I would avenge my father's death. Much like how it had been at a small desk in a small room in Scotland that I had decided I was ready to learn the truth. And as I stood there now, staring down at the desk, I found myself lost in my own thoughts of how my truth had changed.

A gentle knock at the door had me attempting to brush the thoughts away, but at the sight of Serena, I found it impossible to do so. My jaw tightened, ticking, and I looked away, deliberately avoiding meeting her eyes. I moved around to the other side of the bed and to the dresser, busying myself with the task I had originally entered the room for—searching for a clean set of clothes to change into. But the door creaked open further and Serena moved closer.

"You're angry with me," she said, matter of fact. There was little to no emotion in her tone and that right there was the problem. That right there had so much to do with the tension in my shoulders, spreading out and causing my fingers to grip the material of the shirt at the top in the drawer.

I considered denying it or brushing her off, ignoring the anger bubbling up inside of me, but the thoughts kept spinning and the silence between us beckoned those thoughts out, calling them to the surface. They spilled from my lips before I could stop them and I swung to face her, my gaze bearing into her, taking in the angelic light and swirls of what looked like tiny flames circling her.

"You were ready to kill him," I spat at her. "If Charlie hadn't stopped you, would you have actually gone through with it?"

I don't know why I asked. Maybe I was hoping she would argue and defend herself. Maybe I was hoping she would fight and lie and say that no, she couldn't have killed him. She couldn't have driven her blade into Nate's chest, delivering the killing blow for the second time.

But she said nothing, and her silence told me everything I needed to know.

My throat tightened and I let go of a humourless scoff, shaking my head. "You know, when I first met you, I thought you were the most beautiful thing I had ever seen. I thought I could trust you and believe in you, because how could something that beautiful be evil? But now I know you, now I can really see you, I can see the truth.

You might not be evil, but you're not exactly good either."

"Sometimes, when doing the right thing, you don't always have the luxury of being good."

"And killing Nate would have been the right thing?" I took a step forward as I spoke, refusing to back down or turn away.

Instead of answering though, a small smile played at her lips and her eyes fell a moment before meeting mine once again. There was something there, in her gaze, but I couldn't quite figure it out. "You care about him, don't you?"

"Are you saying you don't?"

She moved forward until she was standing in front of me, her hand moving up to gently cradle my cheek. "It was my love that damned him. Amon claimed his soul because I couldn't bring myself to kill him when I was ordered to."

My shoulders sunk, suddenly heavy with the weight of her words. "What are you saying?"

"Death is not the worst fate a man can have."

At that, I pulled back and shook my head. "No. That's…" Taking a breath, I pushed my shoulders back. "No. It's not his time. I'm not going to just give up on him."

"Then we best find a way to save him… before he becomes damned all over again."

She lowered her hand and looked me over once more with that sad smile on her face before leaving me alone to my thoughts again. For a moment, I almost felt sorry for her, thinking about the echo of loneliness she left behind in the shadows of that room. But I forced it down and clung onto the anger. It was the anger I would use to drive me. After everything I had already lost in my life, I wasn't prepared to let go of anything else without a fight.

*****

The first night was awkward and restless. There was plenty of room for us all, from the guest room to the office and even the semi-comfortable couch in the front room. And yet, we all seemed to find ourselves occupying the same space, with the exception of Serena. She hung back, watching us. I half expected to find her gone the next morning, but she stayed somewhat close, even in her distance.

Exhaustion weighed heavily down on us, like a suffocating blanket, smothering us. When I woke to the smell of bacon and eggs and cooked tomatoes, even Nate was flat out and snoring in the chair by the fireplace. Charlie had curled up on the couch and I had taken the floor for the night. My back ached along with the rest of my injuries as I finally pulled myself up, and I rolled my shoulders before turning my attention to the noises coming from the kitchen.

I found Aunt Suzie hovering near the stove, busying herself with cooking breakfast. She had never been much of a morning person, yet here she was, at a time that could be seen as criminally early, cutting up tomatoes and frying up bacon. I could see it written in her face and in the tension of her shoulders, how lost and helpless she must have felt. She may have known about the world of demons and what came with it, but she had never been a Harkanian like my father—for that I was thankful. But that only served to strengthen my worry for her now. I knew my father had never planned to actively involve her in this world, at least not beyond knowing how to protect herself and what to look for, and even now, I hoped to keep her involvement to a minimum.

"You don't have to make us food," I said from the doorway to the kitchen, watching as she worked.

She turned to look at me and her shoulders sagged. I didn't miss the way her gaze flickered from bruise to bruise across my skin, lingering on the cuts that looked worse than they felt. She had already spent the previous night cleaning them up and fussing over me, but it seemed that didn't stop her from wanting to fuss more.

"Daniel," she started, but I shook my head and pushed forward, cutting her off as I spoke.

"I'm fine." And physically, for the most part, I was. I may have ached here and there, but none of my wounds were life threatening. It was the thoughts running around my head that were the issue.

I dropped myself down onto one of the chairs by the table in and reached out for a slice of bread from one of the plates, going on to idly pick at it.

She placed her hand over mine, pausing my movements, and smiled softly. "He would be proud of you, Daniel. He would be so proud."

"But?" I asked expectantly, meeting her eyes.

"He tried so hard to shield you from it in the end."

I let go of a light snort at that. I had grown up on the stories my father had told me. The halls and warehouse that belonged to the Harkanians had been my playground. This life, there was no running away from it for me. But there was no denying that the older and older I got, the more my father had stopped entertaining my curiosity. But I knew now that it wasn't the life he was trying to protect me from. It was the Harkanians.

There was no denying there had to be good people within their walls. My father was proof of that. But when the people at the top are corrupt and the good people are merely chess pieces to be moved and manipulated, lab rats to be tested on, how could the good ever outweigh the bad?

In the back of my mind, I knew I wasn't done with them, just like I wasn't done with Vassago and what had happened with my father. But there were other matters that needed my attention now.

"I need to figure out how to kill a demon… once and for all," I said to the empty air, not expecting an answer, but needing to voice my thoughts out loud, as if by doing so I would clear enough room to think of the answer.

"Well, that's easy," came the lazy voice of Nate from behind me, a yawn interrupting him as he moved forward to take the seat opposite me. "We use Charlie's gift and hit them where it hurts." He grinned at Aunt Suzie. "She can see their weak spots."

"There's two problems with that," I answered. "The first being that it also kills the person they're possessing."

He shrugged as if such a thing was just a minor inconvenience. "And the second?"

"There's no mark for her find on the upper-class demons."

He nodded, thoughtful. "Vassago."

"Not just Vassago," I said, to which he looked puzzled, his brow furrowed. "Amon…"

"Ah… yes." He looked down at his hand and flexed his fingers, as if he was testing his grip. "We should have killed him when we had the chance."

My jaw tightened and I glared at him. "You're an idiot."

"I'm a what now?" He sat back a little, staring at me with his mouth slightly open.

"You heard me," I answered, eyebrow raised in challenge. "What exactly did you think was going to happen when you invoked Amon? Did you think we would just go 'oh well, he had a good run' and just let you die?"

Before he could answer, he let go of a sharp hiss as Aunt Suzie whacked the back of his hand with a spoon causing him to pull his hand up to his chest and cradle it as if such an act could truly hurt him.

"You invoked a demon?" she questioned, tone harsh and reprimanding.

"First of all," he answered, his eyes moving deliberately to glare at Aunt Suzie, "Ow! And second of all, I did it to save Charlie… and yes," he continued, gaze moving to me now, "that was exactly what was supposed to happen."

"So, you've got a death wish?" I challenged.

"I had a plan, and my plan was to save Charlie, and guess what? My plan worked. Charlie is demon free." He rubbed at the back of his hand a little more for effect, but he was earning himself no sympathy. "I'd call that a win, wouldn't you?"

"I'd call it more of a win if you were just a little less determined to get yourself killed in order to save us."

Something flashed across his face, but he quickly hid it beneath a smarmy smile, his posture adjusting and his words taking on a teasing tone. "Aww, Danny Boy, I didn't know you cared."

I didn't deny it, but I wasn't about to give him the satisfaction of confirming it out loud either. Instead, I chose to try and change the subject back again. "Either way, we now have to find a way to get rid of Amon…"

"I may have an idea," Charlie interrupted, no doubt woken by all the noise we were making. She joined us at the table, claiming the seat next to me and fiddling with the sleeve of her jumper. When she saw she had our attention, she continued on. "Myka."

"You think she could help?" Nate questioned.

"If she's alive, yeah." Charlie nodded. "If she doesn't know how to do it, then she has to know someone who does. She was part of the Occultus and the things she could do… It's got to be worth a shot."

"So, the next question is… how do we go about finding a dead person?"

As Nate leaned back, a thoughtful expression falling onto his features, I began to realise that despite my desire to save Nate before things went bad, it wasn't going to be easy. At least when it came to finding the Occultus we had a lead. When it came to searching for the truth about what happened with my father, we had somewhere to start.

But now? We had nothing.

I stared down at my hands before casting a glance toward the doorway where Serena lurked, silent but watchful. I wondered how much she knew and how much of that she was keeping from us. If she could keep so much from Nate, who she supposedly saw as a friend, then what would she keep from us mere humans?

"There was a demon that Myka introduced me to," Charlie said. "His name is Foras. Does that mean anything to anyone?"

"Foras," Nate repeated, thoughtful. "You know, I think I've heard that name before."

"He is one of the old ones," Serena spoke up. "You'll have no doubt heard whispers of him through stories. Some say he was murdered by his own kind, and then there are others who say he deserted the legions he commanded in favour of humans. If he truly is still alive, it won't be easy tracking him down."

Charlie shook her head, confusion lining her words and tugging at her lips. "But Myka summoned him so easily."

"She must be on good terms with him."

"What difference does that make?"

"When you summon a demon, imagine it as a knock at the door. They have no obligation to answer. But there are certain tricks you can use to encourage them."

"Offerings," Nate chimed in. "She's talking about offerings. Animal sacrifices, promising the demon your first-born child, burning an effigy of someone you love, or hate. The list goes on. It all depends on the demon you're trying to summon."

"And what would we use to summon Foras?" I asked.

"Now that is the question…"

One of many, but at least it gave us a start. It gave us something to look for and focus on. It gave us direction.

23

Nate

It was still early when the whispers woke me, like a breath in my ear, brushing against my cheek and calling to me. I groaned at first, attempting to swat them away, but their persistence had me turning to face the direction they came from, forcing my eyes open to glare at the owner. Except, the owner wasn't there. I peered into shadows instead, dimly lit by the remaining embers of what had been a roaring fire hours before.

I had fallen asleep in the armchair beside the fireplace, listening to the others talk about their plans and ideas. In my light slumber, I had a vague memory of Charlie and Aunt Suzie eventually heading to bed, leaving Daniel to take the couch for the night. He had given up what had once been his room to allow Charlie some privacy and comfort. After all, it was only for a short while.

Except days turned to weeks and weeks turned to months. December became January then February, and Winter turned to Spring, and by the early days of April, we were still no closer to finding any answers. In all the searching we had done, all the books we had read, we still had no idea how to kill a high-level demon or how to get Foras' attention. Eventually Serena set off on her own search, checking in with us every so often, but never with any information we could use.

The shadows shifted and I blinked, trying to make them out,

sparing a glance at the empty couch, blanket discarded across the back, showing Daniel's absence. Once more, the whispers called to me, drawing my attention to the shadows at the doorway to the room.

"That you, Danny Boy?" I questioned, pushing up from my seat and heading toward the doorway to follow the thick figure that I swore I saw.

By the time I reached the hall, the thick shadowy figure was standing at the bottom of the stairs. I moved closer, cautious and steady, listening as the whispers grew louder and louder, a familiar voice calling to me from somewhere beyond that dark hallway, from somewhere inside of my mind.

The closer I got, the more familiar the shadowy shape became, and the louder the whispers were. Deep red eyes stared at me from within the shadow, the mark on chest burning deep into my very soul. My head spun, the whispers drowning everything else out until I felt like I was falling into the darkness, losing myself to it.

And then, just like that, it was gone.

The whispered silenced, the darkness gone as the hall light flashed on.

I didn't realise what had happened at first until I felt the hand on my shoulder, and I spun on the spot to find myself staring up at Daniel who was coming down the stairs.

"Nate?" he questioned. "You okay?"

I hesitated a moment before forcing a smile onto my lips. "Yeah, I'm fine," I lied. "I was just thirsty…"

He didn't seem convinced but nodded all the same, his gaze watching me carefully.

"What are you doing awake?" I asked, deflecting the attention, aiming it back at him.

"Toilet…" he answered simply, hitching a thumb over his shoulder and in the direction of the bathroom up the stairs. He moved past me and started his way back toward the front room. "Turn the light out when you're done, will you?"

"Sure," I answered, watching him as he disappeared from my view.

I looked toward the light switch at the bottom of the stairs, studying it for a moment, contemplating turning the lights out there and then and simply heading back toward the armchair I had claimed as my own. But something stalled me, a creeping anxiety tightening my chest and bringing my arm to a halt before I could press the switch. That was when I saw the blood.

Turning my hand over, I flexed my fingers, the feel of the blood tacky against my palm and fingertips. With my other hand, I followed the blood up my arm to the source, the old spell carved into my skin.

Not again.

The self-inflicted wounds there had yet to heal. Not fully at least. And whenever I thought that this time, they were closing up, I'd find fresh blood once more. The whispers scratched at my head again and I pushed forward, into the kitchen and toward the sink, immediately turning on the tap and holding my hand underneath it. The water washed over my skin and I scrubbed at the blood, over and over until it was gone and the only red on my skin was with irritation and the new scars that had begun forming once again over the spell.

"Damn it…"

I closed my eyes, gripping the sink tightly as I kept the water running in the vain attempt to drown out the noises that came from not just the shadows around me, but from within the shadows of my soul. But no matter how much I tried, the whispered words scratched at my mind, digging in and burning, just like the spell carved into my arm did.

"Don't fight me," the voices whispered, and the words made me feel dirty, the mark on my chest burning once more. His mark. "Never fight me, and the world will be yours. Oh, the fun we'll have, little Natty. You will always be mine."

RAY MORGAN

A DEMON'S CRY

ABOUT THE AUTHOR

Born in County Durham, England, Ray Morgan studied psychology before deciding to use what she had learned to torment fictional characters. Obsessed with the supernatural, she spends far too much time engrossed in ghost stories and obsessing about old time lore.

When she's not with family or drowning in caffeine in front of her laptop, she can be found knee-deep in whichever fandom has currently grabbed her attention.

For more information, or for updates on future works, check her out at:
www.facebook.com/RayMorganAuthor

ACKNOWLEDGEMENTS

This novel is dedicated to all those who have been waiting to read since first meeting Nate.

Thank you for your love and for giving me the drive to get this sequel out there. You gave me the courage to believe in myself and my work. For that, I am forever grateful.